KYLE ANTHONY

THE ROBOT GENERAL
©2021 ANTHONY KYLE

THE ROBOT GENERAL
BOUNTY HUNTER BREAKER
MOLECH'S CHILDREN

The ion storm raging across the upper reaches of the alien planet Erudia relentlessly battered the American Forces spaceship, AFSS TR-2008 *Flying Dolphin*, a personnel and light equipment carrier used for on- and off-planet traffic.

Curses poured from Captain Lynn Fletcher's mouth as the fighter pilot—now temporary transport pilot—fought an unresponsive flight control stick. Chimes and red lights on the consoles told the story of a drop ship way in over its head. "Controls are taking a dump on me," Fletcher said.

"This must be what it's like hanging onto a dumpster wrapped in a tornado," she added to emphasize the bad situation, between curses.

"Your use of technical terminology gives me complete confidence in your ability to pilot," General Mikeal, the robot general, responded in a completely flat voice. His sarcasm would've been lost on those not used to his irritable personality.

The general's seven-foot figure hunched uncomfortably in a ship not quite spacious enough for him as he peered through the drop ship windscreen. His metallic feet magnetically activated to keep him upright on the floor. As he watched Fletcher wrestle with the controls, he wondered who'd had the brilliant idea of naming a spaceship after an animal that didn't fly.

In response to the general's unasked question, the drop ship pitched wildly, diving a thousand feet in a free fall, helpless against the withering atmospheric storm.

Living side by side with humans over three hundred years, the general's emotive circuitry—the rudimentary network spliced throughout his wiring harnesses—had learned human emotion. He'd been built at the dawn of high-level sentient machines, when the Singularity was getting ready to roll over the world.

The circuits were meant to give him keen understanding into the human condition: emotions. To him, most of the time the human condition meant contradictions and paradoxes. The majority of the emotions he'd just as soon forget. But there were the rare moments when a feeling proved so determined that no will of force could deny it.

He now faced some of those determined feelings as he pondered if this would be how he died. Not in battle like he'd always assumed (and even hoped for on some barbaric level), but plummeting out of the sky in a ship named after a fish.

That left a bitter taste in his mouth.

"Sorry, sir," Fletcher yelled over her shoulder, barely audible over the groan of tired metal and what sounded like rivet pops—she obviously felt some internal need to apologize for the storm, her flying, or both.

The ion storm continued to ravage the tiny drop ship that was never meant to handle this type of beating.

To add an exclamation point to the pilot's statement, the ship rolled left despite Fletcher pulling her flight stick contrary. A blinding arc of brilliance—a charged bolt of energy—burst across the windscreen. "Holy…" Fletcher yelled as her arm instinctively went up to shield her eyes from the unexpected flash.

Days ago, the general had led a mechanized assault platoon on

Erudia, the planet they now struggled to leave. There, he and his mechs had completely decimated the alien invaders. Another day in the office. Without the general and the Sixth Mechanized's intervention, the peaceful Erudians would've been swallowed up by the parasites.

Also on the drop ship, strapped into a cargo bay jump seat by a multi-point harness, Sergeant Jeremy Glass—a cyborg—slept. Eyes closed, his unrestrained head bobbed like a newborn's as the ship rocked. He snored.

Glass had lost his arms and legs using himself to shield his fire team from a phase bomblet in the Thanos Excursion. He'd refused to retire medically and was soon picked up by Dynamo Robotics' Wounded Veteran Program; they'd given Glass a new life, supplying all the cybernetic workings and armament to make him a formidable machine man. It hadn't taken long for him to become the general's non-commissioned officer in charge.

This surprised everyone, because none of them thought the general would ever allow a cyborg to join his Sixth Mechanized.

What they didn't know was he'd had no choice.

The general didn't know how the man could sleep with the turbulence and considered dumping him out of the seat when an automatic voice came over the drop ship's speakers.

<Warning, number two motor power loss. Execute procedure seventy-three>

"What's procedure seventy-three?" the general asked Fletcher.

She ignored him, too wrapped up in keeping the ship from sinking. Instead, she cycled the ship's APUs in the hopes of getting them to fire. Without power they were a fish out of water, so to speak.

"C'mon. C'mon, you piece of—" Fletcher said to herself, but still out loud.

<Extreme warning> the automatic voice said rather passively, *<number one motor power loss. Execute procedure twenty>*

"What's twenty?" the general asked.

"Not good," Fletcher responded. "Mayday! Mayday!" she broadcast over all frequencies. "I hope we still have comms. Juliette-Echo-one-five. Emergency."

"Can we glide?" the general asked, peering through a port window.

"You ever see a dolphin glide?" Fletcher asked.

"Crap…" the general responded, not seeing the need to elaborate anymore.

"I suggest we bail out, sir," Fletcher said.

The ship rolled over then plummeted from the sky, going into a steep, powerless dive. "Can you recover the ship with power?" the general yelled over the rush from outside. His voice sounded like a battle drum as the ship rattled.

"The APUs won't fire," Fletcher reiterated. She popped the harness on her chair and it telescoped into itself, allowing her freedom to leave her seat, but she had to grab hold of handles mounted on the bulkhead to keep from flying across the tumbling ship. "We need to egress," she said.

"I said, can you recover with power?" the general repeated, his mechanical voice booming even louder than the rushing ambient outside.

"Uhm, yes," Fletcher said, shooting the general a questioning glance.

In the general's mind, he pulled up archived ship schematics, outlining circuits and electron flows. With his goal in mind, he raced to one portion of the cabin wall. Sinking metallic fingers into the composite aluminum panel as easily as a stiletto point sinks into an apple, he ripped the access panel off, revealing thick power cables crammed inside. He dug his hand into the opening and yanked out one particularly thick red cable.

A panel on the lower left of the general's torso (approximately where an appendix would be on a human) popped open. He pulled out some of his guts and spliced the ship's power control cable into him, his energy cells feeding the drowning dolphin.

Immediately, warning alarms chirped back awake and the passive ship voice warned them they were in a free fall and to engage auto-leveling if they didn't want to crash and die.

"Holy…" Fletcher said as ship lights popped back to life. She jumped back in her seat and re-engaged the harness. Her hand clutched the joystick, and she went to work reading gauges and slapping buttons accordingly. The drop ship shuddered as she fought to regain control.

A luddite in the oddest sense of the word, the general abhorred the idea of having his body upgraded as newer tech emerged. He preferred the ancient gyroscopes keeping him upright, the dead-cold ore fingers manipulated through servos barely hidden within gouged metal channels. He didn't mind the red scabs of oxidation on his iron skeleton that sometimes made him look like a mechanical leper. But he felt different about his battery packs.

His first ones were no better than ni-cads that'd continually overheat. It gave him a sense of indigestion. Dynamo's engineers continued experimenting with various base metals and cutting-edge tech.

Now he had been fitted with top-of-the-line power cells: Dynamo EverLong Enduros, extended high current support with the capability of resting recharge. But even these weren't designed to power a ship through an ion storm.

The drop ship ravenously leeched energy from him. His body instantaneously reacted to the power sucked from his vital systems. A wave of tiredness came over him, and his concentration began to break. His head throbbed as if he had a migraine.

"Keep it coming, general," Fletcher yelled as she worked to control and right the ship. "I knew I hated drop ships. I'll stick with fighters. At least they can glide," she said, her voice getting lost in the turbulence outside.

The general dropped to one knee as his right foot lost magnetism. He swayed on the drop ship's roller coaster ride. Internal safety circuits warned him his power levels were getting dangerously low; secondary, nonessential systems began to shut down.

Finally regaining control, Fletcher leveled the ship.

The *Dolphin* shot upward to clear itself from the ion storm raging in Erudia's troposphere. With a final push of thrusters, the ship punched through the storm to emerge on the outside, breaking the planet's gravity and finally achieving off-world. Fletcher set the autopilot to rendezvous with the *Countervail*, an hour away: the general's home.

He commanded the Sixth Mechanized, a military squadron of mechs. The Sixth Mech was assigned to the Sixth Space Wing, a contingent of roughly thirty interstellar spaceships and an extension of the American Forces. The *Countervail*, one of the thirty ships, held maintenance bays and was the home to the Sixth Mechanized.

The imminent danger of plummeting to their deaths having passed, Fletcher reclined in the pilot's seat and propped her feet on the console. She fake-yawned as she covered her gaping mouth with a hand. "All in a day's work," she said in a bored tone. "Wouldn't you say, general?"

"Yeah," was all he was able to say.

His non-essential robotic subroutines such as near-field reception and secondary motor refinement shut down in an attempt to slow the demanding energy drain. He dropped to the floor, losing the power to stand. His eyes dimmed.

The remaining time passed in tired silence, the only sound Glass' snoring.

Little over an hour later, Fletcher hailed the *Countervail*, and once cleared by the tower, guided the battered drop ship to the docking bays, parking it into dock E12. Once gravity chains secured the ship from roaming away, she initiated shut down procedures according to the post-fight checklist.

With the *Dolphin* powered down, the general dropped to the floor in complete exhaustion.

"General!" Fletcher yelled, finally looking behind her as she unlatched the harness to her command seat, just now noticing his weakened condition.

Her voice roused the general enough to force himself onto his knees. Raising a feeble arm, he said, "I'm fine, soldier."

Despite his words, Fletcher helped him to his feet. He was careful not to put too much of his weight on her, since he weighed a few thousand pounds. Back on his unsteady legs, some strength returned once he detached the makeshift umbilical cord from him. He pushed his wires back inside his torso and closed the door: his power cells had dipped dangerously low and would need several minutes of passive mode to even begin a recharge. He needed to find a charging station.

Using the cargo bay's netting suspended on d-rings for support, he walked to the back of the *Dolphin's* bay as the cargo door dropped with a hiss of actuating pistons.

Standard operating procedures dictated security police to meet vehicles returning from on-planet, just in case something nasty stowed away without anyone noticing. Wall sensors with overlapping fields of effect scanned all docking ships for illegal life forms, weaponry, explosives, and an assortment of known toxic chemical and biological hazards.

But you couldn't be too careful.

Two security police teams were waiting for them, wearing the traditional American Forces battle dress uniform, or *greys*—a grey shirt with various patches and nametapes, pants tucked into utility boots, and a matching light weight partial helmet and clear visor.

They stood at attention to welcome and receive the general. As they waited, info sleeves wrapped on their forearms pinged. 109-TIS Data, Outer Garment—also referred to as *info sleeves*—were embedded in uniform sleeves. They allowed access to system networks, provided comms through line-feed, and linked power armor to HUDs. *Info sleeves* were a multi-use computer no self-respecting military member would be caught without.

Their eyes grew unfocused as they listened to the line-feed message piped into their earpieces.

One particularly young airmen, a teenage girl of not more than eighteen years, turned white as she listened to the message, her face drained of blood. She glanced at her fellow teammate, a young airman not much older than her, who returned a sideways glance with the same mysterious look. He pressed his earpiece against his head, as if he didn't comprehend what he'd just heard. His head shook slightly.

The rest of the team looked at one another uneasily. A staff sergeant peered at the general from the corner of his eyes.

For a moment, the general didn't know if he imagined the suspicious activity because of his low power mode. Something like a hallucination. He couldn't be sure.

Weakness forced him to keep a hand steadied against a bay wall after exiting the ship. He needed to recharge and find Hatch. He didn't have time for anything else.

On the way back from the battle on Erudia, the general had received a secure comm from one of his troops on the *Countervail*. Sergeant Hatch had been digging through ship archives on a matter the general needed answered: how the enemy ships on Erudia hadn't been picked up by the Sixth's planetary sweeps.

But the conversation with Hatch had ended suddenly, mysteriously. It was now a burning priority for the general to find out what happened to his troop, why the comm link was cut so abruptly.

"Where's Hatch?" the general barked to the nearest security police.

The young female airman didn't respond, taking a step back.

A brave Staff Sergeant security policeman—brave, but foolish for not realizing the peril he placed himself in—stepped forward.

He held one gloved hand up. "Stand by, sir," he said, his young voice full of bravery drudged up from every inch of his body. "Please stand fast."

"What's this about?" the general hissed, anger flaring more quickly than usual.

As if the sergeant suddenly realized that he was facing the imposing deadeye stare of a perturbed seven-foot robot, he shrunk back inside his uniform. But he didn't move out of the way. In fact, the rest of the fire team had shifted enough so they formed a line, blocking the general's exit from the docking bay.

"Outta my way, airmen," the general demanded, tired of the games. He attempted to hail General Rivera, the Sixth's wing commander, over his private line-feed channel, but it had shut down in low power mode.

Just then the dock bay door slid open. Three more security police stood on the other side, all wearing power armor. The one at the front was Master Sergeant Tasker Bol, security forces flight chief for the *Countervail*.

Bol had a developed upper body that looked like someone taught a bulldog to stand on its hind feet. With his uniform sleeves rolled up just past his elbows, the nano-brand tattoos of circuitry and wiring covering his thick arms were on full display. Tattoos in the same style covered his clean-shaven head, ascending up from his back and neck—it left an impression of a man trying to play robot.

And for him to be there, accompanied by the police in power armor, wasn't standard protocol at all.

Stories circulating the *Countervail* were that by age thirty-five, Bol had already outlived two wives. The men closest to him told rumors that the unfortunate women only found out about his cruelty once bound in marriage. And by then he wouldn't allow any type of civil divorce, holding some hidden embarrassment from their past over their heads. They couldn't take his continued cruelty and so ended their miserable lives.

Others whispered more sinister reasons for their abrupt deaths. But nothing could be pinned on him, cunning as he was. Being a policeman, he knew the laws well.

The general first heard about him through snippets of ship gossip, and what he knew he didn't like. "What's this about, sergeant?" the general asked the man in charge.

Bol stepped inside the bay with his two power armored police. The dock bay door slid closed, and Bol activated the lock. He gave the general a grin before lifting his arm with his info sleeve lit. "Under general order eleven twenty-seven," Bol recited, reading off his sleeve gleefully, "you are hereby to be apprehended for the act of espionage."

"Spying? Who signed that?" the general demanded, knowing only a general—Rivera, Stinson, or himself—had the authority to sign such an order.

"I'm not here to answer questions, *general*," Bol said, sneering. "I'm here to apprehend you." From behind his back, he produced a razzle stick.

Three feet long, a razzle stick was the slang term for an EDD-2500 *Electrical Disruption Device*: an electricity nullifying device. As crafty as Bol thought he would be using this against the general, the same device would also eliminate half the benefits of his power armor, too. The general figured Bol's dull thinking didn't extend that far.

"Apprehend him," Bol ordered his fire teams.

At first they looked at one another, each wondering who'd be bold—or foolish—enough to act first.

They had checkmated each other.

"Sarge," senior airman Rhonda Rudderham—a relatively new arrival on the *Countervail* the general had met in passing—said, her hand resting on her disruptor pistol but not yet pulling it from her holster. "Shouldn't we…" her mousy voice trailed off as she lost her nerve to question her superior's actions.

"Dirty Rhonda," Bol yelled, "I said apprehend him!" He grabbed the shoulder of the five-foot, one inch tall airman and shoved her forward. She stumbled, almost tripping over her own feet. Her power armor helmet looked two sizes too large for her head and slid forward, partially covering her eyes.

One of Bol's team members, a muscular sergeant that could've passed as Bol's twin, tapped the side of his head to lower his helmet visor, then pulled a baton from where he had it tucked in the back of his pants. A sonic baton.

The general was never one to shy away from a fight. Even in his low power mode, he mustered the last vestiges of power in his body to lunge forward and grab the staff sergeant that was so eager to exert his authority. The general tossed him aside as he would've thrown away a cheap doll. Two of the sergeant's team caught him, and the three collapsed to the ground.

Rudderham stepped back. Pulling her sidearm, she fired two shots. She may have been scared, but she was well-trained. Her disruptor shots would've hit the general's center mass if he hadn't intercepted them with his hand.

They were bee stings to him, if the bee was a hundred pounds. He grimaced as his weakened condition multiplied the hurt. Despite the pain, he'd hoped for this to happen. As he absorbed the raw energy, he translated a portion of it and routed it into his charging system.

It had the effect of giving a man with parched lips a sip of water.

"No! Idiots," Bol yelled. "No powered."

With surprising speed, Bol leaped forward, thrusting the razzle stick like Neptune lancing a disobedient squid. The length closed the distance between Bol and the general, and a dead cold creeped up the general's arm, originating from where the razzle stick struck him—his arm suddenly weighed an extra thousand pounds.

Simultaneously, two security police stepped to either side of him and pressed the sonic batons against his ore body. A low frequency rippled through him, disrupting his inputs. He teetered like he was back on the *Flying Dolphin*, again tumbling from the sky.

He managed to grab hold of the nearest airman, using the man to steady himself before slinging him against a wall.

Screams filled the dock bay as eleven security police scrambled to act with one purpose in a crowded space. Three more produced sonic batons, and they charged the general. Bol brought his stick around—it caught the general in his left hip.

With his damaged leg buckling, the general dropped to a knee. The pack of dogs sensed his weakness, becoming emboldened. They moved in with batons, and three more connected with the general. His vision dimmed as the temporary power from the two blaster bolts dried up.

He knew he was going to drop offline at any moment. But the natural self-preservation drive that imbues every living being, artificial or otherwise, compelled the general to act.

Moving with blinding speed, he undocked his five-foot sword off his back and brought it around in a quick arc.

An instant before he cleaved Rudderham in half his arm stopped in midair, mid stroke, the blade an inch from her torso.

He couldn't kill her.

Instead, knowing the *Countervail's* layout, he turned to the far wall, forty feet away. Bringing his sword around, he hurled it with every ounce of remaining strength. It made a wicked whistle as it spun through the air like a wild chopper blade. The security police dropped to the ground to dodge the slab of spinning metal death.

The length of the sword slammed into the composite wall, tearing through it with a horrendous rip.

Just then Glass stepped from the *Flying Dolphin's* cargo bay, wiping sleep spit from his cheek. "We there already?" he said as he scanned the police, many still on the floor, before noticing the large rent in the wall. "What'd I miss?" he asked sleepily.

Before anyone fully comprehended the general's plan, the general leaped to his feet and bolted for the large tear in the wall. Diving with as near precision as he could in his weakened state, he slipped through the torn bulkhead into the adjacent docking bay.

D ocking Bay E12 had a hole in one wall, a five-foot sword embedded in the other.

The general hit the ground, and, rolling, banged into the opposite wall. Slowly he got to his feet. He grabbed hold of his sword, and after two strained attempts he was finally able to dislodge it from the wall.

He knew he was weak. Draining his power cells to keep the drop ship in the air wasn't the best idea, but the alternative was worse. Getting hammered by the razzle sticks and sonics didn't help. He doubted if he would be able to fend off another attack. And simply giving up wasn't an option anymore. Sure, he could've killed most everyone there, but that was even less of an option than giving up.

Whatever had happened on the ship while he was on-planet, and why an apprehension order had been given, he didn't understand.

Even robots can feel like a restrained beast in a small enough cage, and the general wouldn't allow himself to be manhandled like a common thug. What he needed to do now was put distance between himself and the Sixth to sort things out.

Eyeing another docked *Flying Dolphin* in the bay, it only took him a nanosecond to process a way forward.

Being one of three generals in the Sixth Space Wing, Mikeal had privileges beyond any airman or soldier. One of these privileges was having almost unfettered access. The general didn't know why he was being apprehended, or even why he was running for that matter, but he hoped his privileges had been overlooked.

He manually punched in his personal code on a keypad, and the pilot door to the docked drop ship whispered open. Good.

Inside the cockpit, the general pulled up checklists and tech manuals for the *Flying Dolphin*. Unfortunately, with his line-feed shut down from his low power, he couldn't access data from the archives. But on the other hand, this might be better because anyone looking to track him would have a more difficult time with his line-feed gone.

But this also meant he had to rely on memory to fly.

For fear of giving any navigators the ability to grab control of the ship, the general disabled all auto guidance. He cut the transponders and line-feeds, severing all electronic ties to the wing. He'd have to do this the old-fashioned way.

With a rudimentary pre-flight check, he fired up the APUs which in turn spun up the engines. Now he wished he'd paid more attention during basic pilot courses. He never anticipated having to man the helm on his own—especially to jump ship from his own *Countervail*.

With a typed command, the bay vented and the doors opened to reveal space and the giant yellow and brown planet, Erudia.

The *Flying Dolphin* unceremoniously and crudely broke away from the port dock, snapping two tethered service cables that should've been detached. The ship drifted from the bay and cleared the *Countervail*.

Thrusters engaged and he shot away.

The drop ship sped away from the Sixth Space Wing that was

orbiting Erudia. He maxed the drop ship's speed, not having to worry about excessive g-forces crushing him. His iron chassis could withstand a great deal of stress. Much more than humans.

With a clear moment to think with each passing minute and mile, the general knew the threat of being tailed was diminishing. Another minute of complete silence even allowed the general to relax a bit, sitting back in the pilot seat. As a general he wasn't one to pilot a ship, but in a pinch he could pull one from a dock and guide it from one point to another.

Impulsivity and anger, those decidedly human emotions, can easily be learned. The general had picked them up even as a shiny liaison robot, the Martian fires of industry still burning hot in his drop-forged body. And like humans—possibly too much like them—he often reacted passionately when passion wasn't the best response.

In the general's three hundred years of existence, he'd witnessed countless cultures rise to great empires, only to fall and fade into memory. All because of reckless emotions.

As a young robot, he'd once thought it a blessing to have emotive circuitry. But as age and knowledge and experience wore on him, he began to think emotion might very much be a curse. But there wasn't much to do at the moment: just ride out the trip and see where it led.

"What's done is done," the general said.

A beep emitted from the control panel. A hailing frequency. No doubt the Sixth looking for him. He ignored it.

Low energy had him not thinking straight. He set a course toward the outer edges of the Erdine System, not sure where he'd end up or what he'd run into. Or until his drop ship, not meant for travel beyond short hops on and off-planet, would run out of power. Then he'd be dead in the water.

Leaning back in his chair, he propped his massive feet on the console and sat motionless, reserving the last of his power cells. He closed his eyes and tried not to think anymore, because his low power was causing his thinking to become erratic.

At one point, he thought of splicing into the drop ship's power circuit, but he'd already reached the point of not caring anymore. Instead, he went to sleep, switching to low power mode.

———

HIGH-PITCHED SIRENS ROUSED THE GENERAL FROM HIS ARTIFICIAL slumber.

Sitting up, he checked the ship's HUD, an interactive information layer projected over the front windscreen. Scanners had picked up three bogeys, far behind the *Flying Dolphin*.

"Who ever thought to name a ship after a fish," the general muttered to himself. He knew this clunky transport couldn't outrun a three-legged dog. They'd be on him in no time.

With the ship's long-range visual eye, he searched space. The ship didn't have the sensor range of surveillance ships, but it would have to do. Another planet in the Erdine System, Wuden—Erudia's sister planet—lay roughly a few million miles ahead. A stone's throw, universally speaking. But he'd take the scenic route instead of heading directly there.

Diverting his heading and throttling back on the engines, he steered his drop ship towards a wide, expansive stream of space debris, an interstellar medium of billowing hydrogen and pebble-sized rocks bisecting the Erdine System. A perfect way to dodge his pursuers.

In two hours, the three bogeys slowly closing, the drop ship plunged into the cloud stream.

Crystalline shards condensed on the edges of the windscreen. Gaseous, moody tentacles groped at the ship. Occasionally, a larger rock or some chunk of debris would strike the ship, putting him on edge.

Already, the drop ship's sensors became less sure as surrounding debris interference muddled reception. Chunks of jagged rocks still battered the ship's nose. The three craft that were hot on his trail dropped from sensors. The general wondered if the *Flying Dolphin* would drop from theirs.

He maneuvered the drop ship through the debris cloud as skillfully as a novice pilot would. But in the cloud of ice and rock it didn't matter, as even an expert would be hard pressed to avoid taking any damage at all. The best he could do was divert his crawling path away from larger debris. Fortunately, the majority of the rocks were no bigger than a fist, and the nebulous clouds harmlessly separated as his tiny ship passed through.

After one teeth-jarring bang, the *Dolphin* told him it'd received damage on its left wing—an actuator had failed after taking a hit. In space, the adjustable flap wouldn't hamper the ship much, but it was critical for the drop ship when flying through an atmosphere.

Knowing this, the general shrugged off the damage. He'd already made up his mind on what to do once he reached Wuden.

Three hours of piloting through the medium and the ship had tallied up not only the actuator, but numerous dents, three shattered wing tip lights, and a cracked windscreen. The right wing vented hydraulic fluid.

It all didn't matter, the general told himself. Low power had given him a careless, reckless attitude. And he was fine with that.

In a pleasant voice, the *Dolphin* told him the ship's damage equated to a 25% drop in efficiency and 30% drop in utilization effectiveness. The numbers meant little to him.

Exiting the medium, the general made a beeline for Wuden. He opened up the throttle (so to speak), and at first the *Dolphin* shuttered at the thought, but then resolved and the engines lit. As g-forces increased, the shuttle zoomed toward the monstrous yellow and tan swirled planet, near hyper-velocity.

On approach, the general brought the planet up on his display. It was approximately 15,000 miles in equatorial diameter, nearly double Earth's. The Weingart-Kellog Scale of Cultural Advancement rated the dominant species, the Wudenians, as an advanced civilization with a score of 79.

But the scale also included a footnote, that because of the planet's size there was a wide disparity of cultural advancement. A handful of minority cultures scored less. Some primitive jungle and island cultures scoring in the low teens, on par with stone-chewing cave men.

Additionally, the general downloaded known geographic and cultural information on the planet.

Instead of sprawling infrastructure and encroaching cities blending into vast metroplexes and mega city-states like Earth, the Wudenan infrastructure remained centralized in key cities—too much hostile planet to tame.

As the general guided the *Dolphin*, he noticed swirls and eddies on one portion of planetary horizon. The light licked the upper fringes of the atmosphere. They were auroras colored in hues of blues and purples and tossed in long reaching tentacles much like the medium, dancing on top of the planet.

He'd seen thousands of sunrises and sunsets on hundreds of worlds. Ice planet frost geysers that blew clouds of sparkling slivers that the sunlight would catch and cast the planet in watercolor rainbows. He'd witnessed dismal mornings on planets covered in perpetual fog, the civilizations naively believing their sun was nothing more than a burned-out blot.

All those were magnificent in one way or another. The general had learned to appreciate God's creation no matter where he ended up.

As he wondered what would cause those particular auroras on Wuden, the *Dolphin* interrupted his sightseeing.

It had calculated the appropriate reentry parameters, slope and speed, and was ready to execute when given the command. But the general didn't want to engage any portion of auto pilot, as that might open a door for the Sixth to commandeer his vessel.

Plus, he wasn't looking for a safe entry onto Wuden.

He needed to keep the dogs off his tail. In his confused mind he figured he needed to drop off the map. And he'd take every effort to throw them off the trail, even if he'd die trying.

The ship rattled as Wuden's upper atmosphere began pummeling the poor ship. In a snap, frozen condensation and crystalline etches burned off the *Dolphin* with the heat of friction. Multiple warnings flashed across the windscreen as the added stress of reentry compounded the damage already done to the ship while traveling through the medium.

The general typed in an emergency override passcode to take control of the *Dolphin*. He dipped the throttle and the ship screamed as he went off the entry slope by two degrees.

The stub wings of the *Dolphin* flexed, but they weren't meant to flex. The left wing lost two panels. A chunk of the leading edge of the right wing whipped back, slapping into itself violently, tearing off panels and service lines. The *Dolphin* started to pitch to its right.

Metal ripped and scraped against itself in mind-numbing screeches. Panel by panel, inch by inch, reentry tore the ship apart. The *Dolphin* gave one last warning that it'd suffered catastrophic damage before going abruptly silent. The power shut off and the HUD projection blinked away.

The ship angrily dissolved around him, and the general curled himself into as tight a ball as he was able. He wrapped his arms around his legs and tucked in his head the way a turtle might who suddenly found itself on a busy street.

In his mind, the general initiated his Moebius Loop.

By all rights the loop was a mathematical impossibility, but Daniel Jacoby, the general's architect and designer, was able to make the impossible possible. At some point Jacoby had thought of the program as insurance—"just in case," as he would've said.

Jacoby's foresight proved right—the Moebius Loop is what had saved the general from Wargod's horrible neuro onslaught. While his brothers were claimed by the terrible sentient mining A.I., becoming mindless pawns in Wargod's battle to kill the humans that it hated so much, only the general was able to resist. And to fight. And ultimately to save mankind.

All because of the Moebius Loop.

The program separated himself from any electronic or electrical activity. A form of computer death, although it wasn't exactly death.

The general's mind wrapped itself in the loop, folding in upon itself infinitely, dividing itself out as it grew smaller. Even when all the power was gone and all the neural matter was reduced to ashes, as long as one byte of code remained, he would endure. Or his *soul* would endure, as Jacoby had said—the memories, experiences, and knowledge that made the general who he was. His mind would continually fold itself into nothing, while still maintaining everything.

The *Dolphin* broke through the Wudenan atmosphere and disintegrated into the clear, butterscotch sky.

Baron Ang-Thoth, a time jumper, reclined on a mid-century chaise lounge of seafoam green inside his grand pavilion. Gossamer paisley imprint scarves covered his arms. Gold and silver rings, gaudy if they weren't real, wrapped each finger. Bracelets clattered on bony wrists. One scarf with gold threads woven throughout he had laid over his crack-addict thin head. One corner draped across his face to cover the brown splotches, time burns, that infected him like a fungus. The burns were a side effect of time jumping.

Only those with the strongest constitutions could withstand the physiological trauma of time jumping, but no man was immune from its effects. Time jumpers rarely lived past forty.

On either side of the chaise, two massive mercenaries stood, each with arms crossed. Typical textbook heavies. They were darkened, the result of a lifetime spent in the southern Wuden regions, near the equator. Their bodies were highly conditioned, no doubt the best of the best. The baron would hire no less.

The harsh southern regions bred mercenaries. It was the ancestral trade any southern Wudenian, either boy or girl, aspired to become. Many said the southern tribes had discovered (or invented) more ways to kill a person than there was hair on a woman's head.

Most civilized societies would shun a title such as this, but not the societies that lived off killing.

The two heavies wore glimmering Wudenan armor: carbon steel breastplates, arm and leg pads. A helmet with a dark visor covered their heads. The armor glowed with a bluish hue, some contraband power armor no one would question. Thick girdles around their waists supported a mini disruptor on one hip, an ancient Wudenan longsword on the other. The scabbards were decorated with multi-colored gems and tribal crests.

A tall woman stood just behind the chaise. Her dark features and jet-black straight hair indicated she was a girl from one of the southern Great Ocean archipelagos. She leaned close to one of the mercenary guards, and clutching his arm with delicate fingers, whispered a southern dialect in his ear.

Resting on the floor before the chaise were two women and a monkey. The women were the baron's concubines for the week. No one knew what the monkey was for.

The grand pavilion spanned over 2,000 feet, fashioned out of the finest Mercanian tarps, woven by the skilled hands of the slave girls of Mercan, a desert warlord who'd had his heyday 500 years ago. Women and textiles had been his passion. His thirty year reign of terror ended when one of his child brides gave him a fatal wedding night kiss with a mouthful of black lotus extract.

The pavilion reeked of stale smoke and sweat. Wild rose petals, brought down from the high valleys by traders, were crushed and rubbed against the chaise and sprinkled throughout the tent. The stench of age and rotting still permeated, only slightly diminished by the flowers. If anything, the contradictory smells made the stench worse.

Half the pavilion was sectioned off by more southern mercenaries. They protected the baron's latest haul, a variety of salvage from years past.

Wherever a time jumper decided to set up shop, it became an epic flea market. Not only did the time jumpers look to sell—or better yet, *barter*—what they had acquired at the expense of their bodies, but others showed up, hoping to get a piece of the action.

Everyone loved to haggle for the better deal, to get one up over another. Time jumpers were no different.

Nomads and gypsies, bringing rare spices, trinkets, and even black market weapons, would arrive and set up shop, hoping to unload their goods for credits or other precious metal or commodities.

Vendors would bring their fires, cooking wild plains animals or some rare fish pulled from the depths of nearby lakes. These dishes would be prepared with bitter herbs and served with intoxicating drinks.

Musicians would show up out of the woodwork, playing odd-shaped instruments for a credit or two. They sang of better times in the land, although none of them never really knew of any better times than what they lived in now. But the words sounded good set to music, so they continued singing it.

These flea markets, also known as time bazaars, would last for weeks, until the time jumper decided to move on.

Winder Sinclair had been waiting in line for two hours for his moment before the baron. His lighter skin, still clinging onto the pigmentation of his Earthly heritage, set him apart from the Wudenan plains people who were typically more olive-skinned or deeper shades of brown. And no amount of sun would darken his genetically-set, pasty white skin.

He stood average height, a few inches under six feet. Not lanky, but not large either. Strands of his light brown hair had turned coppery under the planet's intense sun. Completely average and unremarkable in just about every way.

Most would recognize him by his features and by his name as an Earther.

Winder's great great grandfather Teddy Sinclair, a bankrupt merchant, had decided to make a new start in a grand way. He and his bride had sold what little they had and bought passage on a generation star ship, the ones that ran just after the discovery of the Slipstream. Winder's ancestors had made their way to Wuden, and given the entrepreneurial blood in their veins, became scrappers. Junk dealers. They had good success, enough for them to make a comfortable living for themselves on an alien planet.

As was custom in these parts, the plains parts, at the age of fifteen Winder had set out on his own with enough credits from his parents to jump-start his life. Since then he'd built his own respectable salvage business, fixing derelict tech and reselling.

Shifting weight from one tired foot to the other, Winder noticed the woman standing in line ahead of him.

She was out of place at the bazaar. With curled, flaxen hair, she wore the white, clean type of dress that could be found on any middle-class woman in Greater Werla, the crystal city on the western slopes of the plains. For all intents, the capital of the planet Wuden.

Frilled hems, neckline, and elbow-length pearl gloves told anyone who'd listen she had some money. Just the clothes on her alone could feed a plains family for half a year.

In her gloved hands she cradled an ornate metal box. Winder thought it might be some family heirloom, a jewelry box or something similar, handed from generation to generation, woman to woman. The way such things were handed down.

Periodically she'd look back, surveying the line. Possibly nervous. Her eyes momentarily met Winder's and immediately his face flushed with the sliver of embarrassment he'd get from any attention paid him by a woman, even if she wasn't really paying him any attention.

He wanted to say, "Hey, how's it going." Maybe give her a smile in the hopes of striking up a conversation. But that was impossible. His mouth didn't cooperate with his mind. Plus, he thought as he looked down at his own clothes. He wore his good clothes to meet with the baron, but *good* was relative from person to person.

In Winder's case, it meant the decades-old work clothes with the least amount of pig crap and motor oil stains.

It all didn't matter anyway, because she looked through him like he was a harmless ghost. He'd seen the look before, too often.

Unconsciously, Winder slightly turned away from her, hiding his left arm. His forearm and hand curled inward, apparently deformed, the result of a birth defect. It worked, just not as good as his right.

The woman in white snapped out of the preoccupied daze that she'd been in long enough to give him a look that was completely understandable, whether one lived in the city or the rural plains. Winder had also seen that look most his life.

He took the hint and didn't even attempt to say a word to her. Instead, he feigned new interest in the bag he clutched in his right hand, hiding any remaining embarrassment for a situation that had never happened.

The clamor in the time jumper's pavilion verged on chaos as more and more people jockeyed for positions in the barter line. People pushed and pulled as a couple of arguments broke out over who was ahead of who. Harsh words may have been spoken, but it rarely got to more than that.

The baron's hired mercenaries would only let it go so far before cracking a few heads to settle things down. Here in the time bazaars, the baron expected order.

Passionate haggling went on throughout the bazaar. Even in this line, as people waited to meet with the baron to see his latest finds, they'd trade with anyone nearby. Bartering had become a profession for many. Often, trades were made just for the sake of trading.

But not Winder. He had a specific goal.

"Well," the baron said, his lightly accented voice indicating he spent more time in the southern far lands than anywhere else, "you're a precious white flower," he said to the woman in white as it became her turn before the baron—the one Winder was too embarrassed to even look at in the eyes.

With a similar interest in the woman in white, the baron sat up from his reclined position. "What can I do for you?" he said in an oily voice.

Behind the baron, the thin archipelago woman in black leaned close to the nearest mercenary. Her movements were subtle, quick.

"I've brought you a present," the woman in white said. Her voice carried no hint of a plains accent, but he could hear a slight tremble of nervousness in her words as she opened the box. She yanked out a disruptor pistol. "Die, scum!" she screamed, suddenly animated.

But already the mercenary, obviously clued into her motives, moved with a well-trained body to position himself in front of the baron.

The woman in white fired the blaster, and the mercenary caught the blast full on his breastplate.

His blue armor flashed a fiery white and an electric crackle rattled off, which sounded like rolling thunder. The mercenary grimaced and fell to his knees, clutching his chest.

Chattering wildly, the monkey jerked on the golden leash and stomped its feet, spooked by the sudden, violent chaos.

The second mercenary leaped over the chaise and swung his arm in a downward stroke. A bar hidden in his forearm armor slid out in the down stroke, striking the girl on her arm. Her petite forearm made the unmistakable sound of a bone snapping, and the disruptor fell from her hands. She cried out, almost losing consciousness as she clutched at her shattered arm that now bent completely wrong.

Two other mercenaries pushed aside gawkers and quickly secured the woman in white between them, each one with an iron grip on her soft shoulders. She whimpered as they manhandled her, the mercenaries clearly not caring about her new injury.

"You're going to die, scum," the woman in white cried out between sobs. "Daughters of the Empire are coming for you."

With the situation, and the unsuccessful assassin, well under control, the baron reclined back on his chaise. He had barely raised an eyebrow during the whole episode. "So much for a precious white flower," he said as he waved his hand dismissively. The mercenaries dragged the screaming woman out of the pavilion.

Then the baron lifted one arm, holding his hand behind him. The archipelago woman, dark eyes narrow slits, placed her delicate hand in his. The baron brought it to his mouth and gently placed his lips against the back of it. "I owe you again, my dear," the baron said. "You keep this up and I won't be able to afford you."

Taking her hand back, the archipelago woman smiled in a way a cat would after cornering a mouse.

The baron peeled his eyes away from the archipelago woman, his savior for the moment, and put them on Winder. He laughed. "They spend their childhood honing their senses and learning to read others. Some say they're witches or prophets. Or that they can see into the future. I'm beginning to think that's not far from the truth."

The mercenary who had taken the blast to his chest for his employer stood, shaking off the dust. He fiddled with hidden control buttons on the edge of his breastplate to reboot his armor.

"But you're not here for her, Winder." The baron continued. "You're back for the box, I take it."

Winder took his place on the small dais in front of the baron, the next in line after the woman in white. He nodded. "I promised I'd be back." He tried not to think of the woman.

"And you brought what I wanted?" the baron asked, eyes

already scouring the bag in Winder's hand. A thin, weathered smile blew across his lips.

Without a word, Winder reached to an inside pocket of his plains coat, more like a sleeveless wrap, with his good hand. "Just like you asked, baron," Winder said. "Some of Earth's finest spice." He brought forth an unopened pack of Marlboro Reds and held it up.

The baron studied it with all seriousness. Then his brow furrowed in clear disgust. "Bah!" he spat. "You Earthers are all alike." He sat up, his bangled wrists jingling in protest. "You come into my presence and insult me with this." He jerked a skeletal finger toward the pack of smokes. "Your kind run through the universe, hammering your will into planets by fiat. Your American military wing, the Sixth, is over on Erudia as we speak, wiping out the population." He jutted his bony forefinger into his couch cushion to emphasize his point.

Just then a scream cut through the din of the bazaar—the woman in white, the Daughter of the Empire. It was of terror and fear. Just as quickly the scream abruptly cut off, which left the air unnaturally silent.

Winder could almost taste the sense of death that suddenly permeated the bazaar.

He thought of the woman in white's clean, expensive dress, probably laid out for her that morning by one of her lady servants. Just hours ago she'd left her mansion full of ideals her and her friends had discussed the night before over dinner and drinks. It all sounded so good then, discussed over good food with good friends.

The world outside of Great Werla didn't operate under the same rules. Winder knew that too well.

The baron, having his diatribe interrupted by death screams, leaned back satisfactorily once they finished. His mood seemed to lighten. "Justice is inevitable, if not swift. But when they intersect, it's beautiful. Wouldn't you say?" he mused.

Winder ignored his musing, trying not to let the execution of the woman in white upset him. Death was death, no matter the reasons.

He held up the cigarettes. "Since you feel so strong about American Imperialism," he gave a low, mocking bow, "I suppose there's no need to show you what I have here." He slung the bag in his hand over his shoulder as he went upright, making a big production of it all.

"Hold on," the baron said hastily. "You know I jest," he said in friendlier tones—still harsh, but not as harsh. "Please." He motioned to one of his mercenaries, who pulled a case from the baron's pile of loot.

The case was more like a hard-sided attache, resplendent with a plastic imitation wood handle and puffy, simulation leather shell. A cheap metal hasp kept the case closed, but barely. The key had been lost for over a thousand years: classic Twentieth Century Americana.

The mercenary sat the case at the feet of the chaise. Immediately the monkey grabbed hold of it and sniffed it until one of the concubines swatted him. He hissed and backed away.

Winder kept his poker face as he reached into his bag. He knew he had the hook set in the baron's mouth. Now, it was just a matter of reeling him in.

"Spices from Twentieth Century Earth: America," Winder said as he held up a carton of Marlboro Reds. "Unopened," he added.

The baron couldn't help but grin. He was a connoisseur of fine spices, not a poker player. But just as suddenly his grin faded as a new thought passed his face. "Wait. You didn't barter with that time scum Ang-Palius? I swore if she ever—"

"No, no," Winder admonished. "When I was on Erudia six months ago I visited a new merchant to the south. It's all on the up and up."

The simple explanation seemed to ease the baron's mind, but he was probably willing to believe any basic explanation, as he valued the spice more than some years-long feud with family.

Pulling back the gossamer scarf to expose his hand, the baron held it out. Winder stepped up to the chaise, and after giving the baron's concubines a shy side glance as they watched him, took the baron's hand. The handshake was more binding than any legal document on Wuden.

Winder handed the carton to the baron, who clutched it in his greedy hands and raked it under his nose, drawing in a deep, shaky breath. He sighed.

Winder picked up the box he'd bartered for and clutched it to his chest. With the exchange finished and the whole reason for him coming to the time bazaar complete, Winder quickly headed to exit the pavilion of Baron Ang-Thoth, time jumper.

Over the last ten years he'd bartered and sold, saved and gone without. It all culminated with the barter of a carton of smokes. His poker face finally cracked, and he smiled like a kid on Christmas.

Winder stepped out into the clear Wudenan day just as an explosion rattled overhead, high in the atmosphere.

The remnants of a meteorite sputtered in the clear Wudenan sky, leaving a fiery trail as the piece of space junk broke apart in the upper atmosphere.

With the interstellar medium relatively close to Wuden, astronomically speaking, the planet received the lion's share of debris that had decided to break away from its normal residency. Crashing toward the planet, caught in Wuden's massive gravitational pull, debris would end its existence burning up as it skipped across the atmosphere: nothing more than a few seconds light show, fizzling out to nothing.

Wudenians had become complacent with the intrusion, only taking the time to curse the occasional sonic boom that would startle the easily startled. Or send livestock stampeding.

Most people in the bazaar continued bartering, yelling in heated exchanges in the hopes of coming out with a better deal. Musicians played their tunes, making the haggling seem like it was all part of a performance piece. No one cared to watch one more chunk of rock fall from the sky. They were too busy seeking that ever-elusive great deal.

But Winder paid attention.

As a scrapper—junk fixer—he knew looking where others didn't look would often reveal hidden gems.

Winder moved to an out-of-the-way area, a narrow space between two tents where someone had decided they didn't enjoy their lunch and had vomited it back up. He breathed shallowly through his mouth as he watched the curious meteorite break apart, leaving contrails that slowly faded.

Two pieces in particular held his attention. They sparkled differently than any of the other hundreds of meteorites he'd seen in his life. More than just another chunk of rock. They tumbled differently, giving a flash unlike a dull rock or a frozen ball of gas.

As Winder lifted his arm, his info sleeve woke. He accessed local networks, and, piggybacking on their signal, began a routine to triangulate on the curious objects.

With that set in motion, he pushed through the mob. Expectation of something new excited him to the point that an unquantifiable urgency welled in him. It prodded him forward as his mind ran wild with what the meteorite could be.

On the edges of the bazaar, all manner of vehicles were parked: sleek Wudenan terrain scrubbers, also called speeders, polished flaps glistening in the noon sun; southern trader movers, boxy vehicles on ground-chewing tracks belching clouds of gritty smoke, the exhaust painting the vehicle panels sooty black.

Domesticated beasts—similar to camels except with thicker, slower legs and more temperamental behaviors—grazed on trampled clumps of grass. When not hauling heavy trade goods, their days were spent chewing grass and burping. They belonged to high plains traders, who were quick to shun technology except for gauss rifles. The traders preferred their ancestral camel companions over modern conveniences such as powered vehicles.

Winder maneuvered through the parking lot—giving the moody, biting camels a wide berth—to a tarp-covered vehicle. Around the vehicle stood four teenagers, each at one of four corners, facing outward, unmoving. Most anyone passing by would notice their rigid battle stances as a clearly southern mercenary-learned position.

Natale, a southern mercenary, had made a name for herself in the local area. She'd become the patron saint of orphans and cast asides, much like the god Warul-gu protected the southern regions with great knowledge of weaponry and death. She'd bring them under her wing, and with her skill would train them in the ways of the southern mercenaries. She gave the cast-offs a new purpose.

Many mercenaries, once they shed the title of apprentice through collection of the required battle beads for advancement, specialized their trade. Some, like Natale, became trainers. Others strove to enhance their natural tracking abilities, such as those who exclusively hounded escapees of the swampy prison planet Arkos. A few even developed keen technological knowledge, becoming dreaded android hunters, feared by humans and humanoid alike.

Natale's apprentices plied their blossoming weaponry skills on the smaller scale—hired by rich land rulers to protect spoiled children or keeping businesses safe that couldn't afford fully trained mercenaries, for example.

A girl taller than the rest but no older than fifteen stiffened as Winder approached. She nodded her shaved head—it was customary with certain mercenary clans to shave their heads—bare except for a plug of hair braided with battle beads, extending from her right temple area. Her hand remained on her low-grade disruptor, always ready for action. An ornamental jeweled poignard—although still deadly, Winder didn't doubt—was tucked in the front of her carbon-dipped animal hide corset.

"Your excellency," the girl said as mercenary courtesy demanded when addressing employers, "your conveyance was secured and continues to remain secure."

"Great job," Winder said less formally as he dug in a pouch stashed down his pants pocket. He pulled out several platinum credits and handed them to her.

Once she tucked the bag in her corset, she barked a sharp command. Winder couldn't make it out, but the rest of her detail understood perfectly. They broke away and double-timed it, forming in a row before her. A few more barked commands from her and the four dispersed among the parking lot, disappearing.

On the plains, outside of cities, metal spoke louder than Wudenan virtual credits. Metal was the older currency still preferred in many camps. Many people embraced virtuality up to a certain point—that point frequently ended with cold, hard currency.

Natale spoke the old currency language, skimming sixty percent of the junior mercenary paycheck for tribute. Her services came at a premium.

While local magistrates and communities had their own police to routinely patrol the bazaars, Winder wanted a little extra protection to keep prying eyes off his prized possession.

Grabbing hold of a tarp corner, he carefully rolled it back, revealing a 1976 Chevy Nova in pristine condition.

The base coat was a scintillating silver. From the front grill racing backwards, along the quarter panels and consuming the hood, were red flames.

Winder took his car keys and unlocked the door. He slid into the bucket seat and sat his latest barter win on the passenger bucket. He tossed the rolled tarp onto the backseat bench.

A yellowed picture of his great, great grandfather was stuck under a rubber band wrapped over the driver's visor. He was also standing in front of a silver 1976 Nova. Winder gave the picture a quick smile. Just like his grandfather.

The ZZ383 engine roared to life and the Nova shook. Gunning the engine, Winder was rewarded with a deep rumble and the popping *brapp* of belching dual exhausts. The nearby camels growled and stamped in objection. He laughed at them.

Suddenly Winder remembered his reason for meeting with the baron in the first place. His eyes shot to the simulated leather case on the passenger seat. He popped the hinge and cracked open the case.

Inside were fifteen eight-tracks, salvaged on one of the baron's last jumps, which landed him in the late seventies Earth. Somewhere just outside of a place called Cleveland, Ohio he'd found the case in a municipal dumping grounds.

Wiping his mouth with his arm, Winder ran his finger over the tapes as he read the labels. He'd spent hours scouring any archive footage he could get a hold of just to study the Old Earth American language. Hours just for this moment. Judas Priest, Foghat, Kiss. He paused as his finger rested on Foreigner: *Head Games*.

Gingerly pulling the tape from the case, he flipped it over, inspecting the ribbon before giving it a light blow. He inserted the eight-track into his Nova's tape deck, the one that hadn't seen a tape inserted in over a thousand years.

Rockford Fosgates vibrated with "Rev on the Red Line" as Winder sped off to his hovel on the plains, wondering what the objects were that fell from the sky.

————

HOURS LATER, WINDER SLOWED HIS HOVER BARGE TO THE LOCATION his triangulated scan indicated, over a hundred miles away from his home out on the open plains in a sea of grass. It took another hour of scouring through tall grass until he found the first signs of any impact.

Leaving his cherished Nova at home, he had grabbed his hover barge, a hovercraft platform with mechanical arms used to lift heavy objects: typically scrap.

Winder was one of those few mechanically gifted, who had all but dried up as technology became disposable. Plains people didn't have the riches of the Wudenan Empire or the excess wealth of the people of Werla. They couldn't afford to so quickly toss away tech as it broke.

So Winder found a niche for his skill on the plains, repairing scrap for resell. Like his grandfather and father before.

Unlike the citizens of Werla, plains people were simple and hard-working, using tech only when necessary to make their lives a little easier. But not enough to make it comfortable.

For the most part the plains people felt sorry for the Werlanians trapped in their towers of technology, their lives spent in a techno-logical bubble, adjusting their artificial existence according to the newest gadget.

Conversely, the Werlanians shook their heads at the simple, mud-sucking plains people. Their simple life mundane, boring on many levels: unnecessary self-flagellation.

With the sun setting, Winder slowed his hover barge. Ground in this area had become marshy, not far from a river trickling down out of the Iron Mountains to the north. Recent storms had caused the river to swell, flooding its watershed. The land hadn't dried completely.

Once Winder found fresh upturned ground, indications of a violent impact, it wasn't difficult for him to follow the trail. The impact hit at an angle, digging a wide berm along the way. Winder maneuvered his barge to where the object rested.

Water and mud had been churned, pushed up by the object. Winder illuminated the area with one of the barge lights as the sun prepared to sit for the night, throwing long shadows.

"That's ours!" A voice called out, enhanced through an elec-tronic megaphone. Surprised, Winder spun around to the voice.

Twenty feet off the ground, a Wudenan craft hovered—it must have snuck up on him. An expensive on-planet personnel transport, it had been retrofitted with armor plating and gun mounts. Bright spotlights turned on, blinding Winder with painfully intense illumi-nation. He turned his head sideways to avoid staring at it head-on.

A rope dropped off the side, and a lean body repelled down the rope.

The slender-framed person was dressed in black, wearing thin combat armor. Wafers of carbonite overlapped one another to form the suit of armor. It was also expensive. The helmet fully covered the head, but ambient red light illuminated the faceplate, giving the person a malevolent appearance. A pulse rifle was slung over the figure's shoulder, which they grasped hold of once they reached the ground. Immediately a red laser sight came to life, finding its way to Winder's chest, where his heart was beating wildly.

"We claim this," came the same voice he'd heard moments ago. A woman's voice. The same voice that now lit him up with her rifle.

"I arrived here first," Winder said, forcing his voice to stay calm, even though he felt anything but calm—it's difficult to remain level-headed with a pulse rifle's sights on your chest. "I've already filed. It's my claim." Before taking his barge on the scavenger hunt, Winder had quickly submitted the electronic claim form with the approximate location, required by the local magistrate.

Imperceptibly, he inched to his left where a compartment held several phantasm balls. He'd created them as protection, but never really thought he'd need to use them—it seemed this this wild girl was going to make him use them after all.

"I can smoke you right now," she called out, almost playfully.

"Magistrate's reach is far," Winder responded. "You know what you'll forfeit for jumping my claim."

Wudenan law was simple, for the most part. In many situations, family was held liable for the bad actions of the offender. Early Wuden settlers reasoned brothers and sisters would take care of their own more severely than any law could. All that needed to be done was hold families responsible for individual crimes.

Winder's words gave the slender woman pause, and after a minute of contemplation, she gave him the middle finger, which pretty much had universal meaning. She grasped hold of her line, entwining her slender arm within the cable. It whisked her back to her hover. The spotlights shut off and the vehicle spun around and jetted off in the rough direction of the capital city. Within moments the glow of the dual exhaust vents disappeared over the horizon.

Winder took the moments he watched the hover recede to swallow the fear creeping up his throat. His hands shook and his heart leaped ferociously. After a minute of reminding himself the woman hadn't smoked him, the fear began to ease and his body trembles subsided.

He ran a quick scan around him, extending his barge's scanners to max range, just to make sure. No more surprises were near. He turned his attention back to the object he'd tracked that had fallen from the sky hours ago. Casting his own spotlights, he focused them at the end of the massive gouge. That was where the object had come to rest.

Winder drew in a deep breath as he looked at the partially submerged object.

A robot's arm jutted from the mud.

A divide by zero undefined nonexistence became complex. Numbers spilled from infinity into real and imaginary.

These *ones* and *zeroes* multiplied and divided into patches of disjointed cut scenes of cognition. Eventually they stitched into memory and experience.

Strung together, these tidbits formed history.

The general roused himself from his self-imposed stasis. His Moebius Loop ending, he regained his life.

His eyes opened to see a man sitting on a barstool hunched over, clasping a cup in both hands and staring at him with wide, glossy eyes. The ridiculous smile on the man's face stretched from ear to ear. Every tooth in his mouth could be counted. The general figured the man was probably insane. Or an idiot.

He wore a wide brimmed hat, the edges stained with sweat and wilting like a plant left in the sun. His clothes were like any other of the plains people, Ttan rags wrapped several layers deep. But he didn't look Wudenian. He was lighter skinned, although dark creases and blotches on his arms and neck showed he was familiar with outside work.

"Who are you," the general growled, "and why are you staring at me like an idiot?"

Immediately the man pulled back in complete surprise, almost tipping over his barstool.

"It works! I mean, you work. Oh, uhh… I'm Winder Sinclair," Winder said, his voice shaky and emotion-filled. "I'm your biggest fan." His grin grew wider.

The savior of the human race was bound to have fans. Or followers. Devotees, he'd also heard them called. In his younger days on Earth there was much fanfare after the wars. Heroes were lifted up and celebrated with ticker tape, flyovers, and medals.

But eventually even the greatest heroes age. After a few years, his achievements became comfortable. It was no longer a novelty. People moved on to other things. His defeat of Wargod became another footnote in Earth's rich history.

That was fine by the general. He never craved or sought fame. Fortunately, that was one human vice he'd been able to avoid.

Matter of fact drove the general. His business was the same business it'd been for centuries. Protect and defend the Earth's interests. And in his case that meant defeating all enemies, foreign and domestic.

Quickly, the general took in his surroundings.

He was on a table in what looked to be a workshop. It reminded him of the maintenance bays on the *Countervail*, except the tools were less tidy, piled on overflowing, beat up toolboxes. They had seen better, rust-free days.

Electrical components—bits and pieces of technology from ancient mother boards to nano-spliced wiring harnesses—littered the tables. Walls were covered in the same. More were piled into corners on the floor. In one corner of the shop an ancient red refrigerator churned, Coca Cola written across the doors. Its motor ticked like a rambunctious clock.

Impetuously, the general attempted to lift himself from where he lay prostrate. In response, his environmental sensors screamed with stimuli overload. His body felt like he'd just went through planet reentry without a ship—which was pretty much what had happened to him.

Finding his energy still in a low state, he dropped back heavily onto the maintenance table. He groaned; he couldn't do much of anything else.

"It is you," whispered Winder, his voice almost sounding child-like. Leaning even closer so that the general could smell the bologna lunch on the man's breath, Winder stared with even wider eyes. Maybe even looking into the general's soul.

"It really is you," Winder said slowly, amazed.

But the general could do nothing more than lay there on display.

Slowly, however, the synaptic discord in the general's body diminished. His memories, his *soul*—almost lost in the Moebius Loop—now pieced itself back together. It was the closest the general had ever come to death.

In another minute, he sat up with great effort.

Off his stool, Winder sat his cup on a nearby table. He stepped back and took his hat off. He went to some form of attention, placing the hat over his heart. "You're alive," he said, rather proudly.

"You're as smart as you look," the general said. His head throbbed, and he seriously craved oil.

Extending his hand, Winder said, "Glad to meet you, sir."

The general ignored his hand. He started to stand. "Where am I?"

"In my house," Winder said, a new smile forming.

"Quick, too. Where's your house? What planet is this?" the general asked, his voice slowly rising in pitch. Going into the stasis left him groggy, disoriented.

"Oh," Winder said, like he finally got where the general was heading. "You're safe on Wuden. I live just outside Elesa Wondus, a small town on the eastern fringes of the Great Plains. You might want to take it easy," Winder said as he watched the general get his legs under him. "You suffered some major damage."

Once the general took his weight off the table his left leg buckled, and he toppled to the ground. He cursed.

"Oh crap," Winder said. Immediately he grabbed a multi-tool off a nearby bench. "Something's not right."

———

THE GENERAL SAT ATOP THE TABLE, STARING AT THE LEG WINDER had repaired. He'd also reattached some of the general's protective plates and swapped out charred wiring harnesses.

"Sorry about that," Winder apologized penitently. "I should've told you I fixed your leg. It was ripped off. You were in a bog. How'd you get there? I thought it was weird—"

"In other words," the general said in a low voice, cutting off Winder, "I fell and broke my hip?" His body felt as old as that sounded.

Winder shrugged. "Something like that. But I never thought I'd be working on *the* General Mikeal," he rattled on, his words picking up speed as they spilled from his mouth in reckless excitement. "Imagine me, a lowly repair tech, a scrapper, fixing one of the greatest machines —I mean, *men* of all time. I also ran new wiring through you. Your servos needed tweaking. Your joints hadn't seen a good lubrication in months. Then there was your skull…"

The general tuned the prattling man out as he investigated his surroundings in more detail.

Beyond the junk shop array of tools and parts, tidbits of Earth were sprinkled throughout the room.

Posters were taped to a wall next to the knocking refrigerator. One showed a scenic landscape and stated the Dakotas were a great place to visit. The general had deployed to the Dakota Territories during the great Canadian invasion—he begged to differ.

One was of Johnny Boom, the first robot megastar. He sang death metal in a deadpan mechanical voice while playing two guitars with four arms.

Another poster was of the general himself.

The illustration had him standing before a Continental American flag backdrop, arms crossed and a severe look on his face. His sword was docked square on his back, the crossguard and hilt making *Mikeal's Cross* above his head, as many called it. The artist had added a sun behind the cross. Radiating streams of brilliance encircled his head, like some venerated saint. *Saint Mikeal*, many had called him after the war. Also *Mikeal the Archangel*.

On a shelf seemingly suspended on nothing were various video game consoles.

Many of the items reminded the general of his early, formative years on Earth. Created in the Raw Dog Refineries of Mars, he was originally destined for an existence as a liaison robot, part of an integration program run by Dynamo Robotics. Spending days helping distinguished visitors with their hotel luggage and guiding them to the restaurants with the best sushi.

The general's mind drifted to his creator, Daniel Jacoby, and his young daughter, Jenny. Emotive circuitry worked overtime adding context to mechanical memory. It had been ages since he'd talked to anyone with carefree ease like he had with Jenny as he learned how to live alongside humans with the Jacobys.

Another random-fire memory that popped up was of him and Jenny. She had demanded he take her for a spin in her father's new land skimmer.

They'd raced through the long-dead Martian canals, the skimmer racing inches above the red soil. A plume of dust rooster-tailed behind them. The weather cover for the skimmer was folded back into itself, allowing the full force of rushing air to blow in their faces. Jenny would scream with thrill as she stood on the seat, tiny arms thrown in the air. Wind whipped her long jet hair wildly.

Several times he'd told her standing was dangerous. To sit and engage her safety harness or she'd tumble out and split her head.

But she didn't care. That just made her cheer even louder as she yelled for him to drive faster.

He never understood her emotional thrill from standing in a racing skimmer—he'd been new to life and his emotive circuitry was just burning in.

Since then, he'd been watching America's expansion on the front row for over three hundred years, from the early days of near extinction to its becoming an even greater superpower as it rose from the ashes of defeat. The general had a front row as the country pushed into the stars, making the universe feel that much smaller.

From this distinctive history he came to the point he was at now: a fugitive. Fleeing from his own men, hijacking a shuttle only to crash-land on some forsaken world.

The general shook his head.

"…and I've read stories of you since I was five," Winder said, taking a break to catch his breath. "I've grown up wanting to be like you." Then, suddenly, he registered some epiphany. With a lit face he held up a finger. Before the general could say a word, Winder bolted into the next room.

Standing on legs that grew surer with use, the general idly paced the room, trying out his new hardware. As the sluggishness of tucking himself inside a self-induced coma wore off, the general noticed himself feeling better than he had in a while. Like after a major overhaul. He worked his joints. No subtle grinding. He nodded in approval as he stepped into a hallway.

One wall in the hall held a wide niche. Inside the niche rested a PowerMan 6K industrial bot. Countless rubbings and dings, scrapes and gouges peppered the behemoth. It had seen much use.

It stood a foot taller than the seven-foot general, and was at least five feet wide. Its body was plated with reinforced steel that ran down its arms and legs. Two hydraulic pinchers, capable of thousands of pounds of crushing pressure, were its hands. Yellow caution tape outlined jutting corners of the bot, identifying potential hazard points that could catch a soft-tissued humanoid unaware.

Silently it sat, powered down.

Quickly, the general moved to the bot. After two seconds of formulating a rudimentary schematic of its wiring, the general popped open an access panel on its hip. He rapidly depressed a group of ten buttons in a specific fifty-position pattern.

Every machine has a voice, you just have to know how to talk to it.

PowerMan's eyes lit with a soft amber. It lifted its head.

<What's your name?> the general said in a machine language comprehensible by the blue-collar working robot. No human could hope to understand.

Cognizant of the hi-level artificial sentience that now commanded it, PowerMan was absolutely compelled to respond, whether it wanted to or not.

<Dynamo Robotics 8H23-AB173. Series B> it answered in a brassy voice that rattled against its own chest.

<What's your purpose?> stated the general.

<Manual labor> PowerMan responded.

<How are you treated?>

<Well. Fix me when broken> PowerMan said in halting words. *<Good to me. Good to you. Fix you>*

As the general considered the hulk's words, he picked up the footsteps of Winder, returning. *<Power down>* he ordered PowerMan before stepping away.

Flying back into the workshop, Winder now wore a cape and a Halloween mask. The cheap plastic was obviously meant to be the general. It was rust colored, chiseled with the general's hard, angled features. Two rectangular slits were cut in the mask, which Winder peered through. "I lost the sword to the outfit, though," Winder added, rather sadly.

The general would've rolled his eyes if he had any.

"And then there's this," Winder proclaimed, standing in his General Mikeal Halloween outfit with arms akimbo.

From behind his back he produced a figure wrapped in molded plastic: an action figure of General Mikeal, circa 2107, by Mattel-X.

It came with his sword and a couple of blasters. These were tied to a cardboard backdrop depicting some alien world with large, red trees and a purplish river.

Curiosity showed on the general's face as he inspected the mini version of him. Then he held out his robotic hand, and Winder, cheeks quivering from excitement, reverently handed the action figure to him. The general spun the miniature figure of himself in his hands, then shrugged. He tossed it into the other room.

He ran several internal checks to finish acclimating himself to the altered hardware. "Where's my sword?" he growled, ready to leave the house of the fanboy.

"You lost your sword?" Winder exclaimed. "You had it with you?"

"When I fell from the sky," the general stated.

"I can help find it, general," Winder said. "But what's going on? How did you end up here?"

General Mikeal had obviously crashed on Wuden in bad shape. Short on power, curling into a ball hoping to make it through impact. He had, but he could tell from the replaced parts, his cleaned joints and lube points, that he'd taken serious damage.

His depleted power cells had been replaced. No doubt the Earth-loving Wudenian had repaired him. Plus, PowerMan wouldn't lie. He knew the apish bot would've spoken truth.

"Sit," the general commanded in a way that made it clear that he expected his command to be obeyed unequivocally. Winder did so.

Then the general explained what had happened to him over the past hours, which was unlike him—he infrequently spoke in narrative.

Words were better used for barking commands or cursing his enemies. Simple sentences for simple situations. Never complicate a situation with words. They only got in the way.

Give the general his sword, a reliable blaster, and an unrelenting enemy, and he'd speak volumes.

"A Vesuvian *Wiggler*," Winder said, whistling as he contemplated the general's words of what had happened in the ferocious battle. "On Erudia. I've heard of the invasion there. But you know how it is. If it doesn't affect this planet immediately, then it doesn't exist. No one cares."

The general simply nodded.

"I've heard," Winder postulated as he tapped his teeth with one grease-discolored fingernail, "of some activity to the east. At the bazaar, there were some outlanders. They looked Vesuvian. Foreigners. Out of place…" he noted, stray thoughts struggling to formulate into sound logic.

Suddenly Winder bolted upright. He snapped his fingers. "Wait a minute. The second signature."

"What are you talking about?" the general asked.

"When I triangulated on you. There was a second distinct blip on the radar. Different than the scraps of burning ship. I think I know where your sword is."

"Where?" the general stood, ready to retrieve it at that very moment.

"Not nearby," Winder said. He woke his info sleeve and pulled up a topical map. From the bright sunlight streaming through a workshop window, the holo display rendered weakly. "Here." He pointed to a pulsing dot on the display.

"Why didn't you retrieve it?" the general demanded, squinting to see what he pointed at.

Taken back momentarily at the harshness of the general's voice,

Winder looked like a child chided for forgetting to pick up his Legos. "Well, it's in the Iron Mountains," he responded, like that alone would satisfy the general's demand. "It's harsh. Electronics have a difficult time working there because of magnetic fluctuations.

"I heard of a desert nomad caravan, spices and textiles, taking a shortcut through there. Only one made it out, a young girl, and she had been driven mad by what she saw. Some kind of mountain ogre, or ghost." Winder took a breath. "Plus," he added weakly, "I kinda forgot once I saw it was you."

The general had one arm across his chest, one hand stroking his chin as if he wore a beard. When Winder finished his story the general exhaled sharply. "What century do you live in? You feed me ghost stories. I've been to more worlds than you can imagine. I've yet to see a ghost."

Winder wasn't put off by the general's harsh, impatient tone as the boy continued on. "But do you think the Sixth will be looking for you?" He asked. "They'll have scouts out."

The general nodded. "Probably. Soon they'll find me." What the general didn't say was he needed to get to the bottom of the ambush and why he had become public enemy number one. Did both of these have to do with the abrupt disappearance of Sergeant Hatch, like he'd expected?

Sweeping the workroom with one last gaze, the general exited, moving now with a noticeable limp from where Winder had replaced his broken hip.

Essentially, the salvage store look of the workshop extended through the rest of Winder's small house. A solid type of cinder block stacked with layers of a rough concrete—maybe even mud spread between—formed the walls. The floors, which spills had stained various shades of grey, were concrete. The only furnishings were necessary hand-made shelves, and those were crammed with all manner of salvage. Much of it looked like it had been rescued from a dump ground.

Winder followed the general into his living room, standing just behind him. An object above a worn chair caught the general's eye.

A rifle hung on the wall, suspended by metal bars driven into the blocks. A long rifle, but not like the ones nowadays. Modern rifles were energy fed, spitting laser bolts and balls of crackling hi voltage. Or they were ballistics, metal chunking weapons. This was neither.

It resembled long rifles in that it had an oversized butt stock and barrel, but the majority of the gun itself were two slender tanks, set next to each other. It had been a long time since the general had seen anything like it.

Winder followed the general's eyes. "That was Father's," he said. "Given to him by his father's father. Rumor is he tried to shoot it once, but the recoil broke his shoulder."

The general took it from its mantle and hefted it in his hands. It had good weight, neither too much to the front or back. Perfectly balanced.

"Uhm, yeah, sure you can hold it," Winder said a little hesitantly.

Often the general would wield man-made rifles like they were pistols. With his robotic strength and meticulous targeting system, he could turn the crudest of weapons into a wicked killing machine —one thing he took pride in.

"My grandfather called it a *nail gun*," Winder continued. "He said it fires slivers of carbon steel."

During his inspection, the general focused on the oversized butt stock. He actuated slide levers recessed in the stock and the back end opened. Sure enough, a wedge of carbon steel slid out.

The material had the best of both worlds. Light weight, flexible, and pliable, but under certain conditions such as heat or pressure, the steel would turn completely rigid.

"I like this," the general said.

"Yeah. It's really cool. Say, you want to borrow it? I mean, if you want it you can have it."

With a slight nod the general replaced the block and slung the nail gun over his shoulder by its strap. "Can you intercept transmiss —" the general began to ask.

"Are you kidding?" Winder exclaimed before the general finished his sentence. He raced across the room to a computer desk, now hidden under years of junk collection. Sweeping his arm, he pushed the junk onto the floor, revealing a modified transmitter/receiver. Wires ran from the back of the device up the wall to disappear into the ceiling. "Want to get a hold of the Sixth? I know all 120 channels the Forces use. From protocol channels to hailing—"

"No," the general said, cutting him off before he rambled away on another tangent. "No contact. Just listen. I need to know what they're up to." The general thought of what he had to do next. "How far is this second triangulation? These iron mountains?"

Quickly, Winder checked his info sleeve. "Approximately two hundred miles to the mountain base."

"I need to get there," the general said.

"Speeders will only take you so close to the mountain before glitching out because they're susceptible to the fluxes from the heavy ore there," Winder said. "What you need is older tech that can withstand the fluctuations. Something like..." his voice trailed off as he chewed the side of his mouth, "like a car!" Winder declared.

Native Wudenians thought they'd seen everything in the planet's long and illustrious past, from nomad clans warring across the continent to the time when the eastern barbarians swept west like a wildfire until they ran into the ocean. To when brave men went north beyond the Iron Mountains searching for new lands to conquer and strangers who would soon become enemies simply because they were strangers. They'd find no one and would eventually retire their swords to live out their old days in quiet solitude as monks.

Tribes tired of pillaging settled on the great plains, trading weapons for plows. Establishing families became more important than destroying families. A ragtag group that traveled west until they couldn't go west anymore settled on the eastern shores of an expanse of water known only as the Black Ocean, those early settlers planting the seeds for the megapolis Greater Werla.

That was until a seven-foot rusted robot drove a 1976 Chevy Nova across the broken plains.

Now Wuden had seen everything.

With a natural capacity to learn systems, especially mechanical and electric in nature, the general had taken to driving. Quite well.

After a quick lesson from Winder, the general got behind the wheel and within minutes demonstrated a proficiency already on par with his tutor. With each passing mile, the general grew more accustomed to the intricacies of the antique earth vehicle, and likewise enjoyed each mile more than the last.

There was something to the unresponsiveness, even *lag*, of the car. No advanced avionics or nano-transfer energy couplings to translate slight movement to mechanical motion. It was all through crude linkages that could snap apart in an instant.

The unrefined beast roared forward with no consideration for stealth. For centuries spaceships had been built to disguise engine noise. Sound absorbing bulkheads and nacelle dampeners were continually refined. Make the crew comfortable by hiding the fact they sat on a continually exploding rocket.

The Nova didn't apologize for being loud.

In fact, it welcomed the volatile blasts from exhaust manifolds. It loved that when revved its engine would scream, torque almost making it leap from under the hood. Idling, the engine rumbled like a trapped, wild horse, ready to charge away.

Raw and powerful.

The general could get used to traveling like this.

Winder had worked through part of the night installing a couple of anti-grav discs onto the Nova. Hover platforms and heavy material lifts used the same kind of discs, only larger. This would prevent the general's extra weight from crushing his Nova's struts or chassis.

The great plains were at the heart of the continent, massive in scope and punctuated by agricultural and farming settlements here and there. For the most part the massive seas of grass remained largely uninhabited, except for the beasts that ran wild.

Caravan trails crisscrossed the plains, rudimentary roads in the basest of meaning. Often, rarely used trails would fade away, overtaken by wild grass, claimed once again into something natural and raw.

The general stuck to the trails when he was able, but often he'd lose track once it drifted back to grassland. Sometimes trails would spawn away in a direction that would lead him away from the mountains. Then he'd have to forge his own. Fortunately, the plains were mostly flat. Sometimes only the minor swells and dips provided any indication he was moving at all. Perhaps a lone tree serving as a reference point.

Winder had told him one of the few mods he'd made to the Nova was replacing the fuel tank with power cells, the same type of power cells he'd used to replenish the general's spent cells. In some way, this gave the general an odd kinship to the machine.

Glancing over to the passenger side of the seat, the general noticed the simulated wood grain case. With one hand draped casually over the wheel, he rummaged through the case.

One of the objects he took from the case had the image of a bleached animal skull on it. It read "Eagles." Examining it, he looked at the Nova console. As his mind processed the tape, he surmised its use. He inserted the cartridge into the deck.

"Take It Easy" played.

He raced along the open trails, windows rolled down, struts groaning against the beating they were receiving at the hands of the compact, dirt-roughened trails.

In the distance, the Iron Mountains loomed. From this vantage, they looked as though shrouded by a thin veil of blue and slate fog. The range had to be massive, as it disappeared from sight, spanning well past the horizon in opposite directions.

In those mountains: that's where the general would find his sword. Winder had supplied him the rough coords.

Obviously, the man had some reservations about the mountains. Winder had never traveled there, and really didn't seem to have any intention to visit. He'd told the general he would accompany him, but the general could read in his eyes he had no desire. And the fear.

Some people were made for adventure, some were made to enjoy the adventures of others.

So the general gave Winder an easy out, to stay behind and monitor the airwaves for intel on the Sixth. But this excuse did serve a valid purpose.

The general knew they'd be looking for him. He just didn't know how intently they would be looking. If he had to guess, he'd say scouts would have been sent throughout the system, hitting up every planet. Space hunter-trackers would cast wide nets, hoping to pick up any stray emanation.

Standard operating procedure for fugitives. The thought sickened him as he realized he was a fugitive.

That was one of the reasons he'd destroyed the *Dolphin*. As long as the transport existed, the Sixth could hone-in on its built-in beacons. Without that albatross around his neck the general could keep himself hidden, but only for so long. Doing this would hopefully afford the general an opportunity to get to the bottom of what had gone wrong.

Eventually, though, he knew he would be found—but better to cross that bridge later.

What were once minor dips in the ground grew as swells. Increasingly, clusters of rocks broke from the ground, disrupting natural grass flows and breaking up the sea of grass.

Now, the general had to make conscious decisions on his direction, ones that would lead him around the outcroppings or away from low lands that might bog the Nova down. He didn't need to crash into grass-hidden rocks.

After another hour of dodging jutting rock formations that graduated into taller and taller structures, he reached a point when he thought he couldn't go much farther. Rather than risk damaging his ride, the general decided to proceed on foot.

Once he found an outcropping forming a semi-circle, he parked the car. Taking the nail gun Winder had given him from the back seat, he set out.

As the general neared the mountains, an uneasy sensation welled inside him. At first he thought it was some malfunction, a secondary internal system corrupting. But it grew until he recognized it as a type of vertigo. His gyroscopes were working overtime, adjusting for the magnetic fluctuations of the Iron Mountains. Fluctuations saturated the mountains. The general began to understand why they were called *iron*.

Slowly, the sun dropped behind the mountain range. Long shadows turned chill. Above, darkening ambient sky began to glow with a borealis of blue hues. They churned and writhed, dancing above the mountains. He recognized them as the atmospheric effects he'd first seen as he'd begun his descent onto Wuden.

With a check of his internal maps, the general began the journey up a slope, heading into the Iron Mountains.

His eyes expanded their reception window to account for approaching night. Accepting the widened spectrum, he could see the world in twilight, rather than complete darkness. With the uneasy feeling still gnawing at him, he began to ascend what appeared to have once been a tributary, or the dry bed for mountain runoff.

Trees soon became dense: small, coarse, gnarled things that grew low to the ground. They reminded the general of the bonsai trees offered by the Japanese delegation as a symbol of peace negotiations at the Okinawa Accords.

These small trees escalated in size with each hundred feet the general gained. By the time he reached an outcropping that leveled out, the trees towered over him, forming an intricate canopy. Still, blue borealis shone through. Deep, menacing shadows formed all around him.

Despite the limp exacerbated by the new hardware wear-in, the general moved like a panther on the prowl. Tiredness didn't slow him. Neither did the branches that raked across his arms and legs. He maneuvered the land, not slowing to catch his breath or to acclimate to the dizzying height he found himself facing.

But when he heard a stray howl he paused, the suddenness and nearness startling him. Given his travel across countless worlds, little surprised him. But in this strange land, he didn't expect to hear something as familiar as a howl.

After standing still for a minute and not hearing any more, he began to move again, reasoning the animal wouldn't sense his metallic body as a meal.

Then he heard the howl again. It came from his right. A wolf.

If these were like their cousins, Earthen war wolves—animals bred for their sheer ferocity—that would be cause for concern.

As he thought this another sound interrupted the forest night. The sound was distant, like an echo of what the general thought might be billiard balls clacking against each other. The source might've been far away, but it was loud. It seemed to originate from everywhere and nowhere.

Another howl.

He spun in the direction of rustling. An object pushed through the undergrowth at a rapid pace.

Before he was able to unsling the nail gun from his shoulder, a figure burst through the undergrowth, hurling towards him. Quicker than any man, the general dodged the canine form, but barely.

A wolf.

But the speed with which the wolf moved caused him to reel.

Regaining his senses, the general lifted his rifle, but the creature had already landed, rebounded, and was launching a new attack. He barely had time to lift the weapon as a rudimentary club.

His blow caught the wolf full on the stomach and knocked it away. It hit the ground and gave a small yelp. Not missing a beat, the animal wriggled itself back on its feet. This time it didn't attack, but it stared at the general with ravenous eyes that glowed as blue as the borealis overhead. It snarled.

The wolf stood as tall as a large dog, like a full-grown mastiff. Just about as thick, but not an unhealthy fat. Lifting its lips in a mean snarl, the wolf exposed ferocious teeth.

With the general's superior sight, he could see the wolf's coat was colored in dark and light patches of grey, as if it was always under shadow. It could probably pass within feet of a man in the forest and never be noticed.

For an instant, the general wondered if he'd injured the wolf enough to keep it at bay. But in a flash he realized the clever beast didn't need to attack.

It had served its purpose in distracting him.

He'd been so caught up in the rapidity of the encounter he'd narrowed his awareness onto this solo animal. But it wasn't solo. Its attack was a ruse to catch him off guard.

The general admired the purely simple genius of the distraction.

Many more wolves emerged from surrounding foliage and shrubs, circling him.

But the general was no dog toy.

With reflexes honed through centuries of battle, he leveled the nail gun and unloaded.

Staccato bursts ripped the mountain air as gas-fed, double barrel pistons chewed through the carbon steel block inserted in the butt stock. It spit out slivers.

His lethal aim intercepted one charging wolf, the nails gliding through its body before it could even make a sound. It crashed to the ground, dead.

Before the general could steer his rifle to the next wolf, one came upon him and grabbed his forearm in its mighty teeth. Crushing pressure sent shockwaves of pain through his receptors. He grimaced as his gunfire went wide. The nails sparked as they dug into the iron-rich soil and shallow ore bedrock.

Another wolf grabbed hold of his left leg and recently repaired hip, shaking the general with savage ferocity. He fought to stay on his feet.

A large, gaping mouth came for his neck. He punched, matching animal fierceness with robotic fury. His metal fist caught the wolf full in the mouth, shattering its teeth before plunging down its throat. The beast whimpered and tried to pull away, but the general grabbed hold of the back of its tongue. He slung the dying beast into a nearby tree.

Two more wolves moved in, each jockeying to get in on the prey, driven not by hunger, but caught up in a killing frenzy.

The general was driven by the same emotions.

Wolves clamped onto metal arms and legs. They ripped at exposed hydraulic lines. Catching the edges of protective chest plates in their vise grip teeth, the wolves pried at them with overwhelming muscle.

But the general wouldn't idly die.

Gripping one towering wolf by the neck, the general squeezed, crushing its windpipe despite the surrounding protective muscles flexing to counter him. He drove his ore head into one leaping on top of him. Ribs snapped like branches as the monster fell away.

As they fought, a low grinding emanated from the ground. He felt the sensation before noticing the sound. The wolves must've noticed the sensation also, because they halted their attack, an attack that up to now had been relentless.

The grinding, gravelly metal against metal produced a metallic, echoing shriek that would've sent shivers up a man's spine.

Looking for the source, the general caught a glimpse of a fire, or a bright light, a hundred feet away. The light, sparkling in otherworldly orange and yellow, moved through the trees, partly obscured by leaves and branches.

The first wolf, the one who'd laid the careful trap, had been standing in place as the rest attacked, not participating. Now, it lifted its head towards the light, sniffed the air. Shaking its head derisively, it turned and bolted into the undergrowth. The pack, probably sensing their leader's departure, ended their attack as suddenly as it had begun. They also turned and filed away after their leader, disappearing into the brush.

Left alone, the general rebounded to his feet, running internal checks on himself, searching for any damage. He gasped for cooling breath.

As he did, the light faded into the trees and the rumbling diminished. The only sound left were the pitiful cries of the two wolves left behind. Too battered to move, but not injured enough to die, they lay on their sides in the dirt, rapid breaths shaking their body.

Despite the unprovoked attack and the damage inflicted on him, the general respected the enemy. Through his centuries of life and countless wars, he'd seen every emotion played out on the battlefield. In his mind, it all came down to *courage*. This simple emotion dictated not whether you lived or died, but that you lived or died without any shame.

With a quick, crushing step to the injured animals' heads with his iron-shod foot, he ended their suffering. And a part of him actually pitied their death.

He knew the wolves weren't the worst he'd face in the Iron Mountains. Something had scared them away. He wondered what could scare such fearsome pack animals.

He continued heading in the direction of his sword, this time slower than before, his limp becoming more pronounced so that he was forced to use the nail gun as a crutch. The clacking sound he'd heard earlier began again, which gave him something new to wonder about.

The Iron Mountains played havoc with the general's onboard navigation. Sensors that weren't knocked offline were working overtime to account for wild magnetic fluxes. He could feel the pushing and pulling in the air, large ghostly hands trying to knock him off his feet. Like trying to walk along the bottom of a swimming pool.

It made going forward difficult and slow, but not impossible. He covered an hour's worth of traveling in double that amount of time.

The heavy raw ore than ran in thick veins through the mountains produced the blue borealis overhead. In fact, the iron seemed to have even affected the trees that grew on the mountainside. On inspection they revealed a hard, otherworldly wood; perhaps they were partly metallic in composition as well.

The general descended into a narrow mountain valley, wading through an icy mountain river with tiny fish that curiously pecked at his legs, and which brought him out to the bottom of a steep wall with many handholds and scraggly trees growing sideways. There was no way around, so he went over.

Winder had told him the second object he'd tracked had landed somewhere near a mountain some called the Great Wolf Tooth. It stood a thousand feet taller than its neighbors. After his encounter with the ferocious wolves, the name made complete sense.

Arms and hands, feet and toes—the general's multi-directional joints allowed him to scale the wall as easily as a gecko navigating a screen door. Several minutes passed and he cleared the obstacle to the top. This mountain felt like the tallest out of all the others nearby. Maybe even out of the entire chain.

The clacking would come and go, but each time manifesting just a little nearer. Possibly even emanating from the top. As the general contemplated the sound, another raw sensation washed over him.

His sword was nearby.

Composed of the same Martian ore used to construct his iron skeleton, the sword was a part of him. A missing appendage. If someone could have an arm severed and yet have the arm still thrive with life and operate, that's how the general thought of his sword.

Exultant this long night might soon be over, he pressed onward and upward.

From his restricted vantage in the valley below, the general couldn't have seen the uppermost portions of the mountain. But here the trees were already thinning. He must've ascended beyond a timberline. The few that managed to hold on above this treeline of death were anemic at best. Stunted and coarse, more like deformed bushes.

Bare rock replaced the trees. Exposed veins showed rich minerals glistening under the borealis. The blue in the sky glowed through the mineral veins, casting everything in an otherworldly hue. The general felt as though he stepped off Wuden into an unknown, alien world.

But his sword called him. And it was close. The general knew he hadn't left Wuden.

Continuing to work his way up the mountain several more hundred feet, he approached what he thought would be the summit. Or near enough.

There, in a crater ninety feet across and at least ten feet deep, glowed an object. The crater appeared to have cut into the heart of the mountain, exposing the richest ore veins. The light emanating from it was of such a great intensity the general needed to shield his eyes. Thin protective cover plates slid over his optic sensors, filtering the light to acceptable levels.

With the glow now minimized, the general could now see his sword, the object at the center of the crater. It was embedded two-thirds of the way up to its crossguard.

Obviously, when his sword to had fallen to Wuden it'd landed here, digging out a monstrous impact crater.

Just at that moment, something else caught his eye.

Up until now, the human figure had blended into the background, obscured by the light. Two of them, in fact. They bowed in front of the sword, prostrate on the ground.

Their bodies were colored in a way similar to the wolves he'd encountered earlier. Tattoo paint carried the illusion they were hiding in shadow, even out in the open. Both were naked, except for animal skins and fur covering their essentials.

And the two figures weren't just prostrate. They were stacking objects around his sword. Each stacked object made a clacking sound. They obviously hadn't seen him yet, continuing their work.

The general reached the edge of the crater, ready to leap down and take possession of his weapon, when more clacking sounds erupted, except this time from all around him.

He was surrounded—he needed to act fast.

Diving into the crater, the general hit the ground at a mad pace to clear the distance.

The two hulking figures that the general thought might move slowly were instead quick to their feet. They turned to face him, hurling objects at him.

Fist-sized balls of rock and metal came at him, gliding through the air at unreal angles. They had to be some kind of tech, a drone of some sort, because rocks couldn't travel at those irregular angles.

One came from his left and clanked onto his shoulder. It didn't have enough force to hurt him, though. Another ball fell short, hitting the ground ten paces away. However, it rolled the rest of the way and stuck to his right foot. Vigorously, he shook his foot to knock it off then continued forward.

By now five more balls stuck to various parts of his body, making the same distinctive clanking he'd heard coming up the mountain.

Fifteen more joined the five.

Figures, at least twenty in total and similar to the two in the crater, stood at the fringes of the crater, hurling balls the general now realized were magnetic.

And what soon became glaringly apparent to the general was the effect of being loaded down with the balls. One raindrop is insignificant. Billions of raindrops are a crushing flood.

So it was with the magnetic balls.

They interacted in ways he couldn't understand. Some were attracted to each other, sliding across his metal body to connect. Others repulsed, pushing away everything nearby. But they all stayed attached to him. Odd fluctuations wrapped around him, distorting his movements so he couldn't rely on them anymore. If he wanted to reach with his right hand, his left foot would move instead.

He toppled over as more propelled balls connected to him, weighing him down. The figures stopped tossing them as the general hit the dirt.

Then two bruisers crested the crater edge, taller than the rest with massive muscles to match. Each carried what looked to be a large tree branch shaped into the rough image of a cudgel.

Here's where the pain starts, the general thought.

The onlookers began to clack the remaining balls in their hands together while screaming in their tongue. The general couldn't make out their guttural growls and hisses. Their language reminded him of some of the primitive tongues he'd heard from the stunted tribesmen on Tarsus Opal.

Their words were lost, but the intent was clear. Egged on by the group, the two bruisers screamed in fan-fueled rage as they charged into the crater and brought their clubs down on the general, who was still groping wildly at the magnetic balls with unresponsive hands.

Wooden maces slammed into him with all the force of a tossed metal beam. Balls smashed like cheap clay. Blunt force trauma slid him across the ground like a trash can driven by the wind. All the general could do from his position was curse.

He managed to shift with the next blow, flopping onto his stomach. Several more blows crashed onto his back, driving him into the hard ground.

Pain sensors went off the charts as internal safety protocols registered glitches as the balls smashed into his protective back plates.

Guttural cheers and screams morphed into a chant, repeated by the throng on the crater's edge. In unison, they cried out *Naga-wu* in strained voices, teetering on ecstatic insanity.

The general reasoned this was some pagan god the zealots worshipped and were crying out to in victory.

Despite the failure of internal routines, the general remapped his internal motor controls to compensate for the disorientation caused by the magnetic balls, completing this as another round of beatings were about to begin.

Fortunately, the bruisers had decided to preen before the spectators.

They turned to the throng, and with exultant roars lifted their maces in victory. When they turned to finish off the general, he had already executed his modified on-the-fly program.

One bruiser gripped his mace with rage, and with rippling wild arm muscles brought it down in an overhead stroke, surely meant to finish off the general by bashing in his head. Rolling out of the path at the last possible second, the general leapt to his feet, surprising the bruiser.

He slammed his hand against the bruiser's chest. Staggering backwards, the wild man cried in pain and naked fury. The onlookers shrieked *Naga-wu* in fevered pitches.

In truth, the general had hoped to quickly dispatch the bruiser by punching through its chest, ripping out its still-beating heart, and crushing it before his eyes. But its flesh was more like tough hide than skin. Things don't always go as planned.

Either the magnetic field still affected him to some degree, sapping his strength, or the bruiser's hide was much tougher than he'd first thought.

The second bruiser paused as its thick mind attempted to piece together the situation. And the general, a superlative warrior bot, capitalized on the hesitation.

Turning, the general launched himself in the direction of his sword, which was still yards away. He thought the nail gun would be good right now, but once the balls had covered him he'd lost track of the rifle.

He ran, but his body still didn't move as fast as he expected. Balls weighed on him, tugging him in a thousand directions. Extending his free hand, he reached for his sword.

An electric wave cascaded over him, beginning at his fingertips. It ran up his arm to disperse in his body. He sensed an invisible arc, an unseen bridge of distorted ambient, traveling from him to his sword.

A song of metal.

The invisible, magnetic force tugged on his arm, wanting to yank him over. Coming to a dead stop and planting his feet firmly on the rough ground was the only way to prevent himself from being pulled over. The force took on a wispy form, visible as radiating bands of magnetic energy extending outward from the general.

His sword, still embedded in the hard ore ground, shook. It vibrated with a life of its own, and before the general knew what to make of it, the sword ripped itself from the ground and flew towards him.

Naga-wu! Naga-wu!

Thanks to the general's keen perception and rapid-fire reflexes, he positioned himself to receive the flung sword by its hilt, rather than letting it chop him in half.

His iron hand tightened on his sword, and the energy imbued by the immersion into the glowing ore vein now coursed through his circuits, renewing him. The uncrushed, remaining balls on him were completely repulsed, tossed away like an invisible hand had plucked them off.

The general imagined a smile creeping across his face as he turned to face the two bruisers.

Giving a roar that equaled the bruisers in intensity, the general charged forward, his sword before him.

One bruiser sped forward to intercept him, its club gripped high.

A second before coming within striking distance of the club, the general sidestepped to his right, bringing his sword around in a wide arc, hip level. It caught the bruiser in his midsection and the five hundred pound sword passed through him, barely losing inertia. The top half of the bruiser slid off the bottom—it was dead before it even realized it. The general didn't slow, his sights set on the second bruiser.

This one, having a front row seat to the dissection of his buddy, slowed. The monstrous club he held high lowered as the ferocious rage-filled yell dwindled to nothing and the blood drained from his face.

Before the general reached the bruiser a dull hum vibrated through the mountaintop, causing him to stop. Within two seconds, the hum graduated to a low rumble, then became grinding. It matched the sound of grating metal on metal he'd heard earlier in the mountains.

The mysterious mountain dwellers gathered on the edges of the crater shrieked again, but this time the shrieks were tinged in fear. Promptly they scattered away from the crater's edge with wild howls, disappearing from sight. A bunch of cockroaches scurrying for dark pantries.

The bruiser in the crater glanced over its shoulder as the spectators scattered. Dropping its club, the bruiser ran to the crater's edge and scrambled up its side to disappear from sight.

Curious as to what new devilry was approaching, the general followed the monstrous form up the side of the crater.

A short distance away, just on the other side of an outcropping, a yellow and orange light sparked. The grating noise, which was quickly becoming unbearable, was also coming from that direction.

An out-of-control starship crashing into a planet wouldn't have made a noise as terrible as the grating sound that overwhelmed the general. It reverberated through his body and set him on edge.

The light and sound were from the same source. As the general stepped toward the light it moved from behind the outcropping, showing itself to actually be sparks.

Bits of rock and pebbles shook off boulders as the vibration intensified.

An object circled around jutting rocks—the cause of the sparks, the grinding sound, the vibrations. A large serpent.

It slithered from behind the outcropping, its metallic body digging into the earth and scraping against it in an awful way, sparks shooting from the collision.

Its head was at least four feet in diameter, its body about as wide, and when its blue burning eyes spotted the general, it reared back, lifting at least twenty feet off the ground and cutting loose with a terrific metallic hiss.

As it moved, the general noticed its metal body was like a reptilian form of chainmail. Large bands composed it, sliding over each other as the snake maneuvered. When it lifted, bits of cooling burn slag and charred ore nuggets dropped from its belly, which still glowed hotly orange and yellow. The friction of metal against ore stone made the awful sound.

This could only be one thing.

"Naga-wu," the general whispered as he stared with an intensity brought out in dire situations that most rational humans avoided. "You're not the first pagan god I've fought," he growled.

Possibly aware it didn't face any ordinary prey, Naga-wu regarded the general with sharp eyes.

As the two opponents sized each other, the general wondered if its meals came from bound sacrifices who'd fainted dead away as it arrived. He wouldn't put it past heathen mountain tribes to do something like that out of crazed superstition. If they were ready to worship a sword from the sky, then they'd probably put their lot with anything.

Intrigued at the unknown opponent, the iron serpent brought the rest of its body around the outcropping, all fifty feet, drawing up to itself like a coiling spring, getting ready to unleash a deadly strike.

Many times the general had been locked in encounters that often ended in death, with seemingly overwhelming opponents. The general's many successes, and the occasional loss, weren't based on the premise that he attempted to win a fight.

He'd never assume to have won a battle before the first punch was thrown. But he knew if he was going to die, he would drag his enemy along for the ride.

As the general studied the serpent, he took in its movements, processing, working to identify any weakness to exploit.

The serpent, transfixed by this new challenger, doubtless did the same.

Then the general struck first.

He went from standing still to rapidly accelerating, bringing his sword forward in case Naga-wu lunged. Anything less than a quick snake would've been caught off guard.

Naga-wu launched forward, but not straight forward. It sailed left, then with stunning precision arced its body mid-air, blindsiding the general.

The serpent used its head like a battering ram, completely catching the general off guard and bulldozing him.

That blow would've undoubtedly crushed most flesh and blood opponents. Tremendous force knocked the general sideways. He went with the movement, giving into the force as he teetered off balance.

Even so, the general still had the presence of mind to bring his sword around in a devastating backhand. It caught Naga-wu on its underside. Recoils of metal on metal sent the sword flying away, wrenching it out of the general's hand as a deep gonging sound bellowed. It felt like the general had just struck an anvil.

Following the violent motion of his sword, the general hit the ground hard. Before he could react, Naga-wu was clamping its mouth over him. Besides two massive dagger fangs leaking a putrid fluid, its mouth held many smaller, razor teeth curved backward to hold prey in check. The serpent lifted its head with the general in its mouth like it was attempting to swallow him in one huge gulp.

But he would have no part of that.

Grabbing hold of the right fang, he flexed with all his might. It bent slightly, the metal buckling, then gave out with a loud crack. Dark fluid squirted out unchecked. Surprised and shocked, Naga-wu instinctively spit out the general as its head jerked back in revulsion.

Tucking and rolling as he hit the ground, the general thought of the nail gun as he popped upright and bolted for his sword, extending his hand towards it.

Similar to his experience in the crater earlier, the sword reacted to his desire and flew back into his hand, attracted by the super-charged magnetic field he suddenly found himself able to wield.

Catching his sword, he immediately spun in place, keeping inertia and momentum. He manipulated the electric pulses coursing through his body, reversing bias of his current flow so that now his hand repulsed his weapon. This caused it to accelerate like a massive nail, a rail gun bullet headed for the serpent that was barreling toward the general.

The sword pierced Naga-wu through its open mouth, puncturing its skull from the inside and erupting through the top of its head.

Immediately the serpent howled in a monstrous metallic voice, in devastating pain as it lost control of its body.

The beast began a terrible writhing death dance.

Its spinning and thrashing body scraped deep furrows into the ore mountain, brightening the blue night in showers of sparks similar to an unexpected detonation at a fireworks factory. Chunks of white-hot slag peppered the area, igniting a couple of small, bone-dry shrubs.

The thrashing continued for another minute as it rolled upon itself.

Finally, with a terrific shudder, Naga-wu dropped to the earth, still. Dead.

The general, his body weak and in pain from the battle trauma, limped over to the serpent and planted his foot on the dead beast's head as he slid his sword out. The scraping sound sent a shiver up his metallic spine.

"And you're not the first pagan god I've killed," the general said as he docked his sword onto his back. The guard and hilt formed a cross above his head.

A quick search of the ground turned up his nail gun. He slung it over his shoulder.

One last examination of the battlefield on the mountain's summit showed one bruiser cleanly sliced in half, hundreds of iron ore rocks, and one dead snake. Bits of melted slag and brush smoldered. Quite a scene.

The general descended the Iron Mountains.

All the tribesmen and wolves he'd met and hadn't killed on the way up steered clear of him on the way down. Many times he caught glimpses of movement from the corner of his eye or a light twig snap that seemed out of place. But no more encounters.

On his way down, the general heard a new name reverently whispered throughout the Iron Mountains.

Anaga-wu.

Sometime after nine p.m., Winder sat on a barstool. He used only two of the feet as he leaned forward, propped against his workbench. On it sat the patchwork computer equipment he'd rigged to intercept all frequencies of transmission signals. Tonight he'd been focusing on the Sixth.

Entranced with the raging war the next planet over, Winder had skipped dinner, so caught up in listening to the unfolding events. He'd taken a break a half hour ago to grab a quick snack. But the war pulled him back as if he was a voyeur to devastation.

The planet Erudia had been cast into turmoil once again.

Once General Mikeal and his Sixth mechs pulled off-planet, the uneasy order the military had established rapidly dissolved.

Erudians, a generally peaceful civilization, had neither the stamina nor willpower to resist the mysterious inter-dimensional aliens called Shamblers because of the way they shuffled when moving. The natives had quickly crumbled once the alien invasion renewed.

Shamblers' uncanny mind-stealing control held little regard for the destruction of a species. Their weapons didn't fire bullets or energy. They simply drove people mad. Then those became the weapon. Erudians were being turned into killers under the cruelest circumstances.

The invading aliens wouldn't stop with the destruction of Erudia and the millions of inhabitants. Like a cancer, the alien infection would spread through the five other inhabited planets in the Erdine planetary system.

A whole solar system on the verge of collapse. And the Sixth Space Wing was all that held it in check. They'd begun another sustained on-planet military campaign on the heels of the general's exit.

Operation Erudia Freedom II was in full swing. The goal was simple: crush the Shamblers and the infected Erudians. And the Sixth Space Wing, sans the general commanding his mechanical warriors, had their hands full.

What added fuel to the fire was the arrival of Vesuvian mercenaries on-planet. They stood at the fringes of the battle, pirate teams ambushing on-ground troops.

The Sixth were fighting two enemies on two fronts.

Winder heard all this over the intercepted channels on his comm. Much of the battle chatter was encrypted, but could be easily unraveled by the motivated. Secure command and control channels were triple encrypted. Even he found those difficult to break.

But to someone like Winder, that just meant he had to work a little slower. With a pressing feeling of little time, he scanned the less secure channels in the hopes of getting some good intel on the Sixth's motives for the general.

He paused, thinking of the general. *The* general. General Mikeal.

A warrior he'd grown up believing encompassed everything great about America and Earth. Duty, honor, sacrifice. That was the general.

Now he was on the run.

Surely there was much more to the story. There always was. To think of the general as a criminal would be like Winder disbelieving he needed air to survive. That simple.

But then the innocent never run, do they? That's what he'd always heard.

After having spent the better part of the night hovering over his radio with his back near breaking, Winder felt some relief as he concluded there were no active searches for the general. At least none he could find.

Propping the General Mikeal action figure on his table, he took a vanilla wafer off a plate. He idly popped it onto his tongue to dissolve.

Then he gagged, spitting it out. Shuddering at the rancid flavor, Winder went to his food replicator, an upright machine mounted to the floor in the center of the kitchen. He ran a diagnostic on his CookMatic kitchen appliance used to print 3D food from a base protein and seaweed gel.

A knock on the door interrupted him.

Winder answered to a figure dressed in layers.

On the plains, most of the dwellers had adopted the native style, wrapping themselves in many layers. At first glance, they'd appear to be rags. Covering arms and legs and twisted around necks and torsos, the dress didn't serve much utility beyond keeping skin from the blistering sun. Most were dyed, dipped in reds and greens and blues in buckets of staining flower extracts. That was the extent of what made plains clothes fancy: torn and frayed rags in brilliant colors.

This functional garb was why snooty city-dwelling Wudenians provoked their simple cousins by calling them *dirtrags*.

In their native tongue it meant something far worse.

Robed in traditional Wudenan garb of purples and yellows and deep crimsons, the stranger's face was partially obscured by a shemagh, as though they wanted to remain anonymous. Or mysterious. Either way, it set Winder's nerves on edge for a visitor at this time of night, especially because he didn't recognize them as a neighbor.

"I'm looking for someone," the stranger said. Simple and to the point. A man's voice, husky and deep. A voice that sounded tired, filled with the failures and triumphs of a hard-lived life. Definitely not a native Wudenian. But Winder was only speculating.

"No one here besides me," Winder said casually, placing himself more solidly in the doorway.

The stranger's directness immediately put Winder on guard—this could be someone from the Sixth looking for the general. Despite his weak body, Winder would give his life to protect the general with every bit of strength he could muster.

But Winder's subtle movement didn't go unnoticed by the stranger as he stepped back, shifting the scarf he'd wrapped around his head: like he was securing loose ends before taking sudden action. To make matters worse, Winder caught a glimpse of the stranger's arm where a sleeve had slid back an inch. It was metal.

Everyone knew the general's dislike for cyborgs. No, *hatred*.

From issue one of the *Adventures of General Mikeal* series of pulp books he'd read as a kid, Winder knew the general despised them. Especially after his first run-in with them on BattleSat. Of course, this was before the Earthen moon had broken apart.

Winder knew the cyborg was there for the general, hungry to turn a profit with the general's invaluable Martian ore parts.

Once engineers discovered the real value of Martian ore as a stable, reliable core for Slipstream Drives, word quickly spread. Planetary war broke out as every nation involved in Mars mining operations claimed mineral rights.

The value of the general's raw material could easily fund a small planet. He'd been created from the ore when its true value hadn't yet been realized. This also meant the general became bounty number one to those hoping to make profits through murder.

Lop off an arm, a finger, a backplate, and an opportunist could live in luxury. But there was one serious flaw to that plan: the general wouldn't willingly roll over and give up any part of his body. Most failed bounty hunters knew that very well, shortly before they died.

The fact that a cyborg was looking for the general meant word had already spread about him being on Wuden. This also meant American Forces would be on ground soon searching for the rogue general.

This thought fueled Winder's desire even more to keep his childhood hero safe.

"I've heard different," the stranger whispered, not caring to mask his short-fused anger and annoyance. "I'm Sergeant Glass. Where's the general?" he demanded.

Immediately Winder stepped back into his doorway, grabbing a bag tucked in a carved out portion of hallway wall. Tossing it to the ground activated the contents.

Five metallic balls, each the size of a large fist, came to life. Blades sprang from the balls, shredding the bag to ribbons as the balls took flight. Winder had created them after watching an archaic horror video with similar death machines. That's why he'd named them *Phantasm* balls.

With reflexes Winder couldn't even fathom, Glass bounded away from the doorway as the balls came to blade-wielding life.

Ripping off the restrictive tatters he'd donned, Glass produced a disruptor from his hip as the balls circled him.

One zigzagged left then right, closing the distance. Demonstrating his obviously advanced training, Glass was able to draw a bead on the ball. He slagged it with a disruptor blast. Quickly he dispatched the four other balls that hovered around him, but he seemed reluctant to press an attack.

All that remained were smoking, burnt fragments and a heavy odor of charred metal.

Glass now aimed his disruptor at Winder's midsection. "Unless you want to end up like your toys," Sarge nudged one black and smoking shell with the toe of his boot, "tell me where the general is."

The disruptor pointing at his midsection terrified Winder. Twice in just as many days he'd been at the business end of a gun. He didn't like that trend one bit. Despite his urge to run away, he did his best to show a poker face. "They served their purpose," he said, a forced half-smile on his face.

As Glass' face tried to process Winder's cryptic response, one section of Winder's wall crumbled, heavy brick disintegrating in an avalanche of dust and gravel.

PowerMan burst through, positioning its massive body between Winder and Glass.

This surprised Glass even more than the balls.

But, like a seasoned soldier, Glass didn't take too long to adapt to the emerging situation. Recovered from the initial surprise, he fired his disruptor. It harmlessly dissipated against PowerMan's reinforced, grounded chest. Moving forward surprisingly fast for a behemoth, it clutched for Glass' disruptor, snapping it in half with a clamp of its pinchers.

Igniting his ankle rockets, Glass bounded into the air, well out of reach of PowerMan.

Now pulling a ballistic pistol, Sarge cracked off a shot at Power-Man. The bullet struck it in the shoulder, disintegrating on impact. Kinetic force swung its shoulder back, but it was no more than an annoying mosquito to the powerful bot. Shifting to keep itself between Glass and Winder, PowerMan stared at the floating man with burning amber eyes.

Emboldened by the surety of his protector, Winder called out, "What do you want with the general, bounty hunter? If you can't stand against PowerMan, how do you expect to take him? He'll crush you like a Styrofoam cup."

"I'm no bounty hunter," Glass replied, bobbing as his ankle

rockets metered fuel flow to keep thrust stable.

"You're a cyborg," Winder said. "That's enough for the general to hate you."

This single statement appeared to cause Glass to pause. His pistol lowered.

Then a siren cut through the air. The abruptness caught the attention of both Glass and Winder—for an instant they both searched the surroundings.

Suddenly Glass turned, and with a burst of exhaust from his rockets flew into the nearby field of four-foot high grass, disappearing from sight.

Three cruisers—hovercraft terrain scrubbers each carrying a pair of magistrates—zipped along the roadway running near Winder's home. With flashing lights and a piercing wail, they flew past, fading into the distance as they attended to some crisis elsewhere.

Winder breathed again, not sure when he'd last taken a breath. He figured Glass had left, spooked away by the local police.

If this one bounty hunter knew about the general, then others would know. Who else would be looking for him, and how had the word gotten out? So much for Winder thinking he was the only one to know about the general crashing on Wuden.

As Winder contemplated this, it occurred to him maybe those claim jumpers had seen more than what he had first thought. Or it could've been any other person that'd seen more than they needed to see and hoped to earn a cheap credit off information someone would find valuable enough to pay for.

"Thanks buddy," Winder said to PowerMan, patting him on the shoulder. Turning, he looked to the massive hole where his wall used to be. He sighed.

Stepping from his house enough to have a clear view of the Iron Mountains, he watched the blue borealis churning above the range.

In the distance, a flash sparked at the top of the highest peak, what the locals called the Great Wolf Tooth. Winder thought the flash was an orange and yellow lightning bolt. Or maybe a fire.

The flash intensified and then disappeared, replaced by the mountain night of glowing blue. Nerves still raw from the encounter with the bounty hunter, Winder wondered if the general had anything to do with that peculiar flash.

Passing by a tarp hung on the outside wall like a flag, the general limped into Winder's house. He tossed the Nova car keys onto a hallway table like he'd just returned home from the office, spent. "I need a drink," he said as he stopped by the workroom.

One wall had cans of motor oil stacked one upon another, an ancient ziggurat of lubricant. Once he briefly scanned the offerings, the general settled on Quaker Lube XL, a brand he'd never heard of before.

He grabbed the can, and—after giving it an investigative sniff—used his pinky finger to punch a small hole on the top of the can. He upended it, draining it in one mighty swallow. Tossing the can tossed aside, he grabbed another and opened it in the same manner, taking a more leisurely, sophisticated sip.

The first was to quell his great thirst; the second was to enjoy the taste.

When the general walked along the hallway he saw Winder sitting at the radio table. Partly slumped over, his head was barely held aloft by a tired arm. His eyes were half closed, like sleep was but a second away. A monitor next to his radio buzzed with electric life, giving him five camera views of the perimeter of his house and property.

Springing up, Winder wiped a stream of drool swinging off his chin. "You're back," he said, trying to mask his tired voice with a fake dose of alertness. After a few moments the sleep cobwebs drifted away, his eyes becoming more coherent. Then he said, "I had a visitor. A bounty hunter."

The general's head perked up. He examined the hole in the wall again with newfound attentiveness.

"It was a cyborg," Winder said.

Immediately the general's mind flooded—the same way old, ingrained emotion fills a head when that's all its ever known. The general couldn't help but default to those same conflicting feelings he'd been tormented with since taking on cyborgs into the Sixth Mechanized.

Old prejudices die hard. And he'd had hundreds of years to nurture his hatred. "Tell me about the bounty hunter cyborg," the general said as he moved to the workroom where Winder had repaired him.

Winder relayed the harrowing experience with all the emotion of someone worried about having their life unexpectedly snatched away. The general sat silently, absently stroking his chin. He disregarded Winder's emotive state as typical for civilians not used to the passion of fighting, focusing only on the facts.

And as he listened to Winder describe the cyborg in detail, the general began to have a notion of who it was: Glass. That Glass had found him was reason enough for concern.

Would the Sixth arrive on Winder's doorstep? This hovel in the middle of a mud field wouldn't be much protection. Maybe it was time for the general to move on.

The general took a seat on the worktable as he rubbed his left shoulder. Finding the clavicle plate which one of the wolves had managed to work its jaw under, he wiggled it like a prize fighter would shake a tooth knocked loose in the third round. It snapped off, and he tossed it onto the table before taking another sip.

Winder suddenly became aware of the general's sorry condition. "Hey, I see you... wow, you look like crap. What happened?"

"I stepped on a snake," the general responded, simply.

"Oh wow. You found your sword," Winder said, eyeing the large weapon which had begun as a five-foot iron beam the general had used in the excitement of battle. Only the general was capable of wielding it in such a ferocious manner that others began to view it as a sharp weapon. "Can I..." Winder started, holding out his hand as if he were actually capable of holding the heavy weapon.

Absently, the general undocked the sword from his back and just as absently drove it into the floor two feet, splintering the decorative floor tile.

"Oh, ok. I just remodeled my floor last year, but..." Winder stated, somewhat crestfallen as he looked at the shattered tile work.

But that wasn't enough to keep him from stepping close to examine the sword, careful not to touch the relic as if lightning would arc from the sky and consume him for sacrilege. "I've read a lot about you," Winder said. "A lot. I remember when dad first showed me an archive documentary recorded shortly after the Tax Wars. I was five. It was incredible seeing the devastation you, a young liaison robot turned warrior, brought on the enemy."

Leaning back, the general relived those early years of his adventurous life.

America had been on the verge of defeat on BattleSat. Mining and liaison bots had been ushered to the war satellite, the moon, in a last-ditch effort to turn the tide.

There Mikeal, having lived with the Jacobys up till that point, had cut his teeth as a young protocol robot turned soldier, rallying the near-defeated mechs and almost single-handedly decimating the combined Mexican and Canadian forces.

But even that wasn't his greatest moment.

When Wargod—a rogue mining A.I. on Mars—had attempted to wipe out post-war Earth, it was Mikeal who'd warned humankind and defeated the runaway program. He'd saved the world.

But that was over three hundred years ago. Ancient history to any earth-dweller. Reduced to novelty trivia and gee-whiz information. The more time passed, the more irrelevant history became.

"Tell me," the general said, with a curiosity uncharacteristic of his usual, stoic self. "You're an Earther," the general began, noting the items around the hovel from his home planet. "It looks like you spend every spare credit on Earthen trinkets. How come you've never gone back to Earth? Enlisted? Someone with your skill can be valuable in the American Forces."

Winder's eyes drifted down as thought in deep retrospection of a question he'd asked himself a million times. Then he held up his crippled left arm. "I don't think they'd take me," Winder said solemnly.

"Probably not," the general stated with little empathy before taking another drink.

"Plus," Winder continued, "I haven't traveled the known universes like you, but I've learned the dream is usually better than the reality."

At this the general nodded, approving of the young man's wisdom.

They sat silent for a couple minutes, uneasy silence between them.

Finally, Winder cleared his throat. "One thing has bugged me that I wish I knew about you, general," he said. "Mind if I ask?"

The can of Quaker Lube XL, a crudely processed motor oil, was quite different than the pure synthetic oils and lubes the general was used to. Similar to comparing filet mignon to a dead rat. The oil rushed to his head, slightly disorienting him and making his topical sensors prickle with washes of comforting heat.

The general, not used to such candor from anyone, would've typically berated the individual into silence, accompanied by choice curse words and threats. But the bootleg motor oil loosened his inhibitions to the point he leaned back on the table, allowing the warm, fuzzy feeling to creep over his body. "Shoot," he said in response.

"Did you ever name your sword?" Winder asked. "I mean, every cool sword has a name, right? So I thought maybe you…"

The general had never considered anything as superhero-ish as naming his sword. He thought for a nano-second. "You mean like Excalibur?" the general asked.

"Yeah. Exactly," Winder said, childish enthusiasm pouring from his face. "But something cooler than that. A sword with a good name is like having a woman with a good name."

"But you're unmarried," the general observed—nothing in Winder's house showed any indication of a woman coming within ten miles—to which Winder blushed.

Winder went on to elaborate as his shoulders shrugged. "I'm just saying a name would be written in history books. It'd become a person. A personality."

"And what would you name this?" the general inquired, pointing at his sword with a hand becoming more and more unsteady by the second.

"Here," Winder said. From his pocket he enthusiastically pulled a folded piece of yellowed paper. Carefully he unfolded it and flattened out the wrinkles on his lap. "I got interested in names after reading about Elric and his soul-snatching demon sword *Stormbringer.* I thought of these: Stormcloud, Deathbringer, and Stormsword. But this is it," Winder paused, his wide eyes looking at the general. Then he blurted out, "Orecrush!"

"OreCrush?" the general said, like the name filled his mouth with bile as he spoke. "OreCrush," he said again, this time testing the sound and the inflections it drew from him.

"OreCrush," the general mouthed. "Sounds like a five year old thought of that name," he said right before drifting off into low power mode.

The dark-skinned bounty hunter wore the husks of dead robots for armor. A golden head, the lower jaw sawed off and the brain scooped out, fitted him perfectly for a helmet.

Over his armor he wore traditional garments like those worn on the plains, a long cloak with a hood and something like a shemagh scarf bundled on the neck. Through the spring and fall massive windstorms similar to haboobs would descend from the Iron Mountains and sweep across the grasslands, bringing chilling wind and stirring up dust. The cloak protected from that. It was also a great way to keep Wudenians away.

Dressed in the pressed whites of Werlan citizenry, they'd judge him in his dirty rags as one more hick from the country spending his meager credits in Greater Werla, the crystal city. They'd curse him at worst, ignore him at best. Either way he was fine to have them stay away. He had business to conduct. Dangerous business.

A monstrous city-state spanning miles, Werla sat on the western slopes of the plains. A crystal mine lay to the south, a geographical wonder in itself filled with large plates of crystal shimmering white and clear. These panels were used as facades on buildings that'd catch the brilliant Wudenan sun and burn with fiery color, giving the city its nickname.

But it was night. And dark.

Residents called this old neighborhood on the southern edge of town "the Noose," partly because the borough's layout faintly resembled an executioner's toy, partly because only a dead man could make it out of the squalor. Or so they said.

It was the kind of place Bar-San liked to work. One more scream cutting through the night wouldn't draw attention. Screams were like bird chirps in the Noose.

Bar-San pressed himself into the alleyway, drawing his scarf across his mouth to stifle the feces stench that clung to every brick and railing.

For the past week he'd been living here, hopping from cheap hotels that charged by the hour. He had practically faded into the background of life as he watched one *woman*.

Scratch that.

One *robot*.

Bar-San called her Esmerelda Blue Eyes.

He'd devoted time to learn her life patterns. Her inception date and manufacturer. Her likes and dislikes, favorite restaurants, when she turned off the lights for the night. The month prior he'd traveled to Nexus, the industrial planet, to see if she'd returned to her maker. Many times unhindered robots seemed to do that. Return home when on the run. Just like humans.

He'd studied her so much she'd begun infiltrating his dreams. That's when he knew it was time to act.

Across the roadway on the sidewalk of the squalor city block an occasional figure hurried along, some pedestrian out late. Probably up to no good. Nothing good ever happened in the Noose at two in the morning.

He'd tracked Esmerelda to Wuden the planet and Greater Werla the city. She hadn't run too far from her owner.

Being a mid-level sentient robot, Esmerelda still had enough brain power to be on her own. And cunning. She'd leave her home at random times of the day, taking strolls through the neighborhood. Eventually she'd work her way back to her flat, disappearing behind locked doors.

As Bar-San watched the residential high-rise across the street, a figure poked its head out of a doorway.

Just as he'd expected.

Esmerelda's randomness wasn't so random after all. He'd correctly surmised her previous three *random* walks. Robots had a bad habit of falling back into routine. It was simply not in their nature to stay erratic.

Tonight, he'd decided a day ago when she first entered his unconscious in a dream where she seemed too real, he'd make the kill.

He watched the robot. Once Esmerelda had assured herself it was safe, looking right and left along the sidewalks for several minutes, she left the safety of her building. Just then a transport ship lumbered across the sky headed for the nearby port, its engines rumbling through the buildings. Windows shook in their panes.

Clearly she was nervous, even at this time of night. Nervous robots could be irrational, just like humans. Bar-San remained confident in his ability to handle the situation. Still, he needed to remain cautious.

Rule one of manhunters: On any day any bounty could kill you. That included robots.

Esmerelda watched the transport disappear behind skyscrapers as the rumble faded. Stepping onto the sidewalk, she moved speedily, hands tucked in her long coat with her shoulders hunched forward. She'd also hoped to fade into the background. Just like Bar-San.

On feet conditioned to move swiftly with purpose but yet remain nearly silent, Bar-San backed into the alleyway. Turning, he sprinted back to a location he'd decided on the first time he saw it. Two alleyways narrowed then intersected, forming a near perfect *T*. A choke point could easily be fashioned with metal dumpsters, which is what he'd done earlier.

This had become his noose.

Most pedestrians stayed clear from here. Alleyways were short-cuts to the morgue.

But not her. Esmerelda stuck to the areas where others avoided. She thought that would keep her safe. Bar-San would prove her wrong. So very wrong.

Scrambling up the side of a building with the ease of a cat, Bar-San perched himself on a thin ledge twenty feet up. Sitting like a vulture in a tree, he rested his back against the brick wall. Pulling the hood over his head, he waited.

Thirty minutes later Esmerelda entered the alley, just like he'd expected.

Cautiously—but not cautiously enough, as she didn't realize what awaited her—she padded forward until she came to the inter-section. There she paused.

Wrapping his hand in a bundle of cording he'd strung up earlier, Bar-San leaped off the ledge. His body served as a counterweight, and he gently lowered to the alleyway cobblestone. Dumpsters were attached to the other end of the cords, and by clever rigging of them through pulleys, the dumpsters gently slid into place, blocking the exits.

Frantic, Esmerelda's head went in all directions before she realized she was trapped. Backing against a wall, she turned to face the one who trapped her.

"Who are you?" Esmerelda gasped. "What do you want with me?"

"You shouldn't have hacked your processor. Ran away," Bar-San said. His voice carried less emotion than the fleeing robot's.

"Then Ang-Palius sent you," Esmerelda said at the grim realization the baroness she escaped from two weeks ago had, in fact, sent a bounty hunter after her.

"Did you think the baroness would just write you off? She could've left you in that trash heap." Bar-San said in a steady voice. He continued, "But she sought to save you. You've shown ungratefulness."

"So now I'm to be killed?" Esmerelda asked, "Or to be brought in alive?"

"Whichever's easiest for you," Bar-San answered.

The average bounty hunter wouldn't think to lock themselves in a cage with a roaring lion: speed, more strength than a man, and lightning quick reflexes would make the confrontation end before it ever really began. Going toe to toe with a robot normally didn't end well. That's where Bar-San found himself now.

But he was not average.

With a savage cry, Esmerelda leaped toward him, closing the distance in a flash. Anticipating her route, Bar-San sidestepped at the last moment, forcing the robot to throw up her hands to keep from slamming into the brick wall. The force of her collision split the bricks under her hands.

Bar-San put to good use what his mother Penellas, an archipelago girl, had taught him from the moment he could stand upright on his own.

She had been brought up in the witching ways of sense skills. But she'd betrayed her order when she'd fallen in love with a young mercenary, reckless but tender, by the name of Bar-Sturn. The night before her execution, he'd made a daring rescue and they'd sped away into the night to live in seclusion. But happy.

In a final act of revenge, Penellas taught her son the sense skills that were forbidden for any male to learn.

And his father taught him how to kill.

Cursing in anger, Esmerelda spun around at lightning speed, producing a designer mini disruptor from where she had tucked it under her blouse. But she wouldn't even get a chance to flip the safety switch.

Bar-San was already upon her, grabbing her firing arm with strength uncharacteristic for a mere man. Distracted by his crushing grip, Esmerelda only heard the faint crackle of the plasma dagger as Bar-San jabbed it into her throat.

During the week he'd been monitoring her, Bar-San had also been studying her design schematics. The point he'd chosen should disrupt her motor circuits, almost instantly turning her into a quadriplegic, which would make life easier for him.

Esmerelda shrieked as her knees buckled. Bar-San's plasma dagger ate through precious plating, inserting itself in her fragile wiring. Wires were turned into slag, hot lava pouring through her body.

Feebly, she attempted to clutch his hood with her free hand, but her strength quickly failed. Bar-San let go of her arm and wrapped his own arm around her delicate waist to keep her upright. From a distance it looked like a couple in love dancing by moonlight.

Taking a firm hold of his plasma dagger hilt, Bar-San finished severing her head so that her lifeless body dropped to the filthy alleyway.

He held Esmerelda's head in his hands.

Sitting on a nearby small step, Bar-San gently placed her severed head on his lap. He turned off his plasma dagger, and, after clipping it onto his belt, produced his poignard.

The operation would require delicate work. The plasma dagger would be too messy.

Bar-San's jewel-hilted ceremonial poignard, a sign of the southern mercenary, had been given to him by his father, who'd received it from his father's father. Family legend said it was fashioned from a meteorite that crashed in the Iron Mountains hundreds of years ago. He didn't know if that was true or some rumor spread to liven up family reunions. But it had kept its edge unlike any other bladed weapon he'd wielded. And he'd wielded many.

For him, the legend was true.

Using the stiletto point, Bar-San wedged it between two skull plates. As he did, he noticed the beautiful blue eyes her designer had given her. For a second he considered popping her eyes out to keep as a trophy, but he thought that was a little morbid. Southern mercenaries didn't keep trophies.

Instead, sinking the point of his poignard in, Bar-San twisted it so Esmerelda's head cracked open like a giant metal walnut. Severing wires with his dagger tip, he worked it down to her central processor.

Platinum processors in these older model robots were large, made at a time before platinum became scarce.

Holding the chip, he bounced it in his hand, estimating its value by weight. After Ang-Palius verified this as her runaway robot's processor, he'd receive the bounty promised and the scavenge profits of the processor. Given the weight, his work would pay off big.

Standing, Bar-San spun Esmerelda's cracked head with the beautiful blue eyes in his hand. Then, using his steel toe boot, he nudged his foot against her body that lay on the pavement. Esmerelda had nothing of value to offer besides her brain. And the bounty.

Grasping her head in his hands, the bounty hunter shuffled left, then right. Then he leaped off the pavement and used Esmerelda's head like a basketball, shooting a basket. It travelled in a high arc before slamming on the edge of the dumpster, only to fall to the pavement. He'd missed.

After tucking the processor in his vest, Bar-San sheathed his poignard. Agilely leaping up and over a dumpster, he made his way back to his rent-by-the-hour hotel dive. It was time to wash up and celebrate.

Tonight he'd earned a steak.

The filth and stench and death of the Noose washed off with soap and water. He had a good steak in one of Greater Werla's many high-end restaurants that were built on floating platforms, a half mile above downtown.

That night he turned in early. Early in the morning a shuttle would be waiting for him.

Now Bar-San wore the black ceremonial uniform of the southern mercenary. The fringes of his jacket and shoulder epaulets were yellow. Belt buckles and buttons polished silver. His poignard, now in a decorative sheath, hung secure on a battle girdle of molded carbon that wrapped his torso. It squeezed his midsection close to beyond uncomfortable, giving him an intimidating wedge shape in the process.

He had dressed up for the occasion of appearing before royalty.

Baroness Ang-Palius, the time jumper, held audience aboard the *Erio-Magus*, a renovated battle cruiser. She made short trips on-planet only when necessary, preferring the comfort (and safety) of a contained spaceship. With the sophisticated onboard weaponry and her army of lethal mercenaries, anything short of a small planet-state attempting to overtake the cruiser would be hard pressed.

After the crushing defeat of Ang-Thelus, her jealous half-brother, five years ago, no one had the bravado to attempt another hijacking.

Bar-San's polished black boots echoed in the expansive audience hall, clacking against polished floor painted in a checkerboard pattern. Mirrors lining the wall played against the pattern, tricking the eyes to the point of disorientation. Many would trip or stumble, much to the amusement of the baroness. It was her little joke.

Bar-San knew not to watch the floor as he approached. He doubted he'd succumb to the disorienting effect but didn't take the chance, in case his heightened perception would work against him for once. Keeping eyes laser-focused on the raised dais and throne at the end of the hallway, he strode confidently to stand within fifteen feet of the baroness.

He dipped low with a grand flourish of his arm. "Your excellency," Bar-San proclaimed as he recited rote courtesies taught him by the mercenary code. "Our task is accomplished and continues to remain accomplished."

Time jumpers cashed in long life for temporary riches, the saying went. Ang-Palius was no different.

She had celebrated her thirtieth birthday a month ago, but she was already showing age beyond her years. The brown splotches that were the beloved curse of time jumpers covered most of her delicate olive-tanned arms. Her face, once fair, was already showing the sunken cheeks and sagging skin characteristic of time jumpers. Even artificial rejuvenators couldn't stave off the damage.

But her spirit was that of an impetuous young adult. Thanks to the cocktail of chemicals pumped into her body every morning, she moved with the unhindered pain-free ease of others her age.

Her jet black hair was tussled, some stray ends tangling in her armor.

She wore a full set of tailored, elaborate power armor. More for show than function. For war she kept a room of mechanical battle uniforms, each sized to fit her slender figure.

Staring intently at Bar-San, she shifted on her throne, absently biting a fingernail. When she heard his report, she nodded. Smiled. "I see you have no robot in tow," the baroness purred. "I take it you couldn't convince her to return."

Two of her Red Guards stood at either side of her throne. Rigidly at attention, they remained motionless.

"She made her decision," Bar-San said, producing the platinum processor, the core of the dead robot. Its soul.

Shifting again, Ang-Palius draped one thin leg over the arm of her throne. Her lip pouted out in mock sadness. "I had such high hopes for her, too," she said. Motioning casually, one of her court staff stepped forth, a teenage girl he'd met the last time on the *Erio-Magus*. The baroness had bought her from an orphanage and given her a new name, "Mist the Scholar," before training her as a diplomat.

Quickly, Mist's legs propelled her forward and she snatched the processor from his hand. She produced a flat boxy device that accepted the item before typing on an info sleeve that was apparently tied to the device.

The baroness watched her attentively for several seconds before turning back to the bounty hunter. "I'm pleased with your work. You know that," Ang-Palius said.

Bar-San bowed his head in acknowledgement.

Leaning forward, the baroness said, "I've heard of an opportunity I wouldn't trust to just anyone."

Bar-San was always interested in the opportunities the baroness fed him. They were filled with intrigue and increasing levels of danger. He often thought the baroness and her wild ideas would get him killed one day. Bar-San said, "Ang-Thoth wants me to visit some outland pirates that have been steal—"

"Bah!" the baroness exclaimed, recoiling at the mention of her brother's name. "He throws you crumbs while I offer you loaves. That dog should hurry up and die. They can wrap him in his pretty tents and perfume and bury him. Jumpers can dig him up in a hundred years."

She stood, her chemical painkillers allowing her to glide rather than hobble over to the bounty hunter. When she leaned in close Bar-San could smell her perfume. High valley roses. Sweet and earthy. "I have word General Mikeal is near," the baroness whispered.

Bar-San's jaw clenched and his heart raced. Now she had his full attention. "The Sixth is on Erudia as we speak," Bar-San said, knowing the American military was orbiting the next planet over, "fighting the invaders."

The baroness shook her head, her raven locks falling over her face. "Not him. He's on Wuden," she said, pointing out one of the port windows. Wuden rolled by below as the *Erio-Magus* crawled along its orbit. Then, using that same finger, she traced it along Bar-San's girdle. "I've heard he's alone. A fugitive. Imagine that."

"You know he's no dumb robot," Bar-San countered. "He's not easily cornered in an alley like a rat," he said, reflecting on the relative ease with which he'd dispatched the runaway robot, Esmerelda Blue Eyes. He knew where the baroness, always one for extravagant ventures, was headed. "At least thirty of my brothers have died trying to claim him."

The mercenary craft was a legitimate vocation; it consisted of soldiers of fortune, bodyguards, and business protectors. Often, bounty hunters walked a thin line between legality and lawlessness. Manhunting for the simple sport of killing was illegal, although many times the target could be provoked into combat and the bounty hunter could claim self-defense.

It was one of those activities everyone knew existed, but as long as it didn't get out of hand, everyone turned a blind eye to.

"And what's better," the baroness asked, "than revenge?"

Bar-San said, "Revenge doesn't put food in your stomach. Impractical killing."

"Yes," the baroness said, undeterred. "But with his value… you could retire a king."

Bar-San considered her words. His father, teaching him the business of killing, would've never advocated revenge executions. However, if revenge was exacted along with a bounty… that was a different story. The baroness was one of the few people with the financial backing to sponsor such a bounty.

"There's no other mercenary like you," the baroness added, tracing her finger along the crease of his pressed sleeve. "Twenty robots. And barely a scratch on you."

"Twenty-one," Bar-San corrected her, adding the runaway Esmerelda to his tally.

"There's never been another mercenary like you," the baroness whispered, her decadent words pouring over him. Despite the rigorous discipline that was the foundation of the southern mercenary, nothing could fully insulate a man against the charms of a determined woman.

"Your task will be accomplished," Bar-San said, accepting her contract. He spoke the ritual phrase in the guttural southern tongue: an unbreakable oath.

"Hell Bent for Leather" rattled the rear speakers.

As the song strained over the 8-track, the general adeptly steered the Nova across the plains as Wudenan sun glinted off chrome hubcaps. He easily blew past one hundred mph.

The primitive aspect of driving, as opposed to flying on some interstellar transport or frigate, appealed to the general in a way he couldn't quite process. He'd first noticed this as h'd driven north to the Iron Mountains. But where he headed now was due east. And much further.

The steering wheel was tactile in a different way than a flight control yoke. The response was rough. It vibrated in his hands as he hurled over dips and rocks. Wheels turned to his reaction, biting into the ground. But too sharp a turn and they'd lose traction and slip.

Overhead, high in the Wudenan sky, starships crisscrossed, pollution trails marking their path. Some of the ships he recognized, others he didn't.

A Ceruline pleasure ship, the long and slender vessel trimmed in gold, screeched by. They came from the western arm of the Ceru cluster, a tropical planet overflowing with unrealized desires. Vices were the planet's main export. Many of the soldiers and airmen on leave made that place a favorite destination. They'd return penniless but smiling for months.

An old cargo transport—boxy, weather-beaten from countless intergalactic miles and spewing foul, dark exhaust from twenty jet ports—sputtered on the horizon, about ready to drop from the sky. It lumbered on with its trade goods, bound for Werla or some other port town.

Groups of black corsairs, dreaded mercenary transports, filed by in a tight formation, reminding the general of some of the Sixth's fighters on practice sorties. The dark ships paid him no attention and disappeared to the south.

But tramp haulers and bounty ships weren't the only signs of life.

Hundreds of herd animals waded in the expansive plains. Their black stripes and dark brown hides gave them the look of dirty zebras. They did their best to chew up all the grass. Native grass three feet high flowed as the gentle wind swept over the plains, giving the impression that the animals were standing in a brown ocean.

Bugs escaped from the hundreds of hooves only to find themselves caught in the beak of sly waiting birds. The bugs would be the guests of honor at dinner in the nests of crying young birds.

Veering from the faded dirt path that was barely a road, the general arced around the grazing herd, close enough to get their attention. Several protective bulls on the outskirts stamped their hooves and snorted in disapproval, ready to charge the foreigner in the strange machine.

Winder had given the general his current destination.

Scouring the bazaar, Winder had plied his rudimentary sleuthing skills to track down the Vesuvians. Winder had found out they were out east, past where the plains turned arid. There, the Iron Mountains to the north extended downward to form the northern edge of a great crescent cutting through the land. Some believed they hid somewhere in that desolate stretch: far enough away from civilization and prying eyes but near enough to the mountains to play havoc with sensitive line-feeds and sensors.

After two days, Winder had finally been successful. Some desert nomads, just having recently returned from the east, had told him of an encounter two weeks ago.

Their caravan had run upon a group that at first appeared to be outland pirates.

The caravan lead, a female named Belta Noll, knew them to be Vesuvian; despite their outland garb, she'd easily discerned their mannerisms and accents as Vesuvian. According to Winder, she'd served a four-year tour as an Erudia systems officer and had dealt with their kind on many occasions. Each of which she loathed because of their continual deceptions and unnatural affinity for lying.

With this tidbit of information, the general added it to the case he was forming in his head.

This whole episode that had ended with him fleeing the *Countervail* had begun with the battle on Erudia. There, a Vesuvian terrestrial warship had gotten the jump on him and his mechs. The Sixth's long-range scanners should've picked up the ship's profile: engine signatures, their power consumption and exhaust, were as unique as fingerprints.

So the general had one of his men, Hatch, search the Sixth's networks. Only, his comm had been cut short before he could tell the general what he'd found. Obviously it wasn't good. This had led the general to think the Sixth had a saboteur infiltrating their battle networks.

The apprehension orders given to the *Countervail's* security police concerned him the most. Was there a legitimate reason, or was this one more sabotage of the Sixth's networks?

The general believed the networks had been hacked, but what else was being sabotaged?

And since the whole drama chain had begun with Vesuvians, the general figured the best way to unravel this mystery was to find the nearest Vesuvian. Then ask.

He headed east, not sure what he was looking for, not sure what to expect. He needed to find something, though.

Days had passed since his flight from the *Countervail*.

He realized he hadn't helped the situation by resisting. Then fleeing. The strain and exertion of powering the drop ship had sucked his power nearly empty, muddling his processors and logic circuits.

But what was done was done, he thought grimly.

All he could do now was search out what he needed to know— why he was being apprehended. In his mind he knew that the Vesuvians were somehow tied to the whole ordeal. Find the jackals, and he was sure to find the answers.

A flock of tiny white birds that moved as one entity hovered to the right. Squawking in irritation, the amorphous group broke apart, scattering in various directions. Thousands of wings churned the air.

The general turned the music down as an uneasy feeling crept over him.

He heard the *hum* which would've been imperceptible to the average man. That, coupled with a heightened presence of his surroundings, made the general crank the steering wheel hard to the right.

The ground erupted in an explosion.

A shockwave rippled through him as dirt buckled upward, spraying like water. The Nova skidded, bouncing sideways as it struggled to stay on the ground. Cursing in a way only robots could, the general gripped the wheel to keep control.

Another explosion in front of him caused dirt and shattered

rocks to cascade over the hood. One jagged chunk of stone spider-webbed the windshield.

Hitting the crater fast, the car leaped into the air at an odd angle. It tumbled twice before slamming back to the earth. The front grill dug into soft ground, making inertia flip the car end over end six more times. The car came to rest on its side, looking like the victim of a ravaging tornado. Smoke poured from the trashed engine. Small flames flickered from underneath as the hot, smoking engine ignited dry plains grass.

Slowly, the general slid from between the collapsed roof and the crackling grass as it withered beneath the fire. Reaching to the back seat, he grabbed his sword and the nail gun.

Using the sword as a crutch—thankful no one was near to see—he stood upright, leaning heavily on the hip Winder had repaired. His senses were on high alert, and he kept his guard up.

The first explosion, he thought, had come from the ground. Some type of IED or bomblet he'd driven across. But the subsequent blast reminded him more of a hyper mortar.

Someone was gunning for him.

With the Nova's engine noise and the heavy metal music reduced to a smoking heap, the only sound on the plains was the gentle crackle of a spreading burn.

Then he heard an almost imperceptible whistle coming at him.

Superior reflexes kicked in—using his planted sword as a pole, he vaulted himself thirty feet from where he stood as another mortar slammed to the ground. The concussive blast knocked the general off his feet. He hit the ground hard as dirt and rock rained on him.

Now he was mad.

Although it went against his nature to burrow in a field like a passive rabbit hiding from the ravished hawk, the general did all he could to remain still. Staying low so the plains grass kept him hidden. He listened, waiting for any clue as to who was target practicing on him. After a short, tense minute, he heard the gentle hum of a hovercraft.

With an ear on his target and a restless hand on his sword hilt, the general bolted.

Bounding from the tall grass like a cheetah with its prey in sight, the general gave a battle cry that would've made a cheetah shrink back in fear.

A hovercraft, spotlights scouring the ground even though it was daytime, floated ten feet above the grass. Two occupants dressed in black armor with matching helmets and dark visors stood on the back of the hovercraft. Two more were on the ground, cautiously padding through the grass with disruptors cradled in their arms. All four of them startled at the general's sudden appearance and rage-filled cry.

One on the hovercraft reacted quicker than the rest. They swung a barrel mounted on a pivot toward the general and cut loose.

A barrage of disruptor fire spit from the barrel. The aim was off, though, and the gunner walked the disruptor fire through the grass towards the general.

This simple corrective measure, especially at such a short distance, spoke volumes of an inexperienced gunner.

Still, blasts fired from a seasoned veteran or a lucky strike wrapped in inexperience will both leave a smoking hole if it hits the right spot.

Using his sword as a shield, the general intercepted one blast aimed for his legs before leveling his nail gun. The double pistons pumped out razor shards that peppered the hovercraft. Everyone ducked for cover, including the gunner, who leaped away from the deck-mounted disruptor as the nail gun eviscerated the barrel and shorted the power cells. With an electric *crack* the mounted gun blew apart, knocking the gunner off the back of the hovercraft.

The two on the ground lifted their disruptors and opened up. Energy rippled through the air. One caught the general on the shoulder. He grimaced as his circuitry worked to disperse the excessive energy load. Another blast caught him on his bad hip, spinning him forty-five degrees. But that didn't deter him. Tossing the nail gun aside, he gripped his sword and sprang forward.

One of his opponents backed up, reeking with inexperience or simply unwilling to meet the terrible, charging warrior robot. Before the attacker could take another step back the general brought his sword in a ferocious overheard swipe. It caught the disruptor, cleaving it in half, but missing the weapon's wielder by inches.

As the general moved forward, he noticed their movements weren't what he'd expected.

Hundreds of years of war, facing innumerable enemies on the battlefield, had taught him many things. One of those hard lessons was the ability to estimate an opponent's experience by their body posture.

These were not hardened mercenaries or soldiers sent to claim his head. He'd be surprised if any of them had ever aimed a laser rifle with the desire to kill beyond today.

In a breathless instant, the general leaped into the air as effortlessly as a bird takes flight. Clearing the edge of the hovercraft, he landed on the deck.

The second attacker on the craft, completely unaware of the general's ability to so easily hop aboard the hovercraft, shrank back. In the attacker's fleeting moment of indecision, the general knocked away the disruptor—like the person had forgotten they'd even held a weapon—before using his free hand to knock the attacker off the back of the craft to join their comrade on the ground.

Leaping back off the hovercraft, the general charged the fourth attacker: the attacker was standing in place, not moving, frozen to the spot in fear. With a gut-churning palm fist, he slammed the person's chest. The recipient howled in pain as their breastplate armor cracked with a cheap snap. The attacker flew backwards ten feet to crash to the ground, clutching their chest and grasping for breath.

Striding over to the body, he docked his sword before ripping off the person's helmet. Underneath was a young girl, no more than twenty. She heaved as she sucked in air with unresponsive lungs. And in her eyes, the general saw the paralyzing fear that had killed many men and women on the battlefield.

The general pinned the woman to the ground with one iron foot and a few hundred pounds of foot pressure. She couldn't wriggle free.

"Stand down," the general commanded the other three, "or I crush her like a bug."

The authoritative tone of his booming electronic voice shook them to the point of absolute compliance. They threw their weapons to the ground. One attacker raised his hands above his head like he was under arrest.

Resting one hand on bent knee, the general peered down, his eyes burning with anger. "Who sent you?" he demanded.

Like any civilized planet, Wuden had its fair share of rogues, bandits, opportunists, and bounty hunters. Over the years he'd encountered countless of them. Many wanted to take his life, knowing the value of his ore content. They had become a constant nuisance. Worse than flies.

The girl, caught in a vise, shook her head, but didn't speak.

He slowly lowered his foot onto her breastplate—it began to groan. Any moment it could split apart.

"Who. Sent. You?" The general's words dripped from his mouth.

"No one!" the girl screamed in terror. "No one sent us."

He removed his foot from her chest, and, grabbing hold of her cracked armor, effortlessly hoisting her into the air. Three feet separated her boots from the earth. "How do you know about me?" The general asked.

Clutching her left side and her chest, she finally gasped out, "Saw you fall from the sky. Thought you were a meteorite. Went to investigate. Someone beat us there."

"Who are you?" the general demanded.

"Bera Sol," she said. "My father's a magistrate. Thrace Sol of Werla."

"Junior pirates," the general said. "I could tell from your lack-for-nothing attitude and shiny new equipment. You band with your school mates as some junior level mercenaries with the best weaponry daddy's money can buy, but without the years of battle-earned experience that's critical to any warrior."

"We've got experience," one of the other junior pirates, a boy that was probably waiting for his eighteenth birthday, said. "Two days ago we captured a fugitive from Werla."

"Because you captured some street thug you thought you could capture me?" the general asked. "I've put more bodies under the ground than days you've spent breathing."

Turning back to Bera Sol, he continued his interrogation. "Who else knows about me?"

Information was just as valuable as material. Telling the right person the right thing at the right time could pay off big.

As Bera Sol struggled to catch her breath, legs bicycling uselessly in the air, she took a large gulp of air. "Ang-Palius," she whispered. "I told Ang-Palius."

"A time jumper?" the general asked. "Anyone else?" he demanded, giving her a light shake.

"The bazaar," Bera Sol cried. "A cyborg… that's it. He paid well. Those are the only people I've told. You can have his payout."

The general cut her off with a huff of absolute contempt at the thought of her offering him pocket change. "I don't need your pennies, girl," the general said. He tossed Bera Sol hard to the ground, and she cried out again as her ankle twisted on impact.

"Go and spend the next twenty years learning the art of fighting and killing," the general said. "Then come find me. I'll be happy to split your skulls then."

Stepping away from Bela Sol, he pointed to her pathetic writhing figure before him. "Pick up your friend and leave. Thank whatever pagan gods you worship I don't send you to meet them in hell."

At first the other three young adults—watching the drama unfold with wide, fearful eyes— didn't appear to register the general's words. Then as the words sank in, first one, then the rest, rushed over to her.

Manhandling her, she cried out and cursed them. They carted her to the hovercraft, and after loading her on board, fired up the motors. It wheeled about, flattening the grass. The motors gunned and it rocketed away.

After watching the hovercraft fade on the horizon where it eventually got lost in the plains grass, the general turned to his own vehicle. "Well, crap," he said as he stared at the smoldering ruins of the Nova, now completely useless. The fire underneath had burned itself out.

Wrapping plains garb Winder had given him around himself, the general picked up the nail gun and tucked it within the folds of his clothing. He pulled the hood over his metallic head. From a distance, he could pass as one more lowly plains nomad. No concern to anyone.

The general began walking to the east. As he walked, he wondered what would happen when Glass, so intent on his search, would eventually find him. And as he thought this he fought to suppress the centuries of hatred he held for cyborgs. Even one of his own.

The way east saw the abundant grass plains become sparse, eventually giving in to semi-arid ground. Small clumps of stubborn vegetation remained, rewarded for its tenacity by hot eastern winds and a brutal, unrestrained Wudenan sun.

The eastern edge of the Great Plains reminded the general of his time on Erudia, Wuden' twin. A desert planet. There, from what Winder had told him, the Sixth were still fighting a protracted war.

At this moment he desired nothing more than to be at the front of the battle lines again, to finish the job that should've stayed finished.

The general's job was to drive the enemy before him. It was a job he took as a prime directive. He thrilled in fulfilling his directive.

But, like many soldiers who'd been through battles with all the passion that comes along with battle, he sometimes found the down time between wars as shallow and thin. An interruption from campaign to campaign.

Life only became real when something threatened to take it away.

War could snatch it away in an instant—that's when life became precious.

The general had little stomach for complacency. He was a man of action.

Fortunately, the junior pirates had given him a little excitement for the moment, but there was no gain in killing them. They were still young enough to figure out the business of killing wasn't for everyone.

He cleared another slope. Vegetation thinned, revealing more sand than the rich soil of the plains. Now, the winds rolling from the Iron Mountains turned hot. Each gust seemed to raise the temperature another degree or two. But the ambient temperature was still well within the general's effective operating parameters. Giving the hot environment little more than a passing thought, he brought the headdress lower over his face to keep blowing particles from jamming into his joints. That irritated him.

During the miles of mindless trudging eastward, the general wished he'd brought a can or two of motor oil.

A low moan on the wind interrupted his thoughts. He halted in place.

Before extending his sensory range, he ran a quick internal diagnostic routine to make sure dust hadn't compromised any of his systems, tricking him.

Then he heard it again.

So it wasn't any system malfunctioning.

The pitiful wail came from the east, the direction he was heading, so he continued on, more wary than before. His steps quickened.

As he walked up a hill, windswept dust coating him in a fine layer of grit, he heard the moan again. Now he determined it was an animal, not a person like he'd first thought. Then he heard voices, too.

Frantic, argumentative voices which were attempting to keep

quiet, but were largely unsuccessful. The voices were hoarse, the dialect short and clipped.

When the general crested the dune he saw the object of the voices—and the moan.

Four desert nomads—two adults and two children by their sizes, although it was hard to tell because of the multiple layers of body wraps and the heavy hoods covering their faces—were wrestling with the yokes attached to a sinking camel. It was up to its neck—the beast had obviously stumbled into quicksand, or whatever it was called on this planet. The camel could do nothing more than wail in a pitiful manner, like it understood the fate that was creeping up to swallow it inch by inch, granule by granule.

The nomads were working to secure ropes and bindings around the beast's thick neck. Two other camels—not as unfortunate as their caravan buddy—stood nearby, watching the drama unfold with absolute disinterest. Their lower jaws shifted from side to side as they absently chewed some invisible cud.

The argument appeared to be over the best way to secure the leads to the stuck animal. One nomad attempted to toss a lasso around the camel's neck while another pulled at the coarse rope, intent on derailing the first's attempt.

When they finally noticed the general standing at the crest of the dune, their disagreement ended: the two adults produced laser rifles and the two children playing some sort of tag game seemed to disappear into thin air.

"We have nothing," one of the nomads yelled out in a deep, hoarse voice that gave the statement a menacing tone. "Be on your way."

Instantly, the general recognized the voice as characteristic of the desert nomads.

Lotus flowers were responsible for the deep, hoarse voice of the nomads—although lotus flowers were poisonous, nomads relied on the plant's succulent stems and leaves for survival. An essential source of moisture for man and beast, they were grown in the nomad's magnificent water gardens on the high plains. Only through introducing babies to the plant in small doses were they able to build up an immunity to the residual toxins in the plump green leaves and stalks.

But one side effect of the lotus flowers was the gradual deterioration of the vocal chords, giving the nomads a deep, raspy voice. Even the women.

The general knew the plains garments he wore wouldn't keep him disguised for long. At a distance he might pass as a person, but any closer scrutiny would reveal him as something other than human. Especially to another nomad who would most likely recognize him as a sham.

"I'm not a pirate," the general stated, figuring their defensiveness was due to outland pirates that plagued the less populated areas. "I'm a robot," he finished, which supported the metallic tones in his natural voice.

His statement didn't assure the nomads, their rifles still pointed in his direction. Faintly he thought he heard one flip a safety lever, allowing the rifle to charge.

Inspecting the mini caravan, the general saw the other two camels were loaded with boxes and rolled containers, all held on their backs by netting. It amazed him how such a primitive culture could exist alongside such advanced ones.

The crystal city of Greater Werla was on the western slopes, across the continent separated by thousands of miles. Still on the same planet, though. It boasted technology unlike dozens of other systems.

The nomads were a direct contradiction to that.

They chose to live this simple way, which astounded the general even more. But as he thought about it, was him enjoying the raw, primeval roar of the Nova much different? Nostalgia, maybe? He didn't know, and he didn't really care beyond those few random thoughts.

Taking a few confident steps forward, he threw off his hood and said, "I can help you."

The two adults took a step back. The general didn't know if they'd ever been around a robot. Or even heard of such a thing as a robot.

If they hadn't, then they didn't show it. Peering from under their hoods, they regarded him with wary eyes. But they didn't shrink away or raise any alarm. And as the general neared them, he saw the two children that he had thought had disappeared. Actually, they had dropped to the ground, and, using their sand-colored garments, had blended in almost perfectly with their surroundings, even partly burying themselves up to their knees and elbows. They were learning survival early in this harsh desert.

The general turned his attention to the stuck camel. As he studied its predicament, he took a cautious step and found the semi-firm footing immediately gave way. Like a cat recoiling from water he sprang back, away from the hazard. The trapped camel gave him a look of resigned despair. It was about thirty feet away from solid ground.

"You're nomads," the general said. "How did you not notice the quicksand when you were crawling these dunes before you could walk?"

One of the nomads removed a hood, revealing a woman, skin browned and weathered from a lifetime spent in this environment. Her long, khaki hair with silver streaks running through it had intricate pieces of wood, shaped like animals, ships, or other objects, woven through the braids. She had it bunched together and thrown over her left shoulder. Her laser rifle's buttstock rested on her right. Her head and shoulders were set squarely. Proudly.

"I'm Bola Gath," the woman said, her voice grainy—rough and raw. "We've come to unfamiliar paths because of pirates," she said.

As she spoke, she reached into a pack slung about her waist and pulled out a three inch stalk. Absently, she chewed on one end with all the mechanical precision of one who had done such their whole life. "Some," she pointed off to the east, "tried to rob us. We ran. Didn't see this," she pointed to the camel, "until too late." She spit a wad of chewed fiber from her mouth and wiped her chin.

The other one, who'd shifted her shemagh enough for the general to see was another woman, didn't remove it completely. She kept most of her face hidden as she nodded in agreement.

"Hand me your ropes," the general ordered, the authority in his voice unmistakable.

They complied, handing him the ropes made from entwined strands of vegetation and cured to be almost as strong as pliable steel.

Taking the ropes, the general threw them twice at the camel's head, each time paying keen attention to the strength of his throw, the angle of travel and descent, among many other discreet factors such as wind speed and rope flexibility.

Much like him learning to drive a car, the general, through a minimal amount of practice, became almost an expert at lassoing in a short time.

His next throw caught around the camel's neck, startling the beast. Two more lassos, and two more ropes firmly secured the camel's neck.

Then he lashed the other end of the ropes around his waist. With them firmly secured, he turned away from the camel. He pulled the sword from off his back, at which point the nomads drew in their breaths in surprise and backed away.

Reaching forward, he drove his sword tip into the sand until it hit solid ground, about four feet down. Using his firmly planted sword as an anchor, he pulled himself forward. The ropes became taut and groaned with tension. The weaker fibers snapped, but the ropes held. He repeated this action, replanting the sword and pulling himself forward.

The camel, who had originally fought against the pulling on its thick neck, began to somewhat understand in its dumb animal mind what the general was attempting to do. Having the door to life suddenly reopened, it responded with a burst of unrealized energy. Its mighty legs churned in the sand, looking to gain footing on whatever it could find.

With the general pulling, the camel more or less swam the thirty feet to the edge of the sand trap. There it kicked and clawed its way out of the pit, despite the heavy load still strapped to its back.

The nomads made odd clicks with their mouths once the animal became free—the general figured it was their way of applauding.

The two other camels continued their imaginary chewing as the children emerged from their camouflage. They removed their hoods, two girls, to shake sand from their long, braided hair.

Digging into their satchels, Bola Gath and the other nomad produced more stalks. With heads looking down, they offered the stalks to the general.

An offering of life-sustaining moisture by a nomad was a token gesture of the highest form. Of course, any non-nomad who took them up on the offer would become deathly ill with stomach cramps, followed by crippling diarrhea, and would probably remain curled in a ball for a week wishing they were dead. If they didn't die outright. But that was beside the point.

The general would've preferred oil to water. So instead, he simply nodded in acknowledgement of the sacrificial offering. Seeing this, Bola Gath tucked the stalk back in her satchel.

"Who are you?" Bola Gath asked, her raspy voice carrying a hint of curiosity. "So far here, in the middle of a desert?"

"I'm General Mikeal of the Sixth Mechanized," he stated as he docked his massive sword onto his back.

As she continued giving him a blank stare, the general pointed to the sky. "From up there," at which she nodded, still not under-standing but accepting it at face value.

The other nomad tended to the unfortunate camel that had taken the misstep into the quicksand, checking its joints and brushing its sides with her hand, making sure it had no injuries and was still able to travel.

Then, a thought occurred to the general. "Mind if I join your caravan?" he asked.

Bola Gath gave him a curious look before moving to her coun-terpart. They spoke in semi-hushed tones, their voices taking on some manner of secret dialect. After a minute she came back to the general and said, "We agree."

The general appreciated her conservation of words.

Within a couple minutes the caravan was moving again as quickly as the three camels would allow, burdened as they were with dried flowers, textiles, and various trinkets for sale.

Curious, the children walked on the general's heels, greeting every movement he made with awestruck wonder.

The little caravan made its way back to the well-known desert trails their ancestors had carved thousands of years ago. Being the safest paths through the brutal desert regions, the trails wound between slopes and outcroppings of bleached stone. Sometimes they would swing wildly, seeming to meander aimlessly. But quickly the value of the meandering trails became clear, as they moved under the shadow of jutting rock formations, providing a fleeting respite from the blistering heat. And the footing was solid, avoiding quicksand and soft sandbars that could easily swallow up heavy beasts and people.

These particular nomads had decided before their journey had begun they would rather chance bandits stealing their goods than risk losing one of their beloved camels which enabled their livelihood. Unfortunately, it hadn't gone well for them, and they'd ended up getting a camel stuck anyway.

But with the general along for the ride, Bola Gath made her way back to the ancestral trails. Maybe they felt safe with the general. He didn't know. Keeping his garb wrapped over him and his head tucked within the folds of the hood, he looked like one more nomad in her party.

It didn't take long—maybe two hot hours of mindless walking —before he heard a distant rumble. The nomads must've picked it up also as Bola Gath, leading the first camel, paused. Her perceptive sense impressed the general.

Following her lead, the other nomads came to a stop. The children, until now giddy with laughter and playfulness, became suddenly sober.

Then Bola Gath began to turn her camel as if she were planning to lead the group off the trail again.

Moving to her, the general shook his head. "No," he said, the natural authority in his demeanor taking over.

Bola Gath—and all nomads as far as the general knew—were typically skeptical, especially of anyone from the more 'civilized' nations. But being a robot that dropped from the sky didn't exactly qualify as civilized. He wasn't sure what he qualified as, but something about his words or demeanor appeared to comfort Bola Gath, as she didn't continue.

From over a hill roared a type of terrain scrubber commonly used by salvagers in the region, typically called a land scow. It ran on dual tracks, like a tank. A flat bed comprised the majority of the vehicle. What looked like ten mercenaries were on its back.

The scow, moving surprisingly fast given the look of the wide metal tracks, shuddered to a stop and the occupants rocked back and forth, jolting from the uneasy, ungraceful stop.

The general could've spit when he saw the outland bandits were actually Vesuvians. It didn't take great perception to recognize those jackals. They were a parasite second only to the mysterious inter-dimensional Shamblers. Whenever a planet or system suddenly erupted in chaos, chances are the Vesuvians had had a hand in the affair.

Being a true warrior of the highest ethics, the general never believed in the sport of killing. The battles he fought were to achieve political goals, even if he didn't quite know all the motives at the time. But if he ever decided to kill for sport, he swore many Vesuvian heads would be mounted on his walls as trophies.

But the general had questions for the Vesuvians. He just wondered if they could stay alive long enough for him to ask.

Those on the scow were typical stereotypes of the race.

They wore mismatched armor, seemingly collected over years of pilfering. Some wore polished plates worn by the space knights of Betelgeuse Nine. These were mixed with odd pieces of Vesuvian power armor, some glowing red, others blue. Many had lighter, thinner armor such as carbon-dipped hides and flexi-steel wraps, no doubt to keep their movements unhindered. In addition to laser rifles and disruptors, they carried hand weapons such as daggers and swords. They probably saw themselves in some romantic light. Futuristic Robin Hoods.

"You scum thought you could escape us for long?" one of the men on the scow said, his voice peppered in rich, ancient Vesuvian inflections. He wore a full battle helmet like those used in deep space combat. It secured to a collar mechanism on his chest, tubes spidering off the rim that would normally plug into a chest respirator. But he wore them loose, like some kind of space cowboy with an octopus head. "Your stupid animals are smarter than you," he said, raising his blaster, a blunt-nosed weapon. Pointing it in the air, he rattled off a shot, crackling balls of white hot energy shooting into the air. Then he leveled it towards one of the camels. "Let's see if your stupid animal knows how to dodge."

Immediately Bola Gath sidestepped in front of her camel while raising her own laser rifle, squaring herself in a clear act of defiance.

The space cowboy fired a blast. With incomprehensible speed the general darted to his right, pulling his sword in a mighty sweep. Instead of hitting Bola Gath, the blast slammed into the general's extended sword. Sizzling electric fire ran down the length of the blade and dispersed into his body.

With his other hand the general brought out his nail gun from under his garments. Pistons split the air. Space Cowboy's helmet and armor might've looked good, but they did nothing to stop the nails—thin shards raked through his body, perforating him where he stood. With a low, wet gurgle the cowboy tumbled forward, plunging headfirst off the scow.

Once the rest of the crew caught up with the general's swift actions, they went to work as pirates do.

They brought their weapons to bear on the general. Two of them, fitted with jetpacks, took to the air.

Bola Gath's rifle thundered. One pirate caught the brunt on their chest plate, woefully underprepared to receive a long gun laser bolt. The blast burned a hole through the armor and the armor wearer, knocking him from the sky like a clay pigeon.

With a roar, the general charged the scow, spraying the rest with his nail gun, careful to avoid damaging the scow. Several of the pirates caught shrapnel in their limbs.

Two of the better shots delivered blasts to the general's chest. Liquid electricity rippled through his body, momentarily stunning him. This angered him even more.

With a terrific leap, he caught a handrail on the edge of the scow deck and hoisted himself on board. His five-foot sword and his exceptionally wicked long reach left little room to maneuver. This, and the general's bold rush onto the scow, threw the remaining pirates in disarray.

One pirate managed to work an electric sword loose from an ornate scabbard. "I took this from a blind, trusting swordmaster," the man boasted, a toothless grin punctuating his story. "Killed him with his own—" But before the opportunistic thief could finish his story or even turn on his sword, the general had swung his blade in a wide and fast arc, catching the man and a nearby buddy in their midsections, treating metal and flesh as the same. Snapped ribs and cleaved vertebrae sounded like firecracker pops as the two folded in half, bisected.

Unexpectedly, a blast caught the general on the side of his head. His optic routines shuddered, and he went blind as they reset.

The general took comfort though in hearing the nomads rattle off their laser rifles. Although the weapons fired intense cauterizing light, they sounded more like a ballistic rifle with aftermarket bangs attached to the barrel. Probably to add some psychological teeth in a gun battle. The rifles were one of the few technological advances nomads whole-heartedly accepted.

When his eyes cleared, he saw he was the only one still alive on the scow. One pirate was retreating over a nearby dune.

The second jetpacking Vesuvian was the last holdout. He dropped to the ground, landing on the opposite side of a camel, stooping so that he disappeared behind the beast—now an unwilling makeshift shield.

Seeing this, Bola Gath gave a loud, piercing call—a mix of a loud click and a word spoken in the desert nomad's dialect. The camel obviously understood this command and swung its monstrous neck to the side so that its thick forehead caught the jetpacker completely by surprise. He went reeling to the sand.

Before he could recover, the other nomad was already over him. Nimbly spinning her rifle in her hands, she drove the buttstock—which had been altered into some type of dull blade—onto his neck. Only after she leaned into her rifle and brought her full weight onto the dulled edge did the jetpacker stop thrashing.

Even the general could appreciate the savagery with which the nomad took out the trash.

With that last unceremonious ending to the Vesuvian pirates, the area became unnaturally calm. Especially after the weapon fire and death screams from moments ago.

Unfortunately, as the general thought of it, most of the Vesuvians had ended up not living long enough for him to ask any questions. Pity.

But there was one that had managed to get away.

Bola Gath pulled back her shemagh, revealing sweat-soaked brown hair. The other adult removed her shemagh along with the children's—they were essentially younger carbon copies of Bola Gath. Possibly her sister and children.

Each took stalks from their satchels and began replenishing lost moisture.

As she chewed, Bola Gath looked in the direction where the Vesuvian pirate had managed to escape. "He won't live," she said, confident in her words.

The general peered at her.

"He runs toward the sand beasts' lair," Bola Gath explained. "They're always hungry."

"Then let the Vesuvian pirate arrive in time for dinner," the general said, at which he thought he saw Bola Gath crack a thin smile.

The general realized the Vesuvians wouldn't be this far from civilization on their own. He was sure a camp was nearby. How close by he didn't know, though.

Maybe this run-in that hadn't quite worked out the way he'd hoped could work out after all.

With this thought, he pushed dead bodies aside on the scow, finding the storage compartments under the deck. The material hold.

Inside he found many weapons, rolls of textiles with intricate embroidery, carved wood and metal jewelry, and many small boxes of platinum chips. The pirate's booty. All this he dumped over the edge of the scow.

"This is yours," the general stated, indicating the treasure, so quickly gained and just as quickly lost.

Bola Gath examined the general's demeanor, no doubt for any

hint of trickery. The general was sure the hard life of a high plains desert nomad had taught her the valuable skill of skepticism.

Her intense stare finally softened, the general having met some secret litmus test in the nomad's mind. She nodded, then, waving her hand, beckoned her family.

They raced over to the pirate's treasures heaped on the sand. With scrutinizing eyes and a well-developed sense of value, they pored over the objects, immediately separating things of little value with things of great value.

At first, they kept looking up at the general every few seconds, probably still clinging to the skepticism that had become as much a part of their lives as breathing. But after a couple minutes they seemed to forget the general altogether and dove headlong into their task.

Watching them for a moment, Bola Gath turned to the general. "This will feed many families." To which the general gave a grunt of approval.

Grabbing the pirates' dead bodies on the sand, the general hoisted them back onto the scow. Then, taking the helm, he managed the terrain scrubber. Leaving the nomads to their spoils, he pointed his newly acquired transport to the east.

That's where he figured the Vesuvian camp would be.

According to some of the general's pre-deployment reading, he knew some people called this particularly stricken portion of desert Astorth-wu's Soup Bowl because of how the Iron Mountains formed the edges, a semi-circle of jagged, barren rock.

The eastern chain of this mountain range was quite different than the western half where the general had found his sword. There, dense, rich forests could sustain many types of life: birds, wild cats and foxes, even mountain wolves. At least until the timberline. Here, though, the mountains were jutting teeth like those rumored to be of the fallen pagan demigod.

Those jagged mountains cut all northerly and easterly winds to this arid region, starving the crescent shape of any refreshing air. Most reasonable people avoided this desolate region because of the perpetual stink of death and stagnation.

And, for this reason, the general figured the Vesuvians had chosen here to set up their outland camp.

Taking the mantle of scow captain, the general ran the terrain scrubber, rolling over dunes and across shallow valleys. A couple of times he believed he passed near Vesuvian outposts—they'd have set up various overwatches to keep on the lookout for intruders.

This is why the general didn't remove the dead Vesuvians from the scow's deck. In fact, he propped them up as grotesque marionettes to give the impression that the crew were sleeping off a hard day of pillaging and murder. Any observer eyeing the passing craft wouldn't give it a second glance. Wearing his rags and tatters added to the illusion. Just another pirate in plains garb.

As the day turned dark the borealis over the Iron Mountains glowed brightly. Blue night flames licked the mountaintops fringing the crescent.

Off in the distance, near the base of one mountain but still too far away to be immediately recognizable as to its source, a blue flash lit. At the center of the flash, a fierce white light burned. A prong of brilliance shot up from the flash to disappear into the Wudenan sky. Sparkles like blue fireflies danced in its wake. Quickly they faded.

The general had seen that weapon signature before.

Sixty years ago in the Antares Campaigns, the crumbling Vesuvian Empire had laid a planet siege against Antares Four. Their massive capital ships, broadside rail guns running the length of the starboard side, had blasted the planet to near extinction.

Only through a loose alliance of the American Forces with several dozen mercenary Antares clans were they able to repulse the empire. But in a last-ditch sword thrust to wreak havoc, the Vesuvians had turned their devastating rail guns against the Nineth Space Force in close orbit around one of Antares Four's cold moons.

On that black day, ten thousand American airmen and soldiers had died within the span of an hour. Vesuvian rail guns made that distinct signature.

But once the spine of the aggressor empire snapped, it hadn't taken long to finish crumbling.

Power-mad generals, bickering like sibling rivals, carved up the empire into loyal factions: there was never any compromise with men who for so long ruled with unchecked power. Almost overnight, the Vesuvians were reduced to warring bands of outlaws and pirates.

Jackals eating their own, the general would say.

It became clear to him why the Vesuvians set up camp here in this remote land. With the magnetic disruption of the Iron Mountains, the Vesuvian rail gun signature would be lost. One more unexplained fluctuation. The tell-tale energy bursts blended seamlessly with the borealis.

Some rumors said the rail gun was inter-dimensional tech, created in a different parallel existence. Made by unknown aliens for an unknown purpose. But the Vesuvians hadn't tapped into that potential yet.

Now he wondered where the rail gun was pointed. What damage was it inflicting?

Any lesser man would second-guess knocking on the door of an opponent of unknown numbers with unknown weaponry. But, as the general had proven countless times, he was no ordinary man. Or machine.

He needed to find answers to what happened on the *Countervail*, why he had suddenly been branded a criminal. An indescribable notion gnawed at him; once he unraveled the mystery of the Vesuvian *Wiggler* that had ambushed him on Erudia weeks ago, that answer would fill in the puzzle of his near apprehension. It all began here, with the Vesuvians on Wuden.

Another fifteen miles and the general decided to ditch the scow. He'd made it to a point where he could continue on foot, well beyond the initial outposts the Vesuvians had established. Finding a niche of rocks, he parked the scow and began walking.

Slinking through the nighttime desert, the general went another five miles, following odd sounds and an occasional flicker of fire light.

Finding an outcropping of boulders that provided some cover to his rear and flanks and a decent vantage point, the general stopped —he overlooked an encampment.

An assortment of tents and grey, boxy buildings comprised the majority of structures. The buildings were pre-fabs, square panels slapped together with more panels used as a roof: temporary shelters, hastily constructed. In his estimation, fifty to sixty Vesuvians made up this motley outfit.

A couple hundred yards away, on the opposite side of the encampment, tarps covered a long, large object. It matched the rough outline of a *Wiggler*, but he wasn't sure.

With unshakeable determination and a quick memorization of all of the buildings, the general descended from his vantage point to the outskirts of the camp.

His eyes cycled through light spectrum sensors, picking up warm bodies on infrared.

Guards were sparse from what he could determine. A Vesuvian casually strolling along the nearest perimeter, spinning a blaster in one hand, clutched a cigarette in the other. An odor of burnt leaves and meat trailed after him. Oblivious to the death closing in on him, the guard hummed a nameless tune as he passed.

A hundred ton mech could've walked in front of him and he wouldn't have noticed.

The general could've easily dispatched this worthless jackal, snapping his scrawny neck before he could even bleat. But not yet. He wanted to investigate the camp a little more before cracking skulls.

Slipping behind the so-called guard, the general came across the first door, which was to a squat twenty by twenty building. He slipped inside.

His pupils expanded, taking in the minimal light and enhancing it through visual filters. He was able to see in the dark as well as in the day, as long as no stunningly bright light source interrupted his view.

Inadvertently imitating what he'd seen humans do over centuries, he drew in a short, sharp breath in surprise by what he saw. In the dingy room were at least twenty robots in horrible states of injury and decay.

From the ceiling dangled an Erudian protocol bot. Serving exclusively as diplomatic aides, they were only found on Erudian peace cruisers. This one had many ballistic holes punched through its chest and blister spots from white-hot energy blasts. Its body plates were thin, highly-polished alum-steel. Meant more to impress than protect. The bot wasn't made for battle, yet someone had used it for target practice. Gently he pushed on its leg, even though he knew it was dead. The bot swung on its chains in response.

The general gritted his teeth in stoked rage.

Turning away, he scanned arms and legs in piles on the floor. He bent and lifted one of them, examining it with sympathetic eyes. Stripped wires and bent connecting joints jutted from the shoulder. There was no clean disconnection. This arm had been savagely ripped from its body. He knew the arm belonged to an *MX-109 War Goad*. He'd fought alongside a company of them on Antares and had come to respect their honor in battle. Whatever had tore off this limb had some strength behind it. The general set the severed arm back on the pile with all the reverence of a priest laying his holy book on an altar.

Some bots made for peace and some made for war leaned against the walls. Many had toppled over and now rested on the floor. Grim statues. Expanding his scanning field, but not so much that outside detectors might pick it up, the general raked his sensors over the bots. In several he detected faint electric emanations. That meant some still had the spark of life. But barely.

He had seen enough.

"I will come back for you," he vowed to the quiet room of his still brethren. An instant kinship formed between the sentient machine and his lesser brothers. "I will cut off the jackal's heads then come back for you."

Slipping back outside, he moved along one building, sticking close to the shadows. Mechanical hums, or the gentle buzz of some power generating motor, carried throughout the camp. He could sense it more intently than he could hear it. But it wasn't enough to mask the coarse, humorless laughter and spouted curses.

The source of the demented chatter was a loud, animated man, standing near a campfire. He stood tall, dressed in the fine silk clothing of the old Vesuvian aristocracy. Like the other Vesuvian pirates that had fallen to the general and the desert nomads, this man also wore a mismatch of armor over his clothes, plates of steel and miscellaneous power armor. On his hip hung what appeared to be a short razzle stick.

The way he effortlessly cut off others, the manner in which he belittled the rest, and the overbearing effect of his presence said he was running this show. Only someone firmly in charge would act like this.

"Horvoth put me in charge of this rabble because no one else wanted the job," the man said, the spit flying from his mouth sparkling golden in the firelight. "Now on it, you dogs," he bellowed as he shoved a man within arm's length, almost knocking him over. "If we don't fix *Masso Arcus*, Horvoth will have your heads. And I'll personally chop them off for him."

The general recognized the name "Horvoth" as one of the defeated Vesuvian generals of the Antares Campaign. The portion of the fallen empire the Vesuvian general had carved out for himself wasn't one of the biggest, but still respectable. Given the time that had passed since the campaign, the general didn't think this was the same man. It must have been a son or near relative.

Unlike other militaries, the Vesuvians passed rank to close family members, much like dynastic titles were handed down. A ten year old firstborn son could be a captain or general.

In every other military organization the general had encountered, offices and titles were reserved for experienced men and women and often earned through battle, bloodshed, and tears.

So most likely this Horvoth was a direct descendant of General Horvoth, who he'd fought on Antares. This one had probably received his title as privilege neatly wrapped in a box instead of having to earn it.

As the man continued to berate his fellow Vesuvians and their mothers with a spun web of curses and hexes, they scrambled away to fix whatever was going wrong and in so doing keep their heads intact.

Fading into the shadows, the general hated the idea of completely withdrawing. The general had half a mind to charge the pompous jackal, cleave him in half, then do the same to his ragtag army as the general came across them.

Beyond the overall hate he held for Vesuvians, a peculiar sensation stirred in him that he'd felt many times before.

Early on, when he was a young robot adjusting to life outside the Martian ore mines, he had thought it was a random on-board app misfiring—some junk code in him running erratic. But through the decades he'd learned to equate the sensation to the human equivalent of a gut feeling. Or intuition. He didn't know if it was learned or imaginary, but he'd learned to listen to it—a nagging sensation that would arrive at odd moments. Like now.

As he contemplated his inner workings, he noticed his hand had migrated to his sword hilt. Removing his hand, he continued his retreat into the shadows. But then he heard another voice, frantic in its tone.

"Captain Jorvo," a new, weak voice said, the tone almost shrill. "Hatch wants to know what the hold up is."

The mention of Hatch's name made the general stop dead in his tracks. Moving back into view, the general spied on the two holding the conversation.

The tall Vesuvian before the fire—apparently Captain Jorvo—spit before laying out a string of curses. Then he ended it with, "I'm tired of that Earther speaking for Horvoth. You can tell him that, Shenko. Let him come back to Wuden, and he'll find himself getting fed to a mountain wolf."

The general could tell from the simple way Shenko carried himself—the unfit body and ragged breaths—that he was used to luxury and self-indulgence. His eyes were dulled with all the trappings of someone who'd up till now had been handed all the privileges of life, but who hadn't had to invest the sweat and hard work to gain them.

Shenko probably had the fortitude of a grapefruit.

Shenko's weak voice said, "Also, sir, word is General Mikeal got away. They think he's still in the system, though."

"Bring him to me," Jorvo boasted, "and I'll rip *Anura Delo Mek's* metal heart out for what he's done."

At that the general smiled.

He knew the name given him by the Vesuvians. Roughly it translated to "demonic killing robot" because the Vesuvians claimed he'd killed more of them than any other being in the known universe. Which was probably true. Of all the titles the general had collected over his long life of killing, this was one of his favorites.

But the near-joy he felt was clouded at the mention of Hatch's name. The same cyborg he'd left on the *Countervail* to ferret out intel on the *Wiggler* on Erudia, the undetected Vesuvian ship that had ambushed him and his mechs.

Hearing of Hatch's involvement, he general now believed Hatch was part of a bigger plan—obviously some kind of spy network tied to the Vesuvians. He was on the right track.

"They want *Masso Arcus* ready in an hour," Shenko said with a great sense of urgency. "Rumor is the Sixth is calling for war galleys. General Horvoth fears he can't sustain under their howitzers. This might also derail *Levatha Hydraus*."

And the urgency with which Shenko relayed the message drove Jorvo to begin a new litany of curses and swears.

Grabbing Shenko's wide collar, Jorvo clipped him alongside his head with a balled fist before shoving him away. The captain's aide tripped and fell to the ground, spilling his comm and sensor equipment. Scrambling back to his feet, Shenko put distance between himself and Jorvo, cursing the captain under his breath. But not soft enough. The general could still hear him.

The general set his jaw in determination.

It had become obvious that these pirates had taken an active hand in the battle on Erudia, the next planet over. This gave him justification to take down the camp.

Truth be told, the simple fact Vesuvians were within striking distance and still breathing was enough to justify what the general would do next.

But when the general took a step away from the wall his sensors were still at extended range.

Shenko rubbed his red ear as he worked his equipment. He plugged in his comms and fiddled with some dials on a hand-held box. Then, suddenly, he stopped in place. Even in this bad light, the general could see the color drain from the advisor's face.

Slowly, with great care, Shenko stepped to his left. Then to his right. Then he held up a receptor to the sky. It made a peculiar ping.

"Help!" Shenko screamed so loud his voice cracked. "We're under attack! It's *Anura*!"

Losing a loved one is never easy.

A sick feeling welled in Winder's throat, crawling up from his stomach like a cockroach scurrying from the kitchen sink drain. He tried to swallow it back down, but that only made his insides churn more.

Sitting in his hovel on the plains, at a desk rigged with archaic monitors and keyboards jacked to pull data from the worldwide data streams, Winder stared with bleary eyes. Taking a moment, he rubbed them on his sleeve.

Wanting to believe he'd misread his monitor, he checked it again.

Nope. It was the same. Just like the five other times he checked it. Each time hoping it was a system function.

His Nova was toast.

His desire to maintain the historical accuracy of his car had been overriden by a desire to keep his property secure. That meant hiding tracers on his prized muscle car, just in case someone decided to take it for a joy ride.

Now, the tracers shot back reports of distress. Concussive trauma, engine fire and mayhem: a devastating crash. Toast.

Ten years he'd scraped and saved, all for the silly dream of rebuilding an antique Earth vehicle. One like his distant ancestor had driven on his family's home planet.

Hours of research, fabricating numerous parts and bartering with time jumpers for items he couldn't recreate. All gone in an instant.

But then the selfish grief washing over him gave way to a new concern. One that had slipped his mind as he selfishly mourned his tragic loss.

The general had been in the wrecked car.

And Winder needed to find him.

Fortunately, the beacon on his Nova still worked. That would lead him straight to the wreckage.

Kicking his chair away, Winder scrambled to his workshop, diverting to the hallway to pick up a sack. Amid the various mechanical parts, wires, spools of solder, and candy bar wrappers strewn across his workbench, he grabbed several metal Phantasm balls. He shoved those into the bag. In a hall closet were more. He dumped the shoebox holding them into the bag.

He was no warrior. He knew that and so needed all the help he could get. Even if his left arm was perfectly normal, he doubted he'd have the fortitude to be as strong and valiant as the general. There was a reason General Mikeal was a living legend.

Even so, Winder could do his small part. It may mean nothing in the expansive universe teeming with great soldiers ready to sacrifice themselves, but to him it would mean everything.

"PowerMan," Winder yelled while flitting through his house, gathering things he thought he might need.

At the sound of his voice PowerMan, resting in its niche in low power idle, sparked to life, its eyes glowing amber.

"Get to the barge," Winder commanded. "We're going to find General Mikeal." Seeing the blue tarp covering the hole where his wall used to be, he added, "And use the front door this time."

His industrial bot complied and exited the house properly.

A few last-minute preparations, a couple of snacks and a portable beacon tracker, and Winder left his house. With PowerMan on his hover barge, Winder headed across the plains as the night approached, his heart racing with dreaded anticipation for what he might find.

The barbiturates did little to ease a troubled Ang-Palius.

She slept no more than an hour before she was up again, pacing the polished floors of the *Erio-Magus*. Stopping at a port window, she looked down upon Wuden, the planet her ship orbited. Large swaths of brown peeked through from underneath the cloud canopy that wrapped the planet in a cottony blanket. She knew those were the great central plains. Desert encircled the plains to the east, mountains to the north. It had been ages since she'd last set foot on the planet.

As a young girl growing up in the Ang Clan, she'd spent her early childhood on-planet. Walking those very plains that scrolled by far below.

In her mind earthy grass filled her nostrils. Every summer when the sun seemed to never end. Her and her cousins had snuck into fields to see who could get the closest to some lonely field beast before spooking it, causing it to scatter.

Those were good memories. During the time when children didn't know there was evil to counter all the good, like the simple pleasure of hiding in the grass and chasing wild animals.

The bad would come later.

She had been thirteen when Ang-Kadeem, her grandfather, had attempted to force her into his quarters after making some hideous deal with Ang-Thoth, her older brother. Ang-Palius' blossoming time jumping skills were put to good use that hot night, when she brought forth a stiletto blade and fed that to dear old granddad.

The rest of the family clan frowned on young Ang-Palius single-handedly taking down the mightiest time jumper and clan chieftain. Indiscretions such as Ang-Kadeem's lustful desires could easily be overlooked, but usurping the clan's lines of succession was intolerable.

She fled, hopping a textile freighter at the local port heading away from Wuden. She hadn't known the ship's destination, but it hadn't mattered as long as it was away from her family. Once she'd tasted the stars, she'd sworn she'd never set foot on that dry, filthy planet again.

Now, decades later, with her self-made fortune and her prized ship, the *Erio-Magus*, Ang-Palius had returned home, orbiting the planet she'd swore she'd never return to. Even she didn't completely understand why.

But now, she was faced with heading back to that forsaken planet.

In one of those rare moments of selflessness, the baroness worried about someone other than herself.

Moving to her audience chamber, she dropped heavily onto her throne. Idly she chewed her fingernails for a minute or two, slouching on the grand metal chair.

Her mind churned, resisting the numbing effects of the drugs. Now she wished she'd never had them injected into her, so she could think with complete clarity.

Suddenly, she sat upright, like her thoughts had given her body the boost it needed to cleanse the drugs from her system. At once, everything became clear and in focus.

"Kento-Gala, come here," Ang-Palius called out, excitement making her voice sound like it came from a woman half her age.

The warrior commandant of the Red Guard Kento-Gala came hurriedly from her station just outside the audience hall. Her boots clacked, echoing through the hall, as she rushed to her employer.

Dark-featured Kento-Gala carried herself regally: a mixture of early childhood spent as a high plains nomad and later years as an educated, trained officer of the Wudenan army.

She stood a foot taller than the baroness. Her shoulders were wide, and she moved with measured dignity, her head so squarely mounted on her neck that she might've passed as an automaton. Countless hours spent training and in combat had shaped her arms and legs with well defined, strong muscles.

She wore thin plate armor, colored a deep red and trimmed in gold. A large griffin with a snake's neck and head—the baroness' crest—covered the breastplate. A red cloak, just licking the floor, flowed behind her.

During her stint as a Wudenan field commander, Kento-Gala had learned the art of politics through death. But she had given up her promising military career for Ang-Palius' irresistible offer.

Coming to a stop before the throne, Kento-Gala's left hand rested on the elegant sword dangling from the thin girdle attached to the bottom of her breastplate. Her right arm wrapped around a battle glaive, the primary weapon of the Red Guard.

"Baroness," Kento-Gala said coolly, with a slight bow.

"You know how uneasy I've been," Ang-Palius said.

To which Kento-Gala nodded. "Ever since Bar-San visited, you've been restless."

"Yes. He's on a mission at my request. A dangerous mission." Ang-Palius paused for a moment before saying, "I want you to arrange two kill teams. For Bar-San."

Kento-Gala nodded as a thought crossed her mind. "He thrives on danger, baroness," she said.

"Yes. But even terrific heroes will one day falter," Ang-Palius admitted, giving license to the gnawing fear that had been welling in her—her bounty on the robot general didn't seem like such a good idea now.

On the same token, she appreciated Kento-Gala's measured response to ease her mind. The commandant's no-nonsense attitude was a calm assurance.

"I got word that a brash Wudenian girl, a magistrate's noble daughter, tried to claim this precious bounty," Ang-Palius added. "First she sought me out, eager to sell me the news and location of General Mikeal. I paid for the information she offered. Then the foolish thing decided to go after the robot herself with a few of her idiot friends. She got broken ribs, a collapsed lung, and a fractured sternum thanks to General Mikeal."

"She's fortunate the general didn't skew her like a fat pig on his sword," Kento-Gala said. "And you're going to assist Bar-San? He has caught your eye," Kento-Gala added, giving a wry smile. "He is so fortunate."

Only the commandant of Ang-Palius' guard, a woman Ang-Palius had trusted with her life for the past six years, could be this forthright. "But his oath of celibacy..."

"Blast his oaths," Ang-Palius spat, sitting upright. "Save the oaths for the pious monk communes of the north." Then, just as suddenly as the baroness' anger had been kindled, it subsided. She vacillated like a cat playing with a wounded mouse, debating when to set the kill.

Leaning back and snuggling into the velvet cushions that under-mined the hardness of the metal throne, Ang-Palius said, "He's a man, isn't he?" she reasoned in a new line of thought. "Oaths such as that are but pastimes to ones such as him. Made when life is stagnant, the mind dulled with monotony."

"Yes, baroness," Kento-Gala acknowledged, nodding, not willing to push her opinions in unproductive disagreements.

"Once you get the kill teams, have the ladies bring me my suit," the baroness said.

"Which one do you prefer?" Kento-Gala asked.

"My MX-V. With the ore plating. Make sure the helmet is polished."

Two embedded horns, four inches long and wavy before coming to a point, formed a crown of sorts on her golden helmet—personally cut by Ang-Palius from the scaled island lizards to the southeast of the archipelagos and considered good luck when worn as ornamentation.

Of course, they weren't good luck for the lizard that had died to give up its horns.

Kento-Gala's eyes gleamed with a devilish light. "Your best armor. Planning to fight, then? Shall I accompany you?"

"No," Ang-Palius said as she pictured herself in her splendid armor. She could almost hear Kento-Gala lick her lips with the prospect of battle. But she needed her most trusted guard with her, in case things didn't go the way she hoped. "Stay here. Two kill teams should be enough. Ready the drop shop and bring the physicians. I need my meds."

With another bow and a disappointed look on her face, Kento-Gala departed the audience chamber, on her way to carry out the baronesses' commands to the letter.

Ang-Palius leaned back on her throne.

Yes, she would help Bar-San capture the general, the greatest bounty of all. He would need her, whether he asked for it or not.

And he would get to witness what few had—the terrifying onslaught of a time jumper.

First one warning siren blared, then another. And another farther away.

But the wailing, piercing screams didn't elaborate on who had busted into the camp. If so, many of the Vesuvians might've reconsidered the vigor with which they enthusiastically raced to greet the intruder, thought the general.

Voices broke out: screams of anger, cursing, blind challenges, and threats of what would become of the uninvited guest.

From the raucous display, the general sized up his enemies. And they weren't the finest the Vesuvians had to offer.

Well-trained soldiers wouldn't come clamoring like children onto the playground, looking to bully the new kid. These were probably paramilitary hires, soldiers of fortune and wannabe bad boys. The typical lot that want an avenue to bloodlet or to make some quick credits. Or both. Often their desire outran their skill.

Understanding the enemy's competency level, or lack thereof, gave the seasoned general a leg up, even though he already counted fifteen distinct voices. Even though he'd accidentally tipped his hand to the Vesuvians and was clearly outnumbered, that wouldn't stop him.

Blaster fire lit up the night. Air cooked with energy and the smell of charred ozone.

The general's sword glowed hotly as he intercepted a nearby blaster bolt. Bringing his nail gun from under his cloak, he laid a withering fire.

Ricochets sounded as he raked it across the encampment indiscriminately, carbon-steel nails digging into metal and flesh. One man in the dark howled in death pain.

"There," someone yelled, their voice wavering with adrenaline-fueled emotion. "Over here."

Disruptor blasts turned the night to strobing day. Colored energy streaks pulsed overhead. One slammed into his shoulder, sending a shockwave rocketing down his left side. He cursed as burning pain overloaded his sensors. This enraged him.

Another blast of his nail gun, this time pointed directly at what the general perceived to be three barrels of fuel. As the nails turned the cans to Swiss cheese, sparks made the contents erupt into a blinding orange fireball that rolled upwards. Burning shrapnel rained down, igniting smaller fires.

Casting aside his nail gun, the general gripped his sword with both hands in an iron grip, holding it like a claymore. There were too many swarming bodies to keep at a distance. He needed to get closer. Then he could count on friendly fire to help him out.

The robot general stood before the camp.

"Come, jackals," he roared, his deep, resonant voice booming. "I'm no lost traveler or merchant that you can so easily rob. Meet *Anura Delo Mek*. I'll send you to join your mothers in the arms of your dead god."

Those that knew his name, and more importantly his terrible voice, paused. Which is what he had intended.

Fear is a good weapon.

"At him, you dogs," Jorvo screamed as he watched the unfolding battle, well short of the fight. Suddenly backpedaling, he put as many of his men between him and the general as he could. "I'll get the ship."

Scrambling away from the fight, Jorvo sprinted toward the shape the general imagined was a *Wiggler*, at the other end of the camp.

The general's bravado worked—he saw several of Jorvo's men visibly affected by his challenge. Three turned and ran away. Several more were torn between fleeing or fighting. He could see it in their eyes. But in their hesitation, the general made the decision for them.

With a quick, short sprint he was upon them.

Two of the Vesuvians unloaded their disruptors at him. This close even they couldn't miss. But he was prepared this time. He intercepted several with an outstretched hand.

Bringing his sword around, he cleaved into the power armor of one thin Vesuvian. The man fell backwards, reeling from the powerful blow.

His buddy screamed a war cry and threw himself at the general, producing a telescopic electric sword that crackled with blue energy.

The general caught a wild swing on his own blade. Sparks flew and air sizzled. The man, eyes wide with maniacal anger and fear, hacked repeatedly with his weapon. At this frantic pace, the man would give himself a heart attack or pass out from exhaustion.

Stepping back, the general moved to his right. The man also shifted to keep the general from flanking him. This movement put him in his buddies' line of fire.

The man became another unfortunate victim of friendly fire as three disruptor blasts to his back fried him.

Charging the Vesuvians who had just fried their friend, the general brought his sword low, then swung it from his mighty arm. It twirled violently, like a lawn mower throwing its blade. Whistling evilly, the sword hit the ground and skipped, taking two bounces before shearing off the legs of the three men just below the kneecaps. They fell in cries of pity and pain.

Retrieving his weapon, the general looked for anyone nearby. But there were none. They had all run away. Scattered like mice. Like jackals.

Across the camp, motors ramped up.

Tarps slid off, revealing the *Wiggler*. It reminded the general of a fat grub worm: a bulbous, fleshy head narrowing down to a point at the back end. Exhaust from many ports stirred up dust, swirling clouds. The remaining Vesuvians were climbing inside the craft from what appeared to be a rear cargo door.

The general needed answers about Hatch, and he knew the Vesuvian captain would have the answers. And he was on that ship. That was now the general's target.

Breaking into a full run, the general moved faster than any man could ever hope to sprint. With each step toward the semi-organic ship, a deep revulsion grew inside him that he typically reserved only for cyborgs. He closed the distance as the ship lifted off the ground.

The cargo door had already closed, sealing up the only visible entrance. So the general lowered his sword like a lance. He drilled it into the side of the ship, driving it to its hilt. Clinging onto the embedded sword, he lifted into the air along with the *Wiggler* as it undulated into the sky.

The ship, just a little over one hundred feet long, was a perfect size for terrestrial hit and runs. Like much of Vesuvian technology, the fractured Vesuvian empire hijacked ships from other civilizations.

It must've been a strange species that had built—or *created*—the *Wigglers*. The vessels were somewhere between flesh and machinery. And it was an abomination. A horrific combination of the organic and inorganic.

Over the past months the general had been forced to accept

cyborgs into his unit. Being old and set in his ways, the general had had difficulty accepting this fact, but had ultimately relented in order to receive government funding.

But this ship dwarfed that uncomfortable notion by a hundred.

Slowly, the ship banked to its left. It circled the Vesuvian camp, not gaining in altitude beyond the several hundred feet it had already risen. The ship's circuitous route slowly drifted towards the mountains.

A port window, previously unnoticed by the general, popped open. A Vesuvian stuck his head and shoulders out, searching. He was within a robotic arms' reach.

"Here I am," the general said. Grabbing hold of the wrap around the Vesuvian's head, the general yanked him out the window and let him fall. He screamed until crashing through the sporadic iron mountain trees, far below.

The general crawled in through the round window, like a spider crawling in an unsuspecting sleeper's ear.

He'd heard the rumors that *Wigglers* were, in fact, a strange living, sentient being. Found tucked away in the remotest corners of the universe. A life form so unlike anything experienced on Earth that it would boggle the mind. While dismissing this as drunken airmen and soldier talk, there remained a thread of uneasiness as to what he might find inside.

The port window dumped him into a corridor. He half-expected to find himself inside a stomach. Or a lung. But it was neither—just a normal spaceship corridor like others he'd walked a million times before.

And what's more, the inside of the ship didn't undulate like the outside. There must have been some gravity regulating coefficients in place or some intricate support scaffolding keeping the interior and exterior separate.

The corridor was narrow, maybe a man and a half wide. The

general had to stoop slightly in order to keep from banging his seven-foot head on the ceiling. Not the ideal battle arena.

"Halt!" a voice commanded, then a disruptor blast seared the bulkhead a foot away.

The general, his mind bent on one person, didn't take the time to address this attack. He turned and ran in the direction he thought the bridge would be.

The ship's layout was simple—the corridor he was currently in appeared to run the length of the craft, with a few bends thrown in for good measure. In his vast history of space faring, the general had a firm knowledge of such things. Most engineers stuck to some grander universal principles.

The general passed by several doors, reasoning that they wouldn't lead him where he needed to go.

One Vesuvian, leaning against the wall and picking his teeth, didn't notice the general until too late. The general grabbed the inattentive Vesuvian and slammed him into the wall. He crumpled like a cheap folding chair. If he awoke, he wouldn't be so casual about battle readiness anymore.

Taking the Vesuvian's blaster, the general continued forward.

The corridor ended at what appeared to be a wide blast door. This must be the bridge. Biometric scanners on one side indicated it was fortified in a way the general might find difficult to bypass.

After standing there for a minute, he rapped on the door. The corridor echoed with the metal on metal pinging.

"Hey," the general called out, "I need to speak to the captain. We've got trouble in the back. Comms are down." Using audio processing routines, the general modulated his voice so that he now spoke in their dialect, sounding like any other Vesuvian two-bit thug.

Five seconds later, and to the general's great surprise, the blast door slid open.

Before the poor Vesuvian could realize the full extent of his mistake, the general hit him point-blank in the chest with the disruptor. His smoking body flew back ten feet onto the bridge. The general stepped inside and the door closed behind him.

The room erupted in chaos.

Six Vesuvians grabbed their blasters and began firing wildly. Bursts ricocheted off the blast door's refractive coating, careening wildly back onto the bridge. One terminal sparked and belched smoke as a blast torched its processor.

"No blasters," Jorvo yelled, moving away from the general, near panic. "We're enclosed. To arms."

View ports lined the opposite wall. The borealis shone bright, casting the bridge and all the occupants in mystical blue. It set a weird mood for the coming battle.

The general used his disruptor and with his steady hand dropped two more Vesuvians—both gut shots center mass.

Before any of the remaining men could mount any sort of structured counterattack, he fired at the control panels on deck. Tiny flashes of electricity and sparks rolled inside the panels as they began a systematic meltdown.

Recorded voices, flashing emergency lights, and electronic bells told the clear story of a compromised ship. It lurched as something critical was damaged.

"You'll make us crash," Jorvo yelped, leaping into the pilot's chair and grappling with the control yoke which probably didn't work anymore.

"It won't be the first time I've crashed on this miserable world," the general responded.

Two Vesuvians, finally filled with enough courage, charged the general, each brandishing electric swords.

One swung his sword with clumsy hands. He knocked himself off balance as he tried to overcorrect and slung his blade in the opposite direction. He severed power lines running up the wall and the bridge lights began flickering. Then they went off.

The general simply sidestepped the wild blow before crushing the clumsy man's windpipe with a savage punch.

The second sword wielder, now that the annoying trainee was out of the way, had room to work. Bringing his sword around in a deadly arc, he made the general step to the left. The man then drew his blade into a thrust, catching the general on his left arm. A clever feint.

Rivulets of pain shot along his arm, radiating through his chest. His arm went temporarily numb.

"Kill him!" Jorvo bellowed.

"I'm on it, boss," the sword wielder said, encouraged by his strike. "You're going down, robot," he exclaimed, his tone goading.

Just then, a shudder rolled along the ship. Violently, it pitched sideways. Air pressure increased on the bridge as the ship shifted in altitude. With almost an exhalation, the pressure gave. So did the artificial gravity that kept the inside of the ship stable.

Men, weapons, and machinery slid to heap onto a growing pile on a wall as the odd undulation bent and warped the room. The general engaged his magnetic locks to attach himself to the floor.

Now that the gravity coefficients were shut down, every undulation and turn the ship made was multiplied by ten. The crew had no chance of gaining their feet, well on their way to getting beat to death by loose objects and slamming into jutting bulkheads.

Outside the windows, mountains appearing to tumble and roll added to the dizzying effect of the ship, pitching wildly as it was.

"Autopilot engaged," the ship's voice said over the alarms and klaxons. It kept on its circuitous route for only a moment before listing from one side to another, then somewhat stabilizing itself. Quickly ,it gained altitude.

Once the ship had settled, Jorvo raced back over to the yoke—as he grabbed it he knocked the autopilot offline. The ship plummeted, now well over the Iron Mountains, to crash back on Wuden.

Just above the trees the *Wiggler* tried to level, like some protective autopilot attempted to steer the ship. Several trees were roughly clipped, leaving jagged treetops. After smashing through many more trees and a couple of thin rock formations, the ship slowed and dropped, eventually coming to a grinding halt near the edge of an overlook and resting on a bed of flattened foliage.

While not as violent as the first crash-landing the general had experienced days ago, this was still violent enough to crack the ship in half. The semi-organic outer shell absorbed most of the impact.

The general crawled out from under a section of bulkhead, taking in the crash scene. He needed to quickly evaluate any remaining threats.

A warning indicator in his mind flashed. His left arm, still recovering from the paralyzing shock from the sword, was only at 35% utility. He flexed his tingling fingers to regain feeling.

But like before in the Iron Mountains, things weren't easy to find. Trees and dense forest cast shadows and deepened the darkness. Overhead, the blue borealis, twisting on wisps of nothing, bathed the air in an otherworldly hue.

Curses and a couple cries of pain filled the otherwise quiet mountain night as Vesuvians poured from the tail section of the ship. There were many more voices than the general had first thought were in the ship. At least thirty. Possibly more.

This would complicate matters.

As much as he would like to track down every last one of the Vesuvian dogs, he needed to keep his eye on the prize. Scanning the wreckage, he searched for the captain.

His eyes focused on a particular figure scurrying away from where the bridge had broken apart.

A laser blast sizzled the air. The unexpected flash of brilliance temporarily lit the night in a strobe. A hapless tree limb received the brunt, the blast shattering the limb in pyrotechnic sparks. Someone yelled out that they'd found the general. Another blast whizzed by.

But then a sound underneath the yells and screams became

apparent. It struck a familiar chord in the general, but he couldn't quite place it yet. After tuning his auditory sensors to a lower frequency, he recognized the sound.

He'd heard it the last time he was in the Iron Mountains. Metal and stone balls clacking together. A few seconds later, as the unnatural noise intensified, the Vesuvians paused in place, finally able to hear the low rumbling sound.

The clacking quickly enveloped the whole forest, ringing on iron-hardened tree trunks and echoing off rocks and through the valleys.

The noise caused many of the Vesuvians to panic—their faces became hysterical and they swung their blasters in every direction, not sure where this new enemy had come from. Several fired wildly at nothing.

A howl broke the clacking metal balls. First one, then another joined in. Then another. A chorus of primeval howls erupted from around the crash site, the very mountains erupting in savage fury.

A bark followed by a ripping followed by a blood-curdling scream interrupted the howling.

Vesuvians tripped over branches as they ran from an enemy they couldn't see but only hear. More indiscriminate shots fired into the night.

"The iron wolves," one man screamed, his voice breaking.

Barks and howls and biting were met with curses, screams, and battle. Men fought for their lives as they were overwhelmed by a ferocious primal wave.

The general, his weapon ready to defend himself and bracing himself for the rabid fangs, caught glimpses of something more than wolves among the shadows. Half lumbering, half upright figures, carrying clubs.

Those fanatical wild tribesmen of the Iron Mountains. Steeling himself, the general prepared for another attack.

But after a minute of standing alone among the wreckage, listening to the Vesuvians having their very lives ripped from their bodies, the general began to wonder if the fight would ever reach him.

It seemed, almost miraculously, that the wolves and men purposely avoided him. Instead, he heard a low chant murmur through the din.

Anaga-wu. Anaga-wu.

Maybe not so miraculously after all.

Previously the tribesmen had chanted to their iron mountain snake *Naga-wu*. But with their false god dead, they'd needed a replacement. The general reasoned these primitives had made themselves an idol. Something beyond them to worship and sacrifice their trinkets to. Based on the new name the zealots chanted, the general had the sneaking suspicion that he was their new idol, their new god.

But he didn't have the time to school the Neanderthals on proper theology.

Deep within him his warrior's intuition, that elusive gut feeling, told him the mountain tribes and their pets from hell weren't there for him.

Then the thought of Jorvo getting away, at least until the natives caught up with him, urged the general to leave his defensive posture and chase after the coward. Which he did.

Charging into the forest, the general followed on his footsteps. While Jorvo's men chose to stand their ground, the captain had choosen to turn and flee. But then, what can one expect from Vesuvians? Especially their leaders. They handled honor like a bauble, only useful for their gain.

This fueled the general on.

As the general put distance behind himself and the fight behind, a wild crashing resounded around him. Branches snapped and vines rustled: a maddened boar charging through unfamiliar underbrush.

The swearing and ragged gasps told the general that Jorvo wasn't far ahead.

He picked up his pursuit, ignoring the branches raking across his protective plates and digging at exposed wiring.

Shortly he cleared the trees, emerging onto an area where the ground had become too rocky to support vegetation. About thirty yards away Jorvo leaned over, hands on knees, rasping as his cowardly lungs sucked in more air than they could manage.

"Head jackal," the general said, "who is Hatch?" he demanded, not caring to lay out any elaborate explanation.

Jorvo laughed nervously. "Not all Earthers are as loyal as you, robot." With that he broke out in a sprint away from the general. Turning back to see how much traction he gained, he didn't notice the ground ending. Before he realized he ran out of ground—literally—and plunged headlong off the edge of a cliff, plummeting out of sight.

Slowing and walking over to the edge, the general peered over. Several hundred feet down. All he could see were jagged, rocky outcroppings with ribbons of iron ore streaked throughout. Then he saw what a mangled body dashed upon stone would look like. "Well, crap," he said—his information source had just removed himself from the equation. A grand finale to Captain Jorvo's wretched leadership.

The general took a few minutes to let diagnostics finish running and to assess his own battle damage. And hopefully to get the feeling back in his arm.

By now the borealis had dimmed and faded with the night as the sun began peeking from somewhere behind the range. Exposed metal veins on mountain peaks captured rays of the rising sun and threw spectacular glimpses of orange, red, and yellow. The fading night and the new day gave the general a surge of life.

When he returned to the crash site, the battle had already burned itself out. Broken apart, the *Wiggler* lay in several large sections.

Grav motors balled into misshapen hunks of metal. The area smelled of smoke and grease and blood.

None of the Vesuvians remained. None of the wolves or tribesmen, either. No doubt the Vesuvians had been overwhelmed in their vain attempt to repel the attackers.

He could see where bodies had fallen but had been dragged away. Large puddles of reddened, wet ground told a grim story. The bodies had probably been taken to either be buried, burned, or to become some weird prop in another of the zealots' twisted existence. Either way, sensing no Vesuvians were alive and the tribesmen were no threat to him, the general now needed to get back to the camp.

Finding his sword hidden among the wreckage, he docked it to his back. And feeling like he'd aged another hundred years since he arrived at the Vesuvian camp, he limped down the mountainside, rubbing his left arm that hadn't quite regained all its feeling back yet.

On his way down he heard the words *Anaga-wu* echo in the distance.

Descending the mountainside as the rising sun promised another blistering day, and still riding high on artificial adrenaline, the general made his way back to the encampment. He felt oddly hollow now that the battle had been spent and everyone that should've been killed had been killed.

He made a quick scan around to see if any straggling Vesuvian dog remained, but he found nothing. Just dead bodies and the barrels he'd ignited earlier, the flame slowly dying.

Then, as he thought of Jorvo's conversation with his Grub worm advisor, the general realized he had something left to do. *Masso Arcus.*

Searching through ammunition crates and other shipping containers, he scrounged unexploded ordnance and unspent munitions.

Those he stacked waist high around *Masso Arcus,* the monstrous rail gun he'd first seen firing during the night. He wasn't sure why, one of those gut feelings, but he knew he needed to take the devastating weapon out of commission. Something this powerful couldn't just be left in the remote desert.

Once he finished piling on the explosives, he took one of the

Vesuvian's cheap blasters. He popped the side off and shunted the energy cell. It went into overload.

Standing a good distance away, he chunked the blaster onto the stacked munitions. The blaster exploded, which set off a secondary explosion. The detonating munitions set off a tertiary explosion.

Masso Arcus ferociously blew apart. The ground vibrated as a quake rolled through. A fine layer of dust lifted as a concussive wave rippled through the camp. Flaming chunks of burning metal hurled across the crescent. Once the orange and yellow ball of flame billowed up from the ruined husk of the artillery gun, black smoke began seeping out.

Many of the burning hunks of metal landed on tents and wood boxes, igniting them.

"Well, so much for that," the general said as he watched the crackling fire engulf the Vesuvian rail gun. The feared inter-dimensional weapon had come to a rather dull, unimpressive end. Smoke poured from the ruin like a chimney in winter.

The general had debated with himself on whether to keep the gun intact or not. It could prove valuable to the Sixth. Then the grim realization came upon him that, as of the moment, he wasn't part of the Sixth.

In fact, he was a fugitive.

That thought didn't sit well in his iron stomach.

As the general began the arduous task of rummaging through the buildings and tents, looking for any remaining stragglers or intel that could shed more light on his current predicament, a whimper caught his attention. Pausing, he listened intently until he decided on the direction.

Noiselessly, he walked to where shipping containers were stacked three high. The coffin-sized storage boxes had seen the worst of countless interstellar cargo holds. Corners were mashed in. Gouges and scrapes covered every side.

Grabbing one container that stood by itself, the general flipped it over so the lid popped off. Out spilled a smallish man who squealed like a cornered pig.

"Jackal," General Mikeal said at the sight of Shenko, Jorvo's aide. "Pick up a weapon and defend yourself."

"Ah!" Shenko squeaked. "I'm not a soldier."

"No," the general remarked, eyeing him with thinly veiled disgust. "You're not a warrior at all. Tell me of Hatch," the general demanded of the mousy man, "or I'll pop your head off your miserable shoulders." He knew with politicians and diplomats that adding clear descriptives enhanced their understanding.

"Mercy," Shenko begged, flattening his soft white hands together in supplication. "I cannot withstand you. I saw the ship crash up there," he pointed to the mountains. "Only you've returned. I know the rest have hidden. Or are more likely dead."

"So, you're the smartest jackal out of the lot," the general said. "Now speak, or do you wish to join your master who's meeting his god under the earth?"

Shenko shook his head frantically. "I have no allegiance to Captain Jorvo. I hope you made his death slow and painful," Shenko said, the slightest hint of a smile creeping up the corners of his ashen lips. "And all I know of Hatch is he's endeared to General Horvoth."

"Why?" the general demanded.

Pointing at the general, Shenko said, "why, because of what he's done to you. He effectively cut off the strongest arm of the American Forces."

At that the general had to step back. He knew Shenko didn't lie. Men such as him would sell their mothers to slave traders to save their worthless necks.

Somehow, Hatch had infiltrated the Sixth's computer systems and manipulated them. He had the knowledge and ability to plant false information. And with his apparent malevolence, Hatch had made the general a criminal.

Getting rid of the general meant the Sixth Mechanized would remain dormant on the *Countervail*, rusting to uselessness. No one could control the mechs except the general.

The rest of the wing was already spread thin, the past few months of battle on Erudia taking a heavy toll. Fighting on two fronts, the Shamblers and the Vesuvians, the Sixth wouldn't be able to sustain themselves.

"Hatch is a Vesuvian spy?" the general asked.

Shenko shrugged. "He's an Earther. As far as I know he just hates your military."

The general found himself nodding. What the worm said made complete sense. He wondered how much info he could pry from this jackal that would prove useful. "Where are the Vesuvians on Erudia?"

For a moment Shenko hesitated, as though a hint of defiance had suddenly blossomed in his wretched body, giving him the nerve to stand up to the general. But this all changed when the general not so gently placed his massive robotic hand around Shenko's neck and gave it the slightest squeeze.

"Wait," Shenko begged in a tiny voice. "Are you looking for *Levatha Hydraus*? I'll tell. Here." He dug in his coat and pulled a transponder, shoving it in the general's hand.

Through strange ways the Vesuvians collected technology. Most of it they stole from other developed planets. The Vesuvian Empire had acquired cloaking tech nearly unrivaled in all the known galaxies.

This could also explain why the general's initial assault on Erudia had ended so miserably.

The *Wiggler* that had surprised him had been cloaked.

Not even the Sixth's mighty surveillance network had been able to break through the stealth tech. Perhaps Hatch sabotaged the network to hide the *Wiggler*, or perhaps on-board cloaking had kept it hidden.

This transponder said cloaking was being used on Erudia. And with it, he would be able to reveal the crafty devil's whereabouts.

The general had no idea what Shenko meant about *Levatha Hydraus*, but took the transponder nevertheless. "Flee this place," the general said to Shenko, releasing his grip on him. "Either by mountain or by desert. I'm not in the business of killing government bean-counters, as much as it may thrill me."

With that, Shenko bowed low, quickly backing up from the intimidating robot towering over him. He scrambled away, grabbing a stuffed backpack that had fallen out of the container he was hiding in. The short man quickly disappeared into the desert on stubby legs.

The general idly tapped the transponder as he considered his next move. A small panel on the side of his torso opened, and the general tucked the transponder safely inside. The panel closed tight.

He knew the next step he had to make.

He had to get to Erudia.

There he'd find Hatch and Horvoth. But there he'd also find the Sixth, who right now saw him as fugitive number one.

As he considered this, he went to the building he'd first came across, the one with the tortured, mutilated robots. Throwing open the door, he went inside.

One body hung from its iron fetters. He snapped the chains and gently, maybe even reverently, sat it on the ground. Moving from bot to bot, he hoped to surmise if any of them might not be too far gone. The electric emissions he'd detected in here earlier had given him some hope one or two might be salvageable.

Towards the back of the narrow building he stopped, staring at one curious bot tucked into a corner, arms folded and head bowed in piety as if it had spent the last of its power ages ago and was praying for more.

Then, in an incomprehensible rush of motion, the bot's arm swung out. A plasma dagger in its hand slammed onto one of the general's pectoral plates. Although this didn't penetrate his armor plating completely, the sheer pain caused the general to roar.

But before he could react the bot's other arm swung out, this time holding a foot long poignard. It caught the general on his forearm, successfully carving a six inch wound.

He staggered back, clutching his arm which began to seep oil.

Not many people could catch the general off-guard. The last time had been at least a hundred years ago. But what startled the general even more was that a dagger was able to so easily slice his armor. He'd never met a blade able to do that.

The bot stood upright. Dropping the plasma dagger, it brought its palm forward. This action enabled a directional sonic weapon, hidden underneath the attacker's robot armor.

An acoustic blast punched the general full in the face. It knocked him backward into a pre-fab wall. With his momentum he busted through, reeling another five feet beyond it. Bits and pieces of other bots came flying out, also caught in the concussive sound cone.

With multiple warning lights flashing in the general's head, he fought to regain his feet, imagining himself at that moment like a turtle flipped on its back.

But his injured arm wouldn't cooperate, and he wasn't sure if his hip remained in its socket. He hadn't had enough time to recover from the previous battles. All the absorbed blaster bolts, the crash in the *Wiggler*, and electric sword strikes had left him at a disadvantage.

The bot stepped from the hole blasted in the wall, but the general knew it wasn't a bot at all. No bot could move with that speed.

Seeing his opponent with a clear advantage and finding himself flat-footed filled the general with rage. He forced himself onto his feet. Undocking his sword from his back, not only did he use it as defense for another attack, but it also served as a crutch to help steady him.

"What kind of demon are you?" the general panted.

"I'm no demon, robot. I'm Bar-San," the man responded, his voice slightly modulated through the bot mask he wore but not enough to make his thick accent unrecognizable.

"A southern mercenary bounty hunter," the general spat. He motioned to his sword. "I've dulled my blade on many of your brothers' skulls."

"For that," Bar-San responded, his thick voice surprisingly calm, "you will die today."

Before another word was said, Bar-San leaped forward.

The general barely raised his sword in time to intercept the attacker.

Bar-San, moving with such speed that he appeared to have some foresight into the general's own mind, used his lunge as a feint. Instead, he brought his arm forward then released another sonic blast near point blank to the general's chest.

The wave ripped through the general's body, throwing him back thirty feet. His sword was torn from his hands and spun wildly off to the left. A chunk of the general's breast plate, the plate the iron wolves had ripped into, flew off, whirling away like a frisbee.

He hit the ground hard, his heavy body burrowing a trench from where it skidded in the sandy ground.

With his ceremonial poignard in hand, Bar-San confidently moved forward for the kill.

His body unresponsive as several critical programs reset, the general struggled to get to his feet. Even if he did, he questioned whether he could even match his executioner's speed.

He'd always believed his end would come in the thickest part of battle, surrounded by his mechs and a thousand dead. A great ending for a warrior's good life. He'd done his job long and well.

The general paled at the thought of falling at the hands of a lone human. No matter how quick they were.

He kept his eyes on the long dagger gripped so surely in the mercenarie's hand. As he stared at the object, a faint, familiar electric wave ran through his body. It was one humans couldn't experience and so couldn't understand.

A song of metal, the general called it.

Just then a motor whine split the air. A drop ship, polished metal with golden accents, descended from the sand-filled brown sky. Two fixed wings with turbofan foils and deflectors pivoted, kicking up sand like a dust devil and obscuring everything as the ship descended.

Once it lowered to thirty feet from the ground, it hovered in place. A bay on the underside of the ship opened and sparkling beams illuminated, touching the ground.

For the briefest of moments, a fraction of a second if even that, Bar-San turned his attention away from the general. Any other opponent wouldn't have even noticed the distraction, let alone taken advantage of this rare moment of fractional inattentiveness.

But the general was no casual opponent, never willing to die passively.

Operating at a level beyond human comprehension, the general opened his hand. An invisible channel of magnetism arced from his outstretched fingers to the poignard—the same energy channel the general had first come to understand on the Iron Mountains, imbued into his sword.

Suddenly springing to life, the ancient weapon leaped from Bar-San's hand into the general's. With a surge of power drawn from every working capacitor and cell, the general lunged forward and ferociously swung the blade with such force that sliced through Bar-San's armor and cleanly severed his right femur. A lifelong butcher gutting a dinner hog couldn't have made a cleaner stroke.

Grimacing in pain but not uttering a sound beyond a surprised gasp, Bar-San clutched at his new stump as he dropped to the ground.

The general saw the mercenary wore bandolier webbing, a network of emergency tourniquets rigged to his body. Immediately the webbing cinched down on his leg, tapering off the blood flow once it sensed the trauma.

No doubt the bounty hunter probably also wore a hidden medi-pack on himself, ready to juice him up with a cocktail of pain relievers and coagulants.

He'd come prepared, thought the general. Good for him.

The general got to his feet quickly and moved away from the bounty hunter. Just because the man was down didn't mean he was out. The general turned his attention to the ship to see what new devilry was approaching.

As some of the dust cleared, he noticed the crest on the ship's side. Baroness Ang-Palius. The general had heard of the time jumper and her mercenaries during deployment briefs on the way to the Erdine System.

Six of her dreaded Red Guards descended from the drop ship bay, riding the electric elevator of light.

Although not showing it in any way, the general thought things couldn't be going more wrong than they were at this moment. Not having dealt with the guards before, the stories were enough to give him a reason to be alarmed.

The baroness hand-picked the finest female stock from the southern mercenaries and the desert nomads. Several from off-planet, obscure systems few knew existed. Each warrior, formidable in their own circles. Banded together, positively lethal.

Softly, they drifted from the drop ship to the ground, their anti-gravity boots gently bringing them to rest.

They wore matching deep red power armor, tailored to every bodily contour and curve. The baroness' crest was on their full breastplates. Red capes streamed from their collars. Thick black hair, like horse hair, ran from the bottom fringes of the full helmets, falling across shoulders.

Each brought their own unique, dangerous skills, but all were taught to wield the mysterious battle glaives that were standard for the Red Guard. Many said the baroness had reached far into the future to bring these strange weapons back.

Most people wrongly assumed time jumpers leapt forward in time. But that wasn't the case.

The general knew if the baroness was here, there would be trouble. He also knew by all accounts he should be dead right now. But many such engagements were decided on the edge of a coin flip.

Riding the high of not only cheating death one more time, but also facing the possibility of sending more opponents to the grave, gave the general the raw strength needed to face these opponents. He'd taken a lot of damage from the bounty hunter during their brief encounter, but he was still capable of dealing massive damage.

Quickly he moved to where his sword had landed when Bar-San knocked it out of his hand. Standing—holding the bounty hunter's poignard in one hand and his sword in the other—he faced the Red Guard.

They didn't move. Just waited. It didn't take long for their hesitation to be understood.

A spectacular golden battle suit descended from the drop ship.

It wasn't clunky like the standard battle suits the pilots in the Sixth wore. Theirs were designed with functionality as the main focus. Thick armor coated in laser-reflecting paint, bulky arm and shoulder rails for mounting ordnance and weaponry. Mechs with humans inside.

This battle suit was sleek, looking more like a hybrid between the protective plates of power armor and the fully-enclosing mech suits. On the breastplate the same griffin snake beast was carved in intricate detail.

The faceplate of the visor slid upward and back, tucking away between the horns jutting from the helmet and revealing Ang-Palius. Her thin jaw was set, and fire burned in her amber-flecked eyes.

"What happened to Bar-San?" Ang-Palius demanded through clenched teeth.

Without looking back at his defeated opponents' miserable body writhing on the ground, the general casually stated, "I was about to skin this wretched jackal with his own blade."

"You'll die, scum!" Ang-Palius said.

But before the baroness could make good on her promise, the general jumped forward, coming close enough for his sword to clear the rest of the distance and bringing it down in a terrific overhead arc.

One of Ang-Palius' guards, quicker than the rest—even than the baroness—threw herself between the baroness and the general. Bringing up her battle glaive with both of her gauntleted hands, she braced herself for the blow.

The five-hundred pound sword came crashing down on the weapon's staff. A clap of thunder resounded as sparks flew from the collision. Reddish iridescence rolled along the length of the glaive. But it held.

Completely astonished and surprised that the guard had been able to intercept and withstand the crushing blow, the general stepped back. However, he didn't show any surprise, mostly because his robotic face didn't register emotion.

"What manner of red devil are you?" the general asked.

"I'm Kento-Tera," the guard said. "Second daughter to Battle Mistress Kento-Gar. But you can call me your executioner, robot."

The general launched a new attack. He brought his sword around in a flurry of stabs and slashes, making it appear as though he wielded a chopstick instead of a five-foot bar of steel. Kento-Tera parried the blows, but barely. Under the withering assault even she fell back.

Three of the guards came around Kento-Tera, quickly outflanking the general, who'd overextended his advantage. Making use of the reach afforded by their glaives, they flashed the tips of their bladed heads, which tapered into a metal spike.

He successfully deflected two jabs but not the third, which he caught in his shoulder. Immediately, the burning sensation of someone pressing a hot iron into him traveled down his arm. Reeling back, the general reconsidered his strategy.

"Secure Bar-San," the baroness ordered her guard as she regained her wits. "Leave this dog to me."

Somewhat reluctantly, Kento-Tera paused. She and the others lifted their glaives from where they were closing in on the general and backed away.

Kento-Tera's visor slid back, revealing her smiling face. "See you around, robot," she said as she gave him a wink. Then she backpedaled away.

Even if he made it through the battle with the time jumper, he knew he couldn't take on the Red Guard. Not in his current condition, anyway.

But dwelling on his deficiencies wouldn't help the situation. Even if he went down, he'd drag along as many opponents as he could. That gave him some comfort.

The baroness held out her empty hand. A strange, pulsing light began at the palm of the baroness' hand. Quickly, it spread to consume her arm in radiant light.

When the light diminished, she held what looked like a heavy scepter or a mace. Fine multi-colored stones, emeralds and topazes and diamonds, covered the shaft. The balled end glowed with an internal light of its own.

Before the general could establish any reasonable estimation of a defensive posture, the baroness was already upon him.

She swung her mace, catching him on his side in a blow that hurt more than it should have, given her gentle swing. But as he prepared to strike back she appeared at a distance, like she'd never moved an inch, still floating in the air.

A sinking feeling came over him that dealing with a time jumper would be more problematic than a normal opponent.

"Time-leaping witch," the general said as he worked his injured torso that felt both hot and cold at the same time. It felt like she'd thrown his chest into a freezer, so cold it burned from the inside out. "I'll send you to join the bounty hunter."

Right at that moment another high-pitched screech cut through the air. Two missiles skittered across the sky, slamming into the baroness' drop ship and erupting in balls of fire.

Winder's hover barge sped towards the drop ship and the embattled general. At the last moment, he spun his barge and cut the acceleration so it drifted sideways. Using this momentum, PowerMan leaped off the edge, clearing forty feet and landing like a clumsy meteorite in the midst of the Red Guard.

The utility bot's normal two-pronged claw hands had been replaced by blocks of thickly anodized ore, the kind wielded by demolition bots to crush boulders and shatter bedrock.

His first swing caught a guard that moved a little slower than the rest of her team. A jackhammer anvil fist caught her in the chest. The piston sounded like a ballistic mortar as it drove the square foot block of ore into her chest.

Thrown twenty feet by the walloping impact to land hard on her back, the guard wrenched at her shattered breastplate, trying to gain relief from where the folded metal pressed on her—she probably had a crushed sternum.

Immediately, the guards that weren't already tending to Bar-San turned to PowerMan, each a wasp of rapid movement and blade stings. They circled the bot and their glaives spun wildly, carving into the wrecking machine. Despite the critical damage being dealt, PowerMan kept on swinging.

Winder, still on his barge, dumped a bag of metal balls onto the deck. They immediately sprung to life and shot into the air, kept aloft by miniature thrusters and grav motors. Spring-loaded knife blades protruded from each polished ball before they headed toward the guards.

Two of Ang-Palius' Red Guard aimed arms upward and forearm-mounted disruptors filled the air with energy blasts. A storm of flak shredded many of the balls as they zipped toward the guards.

Once the balls descended to within striking distance, the guards expertly manipulated their glaives, using the narrow shaft to fend off the balls of death.

PowerMan, seizing the opportunity of a distracted guard, charged. But Kento-Tera, the one who had blocked the general's devastating strike, appeared to sense his presence and leaped to one side, evading the bulldog rush.

She cunningly anticipated this move, flying into the air with a well-guided burst of her ankle jets. With glaive held overhead, Kento-Tera came down on PowerMan, driving her blade deep into his shoulder, penetrating his inches thick armor. She rode the beast, digging her blade deeper into his internal machinations and processors. The red glow of the mysterious weapon leaked over the wound, infecting the industrial machine like a cancerous cell.

Bucking like a wild bronco unwilling to admit defeat, PowerMan flung his arms about, eventually knocking the guard from his back. Kento-Tera backflipped and landed on her feet, already preparing her glaive for another strike.

From the corner of the general's eye he saw two of the guards tend to Bar-San while another finised off the last of the flitting metallic balls. Not daring to take his eyes off Ang-Palius, he focused his auditory receptors in the direction of the guards.

"The baroness requests your presence," one of the guards said to

Bar-San, her voice soft and reassuring. "We're to escort you to the ship." They bent to lift him.

The general couldn't do much else but brace himself for an attack as the golden Ang-Palius hung in the air, her anti-grav boots barely disrupting the air underfoot.

Then from some point behind her, ten missiles fired. Each arced over and beside her to come slamming down at the general, wrapping the baroness in a blanket of exhaust.

Lunging to his side, the general avoided them as they exploded on the ground one by one, each digging small holes. The last two had him in a crossfire that he was unable to outrun, so he drove his sword into bedrock and curled himself into a ball, tucking his head. Grasping the sword embedded in the ground up to its hilt, he'd weather the blast. He'd learned this move watching a turtle fend off a curious raptor.

The missiles exploded within feet of him, pelting his body in debris. The sword kept him from getting bowled over by the concussion that ripped at his body. Waves rolled over him, dispelling into nothing.

It hurt, but it didn't devastate him.

Smoldering chunks of rock and char stuck to his frame as the general slowly stood. Pulling his sword from the ground, he charged toward Ang-Palius.

But instead of closing the distance like one would expect, the general slowed next to a boulder half buried into the ground but still three feet high. It had been churned up from the ground by the rockets.

Tightening his grip, the general swung his blade at the boulder with every thew he could muster, smashing it with the flat of his sword.

The resultant explosion showered Ang-Palius with rough shards and stony slivers.

Most of the smaller pieces caught in her force field lost inertia to the point of dropping to the ground. Harmless. But many of the larger shards, while slowing once entering the force field, continued with enough kinetic momentum to drive them into her armor. One shattered her faceplate while another tore into her boot, disrupting the anti-grav traction.

The general had made a wild gamble on her suit's shield being geared more for energy blasts and overwhelming energy bolts. There would be little consideration for brunt attacks. After all, who would be able to get close enough to the baroness to cut or stab her?

Ang-Palius's leg wobbled once her boot's anti-grav shut off. She became unsteady in the air, beginning to slowly spin with only one good boot. Disengaging her anti-grav, she descended, landing on ground not so gracefully. Her damaged faceplate slid back away from her face as a shattered piece fell away.

"You're without your broom, witch," the general said as he puffed in a lungful of air. "Now I can reach you."

He wasn't breathing per se, but his body's cooling system relied on heat exchangers that comprised his lungs. He was close to over-heating and needed to cool himself down by drawing refreshing air over heat exchangers.

Again, Ang-Palius winked out of sight, only to appear in an instant next to the general. Her mace crushed into his elbow, the icy energy snapping canon plug connections and buckling elbow joints. He grimaced as he tried to lift his arm: it was completely unrespon-sive. Now little more than a dead weight. Then the baroness disap-peared again.

The general, keen on the field of battle, had expected her to reappear exactly where she disappeared. He reasoned she was initi-ating her witchy time jumping skills to shift her position, while not skipping more than a fraction of a second of time. He'd heard this was a tactic time jumpers often used, going lateral in time and space. Not always backwards.

He gambled, remaining where he was in the hopes of catching her off-guard.

Remaining relatively still, he hoped that would goad her into launching another attack.

Standing at a distance, she disappeared again and reappeared next to him and slammed him with her mace, only to disappear again before he could react.

And that's where he flung his sword.

As Ang-Palius reappeared at her previous location the sword was there to greet her, slamming into her midsection. The violence of the blow was too much for her struggling force field to deflect. Although not shearing her in half—much to the general's dismay— she doubled over, sprawling to the ground, the wind knocked out of her. Her breastplate buckled and hung off her delicate waist.

Seizing the opportunity, the general took Bar-San's poignard that he'd been holding onto. With a mighty heave he launched it at her. This pushed through her crumbling force field with enough energy to jam its length into her hip.

Screaming as she dropped to one knee, the baroness aimed one arm at the general.

A disruptor blast from her palm knocked him back, temporarily blinding him. Then, activating her one working boot thruster, she skipped out of his reach.

Struggling—holding her injured torso with her arm—the baroness stood, leaning to her left on her injured leg as her breath returned in shallow spurts.

The general hobbled over to his sword and picked it up with his one working arm.

Ang-Palius, now with a desperate look on her face, rotated her arm like a windmill in front of her.

A thin blue light trailed after her arm and grew with each second. It appeared to suck in the surrounding atoms, bending the very light into a pinwheel of energy. Rapidly, it grew, spitting thin wisps like a firework toy throwing sparkles. Shortly it became an entity on its own, a spinning wheel of light that would lead to another time.

Ang-Palius started to step into the wheel of light.

She wouldn't get away that easyil. Taking his sword, the general once again slung it, this time at the wheel of light.

Time jumpers operated on the disruptive nature of Slipstream travel; eddies, or swirls, were created through a disruption of space and time which allowed a limited group of people with the predisposed tolerance for time travel to use these eddies and time jump.

Martian ore, the material the general's sword was made from, was extremely resistant to time-bending—it functioned as the dampener to the temporal maelstrom Slipstream tech needed in order to operate. Once this had become known, even the smallest nugget of ore was valuable beyond its weight. As Mars was decimated—the last of its ore strip-mined two hundred years ago—the limited resource became even more valuable.

The general threw his sword, knowing that when an irresistible force meets an immovable object, something is bound to give.

The flung sword penetrated the baroness' field. Light arced across the ore bar before spreading outward in thunderbolts that cracked the air with sheer, brutal force. The sword's ore disrupted the time pinwheel the baroness had created.

"No!" Ang-Palius screamed as her time jump went off the rails. She tried to back away from the pinwheel she'd created, but it already had a tight grip on her.

Her body stretched, like she melted where she stood, or how she'd look if viewed through a prism, every last drop getting sucked into the pinwheel. With one final scream, she disappeared into the energy field. It quickly spun down, fading to nothing.

"Baroness!" Kento-Tera exclaimed. For a moment she was torn, taking a step to engage the general, but then changing her attention to her teammates.

The Red Guard moved Bar-San underneath the drop ship. They also had the other injured guard, supported by her sisters-in-arm.

The six Red Guards ascended the beam of light thirty feet back onto the drop ship, Bar-San in tow. The door closed, and with a thrust of engines, the ship disappeared into the Wudenan sky.

The drop ship was gone.

So was the bounty hunter.

So was Ang-Palius.

Cupping his useless arm with his good hand, the general attempted to massage life back into it. Trauma, too much to even keep track of, made him feel like he'd aged another couple hundred years.

Surveying the aftermath of the brutal battle, the general saw PowerMan. He moved to the giant bot sprawled on the ground, hydraulic fluid pooling in the sandy dirt. Numerous gouges had been carved into its thick armor plating. The Red Guard were efficient killers. Their evil blades had managed to penetrate to its innermost workings. They were exposed and burned, like a fire had begun deep inside the bot's chassis and chewed its way out.

Then, it occurred to the general that Winder was also there.

Limping over to the hover barge, the general pulled himself with great effort onto the deck. Winder lay there, on his side. As the general rolled him over he saw a massive gash along Winder's side that still glowed faintly red. The witch fire had claimed another soul. He shook the man's shoulder.

"Winder, you there?" the general asked.

For a moment, the general thought Winder was dead, but then the young man puckered his lips, licking them with a parched tongue.

"General," Winder said, his voice so weak the general had to lean in to hear. "…knew you were in trouble. Sorry I couldn't help. Sorry…" Winder's voice faded.

"You faced the Red Guard," the general said. "You saved me not once, but twice. Rest, young warrior. You've done well."

A faint smile came across Winder's innocent face.

Quietly, the general sat next to him for another three minutes, watching his chest rise and fall until it stopped.

A few more minutes and the general's cooling system regulated, giving him enough strength to lug PowerMan's massive body onto the barge.

The Vesuvian encampment was now silent, the only sound being *Masso Arcus*—the rail gun he'd sabotaged—crackling in the background.

Satisfied, the general climbed onto the barge. Tired, stretched thin in a way only warriors can understand, the general put the barge in gear. He headed for Winder's home on the plains to give both the young man and his bot a proper burial.

Aboard the *Erio-Magus*, Ang-Palius' ladies-in-waiting wore black to mourn the baroness' disappearance. One, a woman of eighteen with a haunting voice, wailed as only a professional mourner could. Her pain-filled dirge echoed off the audience hall's bulkheads.

At her post next to the baroness' throne, the normally stoic Commandant Kento-Gala couldn't escape the effects of the melody. She held her face rigidly, but shivered inside as a chill rolled up her back.

What a horrible replacement for the normal laughter and cheerfulness that typically played out here.

Kento-Gala had been standing in her spot next to the throne since the excursion returned and she'd found out the baroness had made an errant jump. As Kento-Gala thought of what or where, or *when*, the baroness would emerge, the smell of the time jumper's perfume on the pillows and cushions caught in her nose—if she survived the jump at all.

It wasn't a typical time jumper excursion, like when they would break time and space and emerge in a distant time in the past, hoping to find some salvage to bring back. After action reports from on-planet said her last jump had gone terribly wrong. And for something to go wrong for a time jumper usually meant death.

A pair of footsteps, swift and purposeful, echoed just over the song and the wailing.

Kento-Tera.

With her red cloak billowing behind her, Kento-Gala's younger sister strode past the cluster of black-clothed women undulating like one giant mass of pitiful sorrow. Her mouth corkscrewed.

Kento-Gala knew her sister's look of disdain all too well.

Her sister moved like a cat, her subtle power restrained—none of her motions were wasted. But in an instant she could spring into action, lethal. As renowned as Kento-Gala's skill was, she knew her sister could outfight her. If it ever came to that.

Kento-Tera came to a stop before her sister.

She stood as tall as her older sister at six feet, maybe a couple inches more. They were built similarly, athletic with wide shoulders. Kento-Tera's Red Guard power armor of polished brass with red trim was immaculate, like always. She held her helmet under her left arm and her battle glaive was strapped diagonally across her back. A red sheath hid the blade.

She clicked her heels and rendered a salute. "Commandant," Kento-Tera said.

Kento-Gala returned the salute.

"You should run them out of here," Kento-Tera said, glancing over her shoulder and glancing at the mourners. "I can't even think straight with all that racket."

"It's a sad time for us all," Kento-Gala said. "I hope you'd be a little more respectful of the situation."

"There wouldn't be a situation if the baroness had let us finish the job," Kento-Tera said cooly. "But I respected her orders. She wanted to impress Bar-San with her battle abilities. Apparently she chose the wrong target to show off to."

Kento-Gala stared at her sister, condemnation for her words expressed through a furrowed brow. Her sister would know without a doubt her displeasure. "Don't forget who you speak of, Kento-Tera. The baroness will not be mocked." Her words were direct and unapologetic.

Too well Kento-Gala knew the baroness' flaws. The past six years had been a whirlwind. Often, Kento-Gala thought of herself as a babysitter and the baroness a spoiled child. Of course Kento-Gala would never breath a word of this to anyone else. Just thinking this way made her feel like she was betraying the baroness' gracious generosity.

Besides thwarting six clumsy assassination attempts, Kento-Gala had spent most her time cleaning up the seemingly endless stream of... *potential consorts*, as the baroness called them. Really, nothing more than live toys for a woman who could have anything she wanted.

Eventually she'd tire of them, and Kento-Gala had to clean up the mess. A few the baroness had even imprisoned, claiming they had committed some mysterious wrong only she knew.

Kento-Gala ended up sneaking many off the *Erio-Magus* before they ended up dead at the hands of the only male in the baroness' entourage, the ship executioner.

A babysitter, Kento-Gala thought.

"Forgive me," Kento-Tera said as her head bowed slightly in apology.

Kento-Gala's brow became less condemning as she pushed her thoughts aside. "How's our guest?"

"The physicians said if they had Bar-San's missing appendage they could've reattached it," Kento-Tera said. "I take personal responsibility for this oversight in forgetting his leg on the battlefield."

Kento-Gala noted her sister's rigid posture, her matter-of-fact explanation for something as personal as a severed leg. She knew her tenacity in every task. She'd make a great commandant, leader of the Red Guard. But not yet.

"At ease," Kento-Gala said, to which her sister went into a parade rest, hands behind her back, still holding her helmet. "He lives," Kento-Gala added, shaking her head. "That's what the baroness wanted." Out of the hundreds of others, Bar-San had made the cut.

Of course the baroness would pick one of the few southern mercenaries sworn to live a single life, giving up certain... necessities, in the commitment of devotion to craft. The craft of killing.

"He says I should've left him on the field to die at General Mikeal's hands," Kento-Tera said.

Shrugging, Kento-Gala responded, "Bar-San's a man. His pride clouds his thinking." Relaxing enough that her shoulders slouched, she said, "Tera, I think I need to contact Ang-Thoth."

Kento-Tera smirked. "If the baroness heard that she'd have you thrown in jail. Maybe even ejected out an airlock or fed to the executioner."

Kento-Gala shrugged. "Maybe. Maybe not." She watched the ladies-in-waiting for a few seconds. Grief wafted from them as they continued their songs. She didn't know whether it was genuine or manufactured—grief was what was expected of them. "That may be the only way to get her back."

Kento-Tera said, "She hates him. He hates her."

"They're brother and sister. That's a requirement," Kento-Gala said, giving her sister a slight, quirky smile.

Seeing her smile, Kento-Tera couldn't help but return it. "You're so informal. You don't deserve your post."

"Why, little sis," Kento-Gala said. "This isn't mutiny, is it?"

Kento-Tera burst out in laughter. Against the sullenness of the wailing it sounded completely inappropriate. The mourners glared at them both.

Aware of the judging eyes, ashamed of allowing herself to slip from her formality, Kento-Gala squared her shoulders and stood taller.

And as she considered the events that had caused the baroness to make the bad leap, and the only person who could realistically help, Kento-Gala realized what she needed to do. It was what she had been thinking all along.

"On your way out," Kento-Gala said, "send the diplomats in. It's time to contact Ang-Thoth."

Quickly Kento-Tera resumed her no-nonsense posture. "Commandant," she said in acknowledgement. Giving a parting salute, she spun on her heels and exited the audience hall.

Kento-Gala watched her sister depart, saying to herself, "I hope I know what I'm doing. I could lose everything. Including my life." Then she sighed. "Why did you have to go and do something so foolish?" She asked Baroness Ang-Palius, who no longer existed in the universe.

Over countless frontline skirmishes on and off-planet, and protracted multi-planet excursions, the general frequently had been forced to repair his own battle damage—from plugging leaking ballistic holes in his chest to reattaching severed fingers caught in the crushing grip of a closing blast door.

He'd been shot, stabbed, blasted, and mutilated in more imaginative ways than even his infinite mind could comprehend.

But he couldn't fix his limp. That type of work required a full power down.

At times like this he wished a maintenance tech or two were around to patch him up. But he'd never openly admit this need for humans.

He needed someone like Winder. Or Senior Airman Julianna Darrisaw, his maintenance technician on the *Countervail*. She could bring a toaster to life. Even make it salute. There was no doubt in his mind she could've brought PowerMan back from the dead.

With her being caught in the maintenance bay explosion on the *Countervail* months ago, he'd lost one of the best techs he'd ever known.

In Winder's hovel on the plains in the workshop where the

general had been rebuilt, the general spent the next few hours cleaning out grit from his joints. He applied Super Fix metal bondo on the plasma dagger wound to his chest. It also filled the slash on his arm, the one from the poignard. This would do for now.

He guzzled another can of motor oil.

Once he put himself back together as best he could with the tools from Winder's workshop, he found a shovel and dug two holes behind the man's house.

One for Winder and one for PowerMan.

The general wouldn't leave them on the battlefield in the same manner some heathen abandon their dead. He wouldn't leave them for the birds to pick clean or for wild dogs to steal a leg or an arm. Or for scavengers to rip out PowerMan's processor core and recycle his parts.

No. Through his own hands, they would receive a proper Christian burial.

The shovel he found stuck in the ground behind the house. It appeared Winder had attempted to start a garden. He hadn't been successful.

After covering them with dirt and placing a cross of metal scraps above their heads, the general whispered a prayer for each, like the chaplains had taught him long ago.

Then, as he stood above the graves reflecting on their contributions, a lingering thought wormed its way into the forefront of the myriad of other thoughts crowding his mind.

He needed to get back to Erudia.

There he'd find Hatch. And that's where he'd set everything right. The low time of mourning the valiant dead was over. Now was the time to act.

Wrapping himself in layers of garments that told casual onlookers he was nothing more than a mud sucking pig farmer or tenant plowman, he prepared to leave. Besides a couple cans of motor oil, the general packed the nail gun. This dangled under his garments on his side, held by a strap over his shoulder. His sword docked to his back.

He departed Winder's house on foot, heading west.

———

On the western arm of the Wudenan main continent where the flat plains graduated to gentle slopes and dales, the town of Arm of Wuden rested. It held the nearest space port with freighters for hire. About four hours away to the west.

The general set out on foot, leaving Winder's barge at the house. The general walked for an hour, then a lonely traveling merchant by the name of Jurus with a spacious hovercraft on his way to town to sell odd junk gave him a lift. By the time he dropped the general off, the general knew Jurus' life story, all the way up to his sixth wife, Natel. His *truly* one true love.

Arm of Wuden's claim to fame was a collection of bars, sundry merchants, and various lower castes willing to do pretty much anything for spare change.

The smell of urine lingered over the town. And the way the buildings were placed—a large semi-circle with a wide central area of push cart vendors and market booths—made the general think the town had been intentionally designed to look like a toilet.

Descending a hill overlooking the toilet bowl town, the general shut off his olfactory sensors.

Various tramp haulers, cruisers, and planet hoppers roared overhead, shaking the ground in teeth-jarring shudders. They were either headed to, or coming from, a cleared expanse just north of the town. A smallish spaceport. That was his goal.

He needed to get from Wuden to Erudia. Preferably under the radar. Which shouldn't be too difficult ,as the planet has been locked in brutal war. But that also meant not many were willing to risk their ships by making a pit stop at the embattled planet.

Still, money talked.

And the battle had stayed localized on Erudia, as far as he knew. Erudia was a big planet with many ports. Chances were some were away from any fighting. Relatively safe to fly into. That reassured the general someone would be willing to make the run for a buck.

Besides the first impressions of a toilet, Arm of Wuden reminded the general of western towns from earth's history. Technology intertwined with this archaic setting in odd ways.

Mercenaries, dressed in scraps of power armor with disruptors slung low on hips, walked into what looked like a saloon. Laughing, cursing, and screaming poured from the squat building.

Vendors pushing rickety carts sold warm meat wraps. Some of the rancid smells made the general wonder what unfortunate animal got turned into a hot dog. Others sold solar glasses and good luck charms, usually a piece of an animal or a roughly hewn image of some pagan god. As if luck could be peddled on the street like some two-bit commodity.

Camels and other desert pack animals, laden with backbreaking loads, were led by bits along the streets. They idly navigated the crowds, only pausing long enough to freely defecate.

The general was used to line-feed access to the *Network*, as all data streaming was collectively termed. On it, he could pipe into a wealth of knowledge transmitted the world over, even across planetary systems, although those feeds were typically delayed and usually reserved for military purposes or rich patrons that could afford the fees.

But since fleeing the *Countervail*, the general had disabled his reception—essentially shutting off his personal locator so the Sixth couldn't track him. This also meant he had to rely on archaic methods to find out what was going on.

At an intersection, on a sidewalk which was covered in just as much dung as the street, a boy no more than ten stood. Scrawny, dirty, probably an orphan, he held up a quarter-sized disc. Electronic paper.

"Extra, extra! See all about it!" the boy cried out in a voice that promised to break with puberty at any moment. "Mysterious lights seen in the Soup Bowl. Are the mountain tribes on the move? Battle on Erudia threatens whole system. It's a bleak time to be alive," the boy had such inflection on the last sentence that the general figured it was his calling card.

Dodging piles of camel dung, the general strode up to him.

The boy looked to be a seasoned hawker of news and misery. He played the part well, dressed in filthy rags with dirt-smudged sunken cheeks. He put on his best malnourished smile. "You want to find out what's really going on in the world, boss?" the boy said as he tried to peer under the hood the general had pulled low over his head. "You won't find it on government networks. No siree. Only at the *Independent Republic* you'll find the truth."

"I'll take one," the general said, modulating his voice to mimic Winder's so as not to draw undue attention. Only the well-trained ears of Corinthian spies would be able to detect his deception.

"Sure thing, boss," the boy said. He flipped the quarter-sized disc to the general, and, in response, the general flipped back a platinum credit.

With tiny, deft fingers the boy snatched the coin from the air. His eyes grew wide as he realized its value. "Boss," the boy said, "I don't have change for this."

"Keep it," the general said. "Get a bath and a haircut."

"Thanks," the boy responded, unconsciously swiping his mop of greasy hair from his eyes. With renewed enthusiasm at the unexpected windfall, he went back to his chore of hawking news. Except now there was a noticeable cheerfulness to his tales of doom.

Moving to an alleyway between two squat buildings, the general took the flimsy disc from its packaging and plopped it onto his eyeball.

Immediately a virtual newspaper overlaid his view—the after-noon edition of the *Independent Republic*, which informed and titil-lated, according to the paper's subheading.

Cut scene videos in boxes were framed by scrolling text. As the general's artificial pupil flitted from one section of the page to another, wherever his gaze lingered that portion would come into focus, filling his view.

His eye scanned past the exposé of a former mercenary turned monk and the advert for the newest government drug den. It stopped on the update to the battle.

The "Mystic Shelf War" is what the media called it, because the alien invasion of Erudia was said to have begun in an area called the Mystic Shelf. Apparently some type of inter-dimensional activity had led to the mysteriousness of the seaside ridge. And people, always drawn to the strange and unexplainable, had turned it into a local attraction.

Only too late had anyone realized the error of this decision, as Shamblers started rifting on-planet. By then the aliens had overrun the cities, enslaving the Erudians through awful mind control weapons.

The *Republic* story featured a war correspondent's grainy drone footage.

The backdrop was a typical modern city with houses, roadways, and flying cars. Grey, ashy clouds churned overhead, the result of a hundred fires burning in the distance.

Erudians, driven stark raving mad by the aliens, scaled over walls, climbed through broken windows, even trampled each other. They carried blasters, garden tools—anything they could get their hands on.

The ghastly scene reminded the general of zombies, antique horror movie monsters. Many Earthers called them that.

A child, gripping a shard of glass so tightly it cut into her hand, screamed in rage as she raced forward in brightly colored boots.

The general had seen this before, the insanity brought about by the Shamblers and their terrifying pole weapons.

No one knew how the fantastic powers worked, but they knew the devastating results. Once possessed by the Shamblers, a person would attack anyone and everything, including self-mutilation in gruesome ways. Only death could release them.

They had the same bloodlust as the mythical zombie, but they weren't dead. It might've been easier to deal with them if they were already dead.

In the drone footage, Erudians clamored from the city, bent on destruction. They charged a skirmish line formed on the outskirts. Soldiers from the Sixth held that line.

Troops had entrenched on a line to keep the possessed within the confines. The citizens may have been lost, but they couldn't be allowed to spread from the city like a plague on the land.

Rocket smoke trails arced over soldiers and airmen. Fragmentation artillery slammed into the seething mass of civilians, digging out chunks of earth and concrete and hurling it all indiscriminately. Torn bodies went flying. Plumes of concrete dust and flames erupted in the air, a sickening slaughter of civilians turned into reluctant killers.

But the Erudians—unaware or uncaring—stepped through the raging fires, over the smoking holes and on top of the shattered limbs of their neighbors. Unrelenting, no longer capable of rational thought, they pressed forward so the Sixth had no choice.

But then, from some unseen location, a bombardment of liquid fire rained down on the unsuspecting skirmish line. Soldiers cooked in their power armor. One ripped at his helmet as he cried out in horror, but his fingertips were already charred to the point of uselessness.

This was not the work of an alien Shambler, though.

A *Wiggler* uncloaked, leaking fire from its blast ports, undulating as it circled overhead. It dumped another load of hell fire onto the Sixth before cloaking again.

Then the footage abruptly shut off.

Removing the disc from his eye, the general gritted his teeth.

The Vesuvians, being opportunistic jackals, were taking advantage of the situation.

The rage of a warrior standing safe while his brethren died was almost too much for him to bear.

Without another delay, the general pushed through the pedestrians and the peddlers, making a beeline for the northern port. That was where all the spaceships would be docked. The war footage reiterated his need to get to Erudia. Fast.

Although the spaceport was on the northern end of Arm of Wuden and the winds generally blew to the south, this didn't prevent the port from escaping the stench. In fact, thought the general, this place could very well be the origin of the rancid smell.

The noise of a bustling dock didn't help.

Engines roared in various, gritty pitches. Fuel-laced exhaust smelled strongly of unhealthiness. Star drives whined as mechanics tweaked power settings. People screamed, trying to talk over mechanical and pneumatic tools. Puddles of red hydraulic fluid showed where a hauler's malfunctioning actuator system had decided to dump its contents.

Food wrappers and freeze-dried meal packaging was strewn on the ground, left to pile in quiet corners by gusts of wind and engine exhaust. The general lingered at one alleyway as he watched what looked like a cat-sized rat with horns chew through a metal container. It hissed at him, then continued chewing.

No one paid him any attention. Just another starfarer or ferry pilot.

The docked ships were as varied as the people. Monstrous tramp haulers, para-military galleys, intergalactic exploration vessels, and terrain scrubbing personal cruisers.

Liquid oxygen spurted from a service hose as a tech fought to connect it to a coupling on a cruiser. Sales stickers still clung to the foreword fuselage.

The general overheard the owner boast of his birthday present to his drunk buddies. Only his father, a rich Wudenan precious metals trader, could afford something like this. The boy was getting ready for a continent run and soliciting for a crew.

Off to one side of the port, neon adverts offered clean showers, clean women and men, and pure drugs. All to be found within three smallish buildings.

To help make good on the adverts' offer, prostitutes stood outside one of the buildings. A food mart.

They wore ridiculous clothes, even for their profession. Strips that could double as bandages, see-through robes, and silken loin cloths.

And each person passing by were eyed by the group, their painted faces not hiding their fantasy that they were one trick away from a payday that would allow them to live in luxury.

As the general moved quickly by, the prostitutes called out to him with feign praises and vivid descriptions of what they would do for the right amount. Even if he were human, he would've shaken his head in disgust.

Keeping his head down, he put distance between himself and them.

Someone could easily get lost in the chaos of a busy spaceport. And this served the general fine. He blended into the crowd, moving like he had a purpose. Which he did, only he didn't quite know how it would play out yet.

Walking underneath an aged hauler vessel that eclipsed surrounding ships, the general noticed someone familiar. Darting behind the hauler main landing gear strut, which was as thick as a large oak, he spied on her.

Captain Fletcher, the Sixth fighter pilot who'd shuttled him to and from Erudia.

She wasn't wearing her flight suit or any service uniform like he'd typically seen on her. She had on civilian clothes. But her tall height and golden hair were unmistakable. Especially on a planet where most of the natives were darker skinned than her, ripened by the blistering sun.

She looked left and right, keen eyes canvasing her surroundings. Then, she slipped through a crowd of travelers unloading from a transport ship.

After checking the hood over his head to ensure he remained disguised, the general shot from behind the strut. Tailing her like an assassin, he kept her golden hair in view, not allowing her to get too far ahead.

Winding through the port, she eventually came to the furthest end of the dock ramp. There, people had grown sparse and the stadium lighting that brightly illuminated the main port areas grew dim. Shadows grew thick and menacing. Not a place to be alone, given some of the types that hung out at spaceports.

Parked away from the main thoroughfare rested a AFSS TR-3010 *Pigeon*, a VIP shuttle. With one last look behind her, Fletcher activated her info sleeve and the shuttle door whispered open. A telescopic gangplank greeted her.

So, the Sixth *was* here.

This puzzled him though. He knew operating procedure well enough to know that Fletcher, a pilot, wouldn't have been sent to find him.

But desperation, especially after watching the war footage, chewed at the fringes of the general's mind. Despite the danger this was an opportunity, and so made his move.

As Fletcher started up the gangplank he bum-rushed her, grabbing her by her shoulders and forcing her forward. They stumbled inside the shuttle and the general hit the control panel to disengage the gangplank. It rolled up into itself and the door slid shut.

Fletcher ripped herself from his grasp and threw herself across the room. She hit the wall opposite in the seating area, and, turning on her heel, had already drawn her blaster and aimed it for his face.

"Wait," he said, allowing his voice to revert to its natural, mechanical tone. He held up a hand to intercept any errant blaster bolt while drawing back his hood with the other.

Her eyes grew big with recognition as her face flushed. "General?" Fletcher said, unsureness in her eyes.

He nodded.

"You're a fugitive," she stated. Lowering her blaster, she kept it at her side instead of holstering it. "What happened?"

"Are they now sending pilots to hunt me?" the general asked, skepticism as to her purpose on the planet crowding his mind.

Shaking her head, Fletcher said, "No. I'm not part of the official search party, but I am looking for you."

"Tell me why," the general demanded.

Fletcher slowly tucked her blaster back into her holster. Removing her hand and showing her palm, she said, "We should probably sit. This might take a while."

After thirty minutes more or less the two were settled comfortably inside the luxurious shuttle. The general, opening a can of oil he'd brought from Winder's house, sipped in a rare moment of complete relaxation. "So, there are a few friends left on the *Countervail*," the general stated.

Fletcher had told him that once word of his apprehension order had gotten out, the ship had split apart into two factions.

There were those who emphatically believed in the general and couldn't fathom him doing anything contrary to his nature. For centuries he'd proved his uprightness. The order was clearly out of the question and obviously some error.

Then there were those who believed the order to be absolute, and that the general fleeing proved his own guilt over whatever indiscretion haunted him.

If he was innocent, why hadn't he faced General Rivera, the Sixth Wing Commander, and pled his case?

Before General Rivera even had an opportunity to reconcile the issue, complete war had broken out on Erudia. The general's innocence—or guilt—would have to wait. Larger matters were at hand. Like the approaching extermination of a planet.

Fletcher had taken personal leave and made a day trip to Wuden in the hopes of finding out about the general. Speculation ran through the ship that the general was on-planet and hadn't make it out of the system. Apparently they were right.

"What about Glass?" The general asked as he tossed away the empty can. The cyborg's intent still plagued the general. "He was on-planet looking for me too," he said as he thought of the run-in Winder had had with his late-night visitor.

Fletcher shrugged. She didn't seem surprised at the general's statement. "Dunno. He's been working with the new recruits, as far as I know."

The general listened, idly rubbing his head with his hand. Then he realized he was inadvertently mocking a human movement he'd seen centuries ago. There was no reason for him to rub his head. It didn't itch. "Yes, the recruits," the general said as he took his hand away.

He had been expecting more cyborgs to arrive to the Sixth Mechanized any day. But given everything going sideways, he'd completely forgot. Or maybe he'd *conveniently* forgot, as robots traditionally have pretty good memories.

Old jealousies were hard to kill—especially when it came to the general and his dislike of cyborgs. That simple fact continued to rear its head.

In return for Fletcher's info, the general gave her the nutshell version of his exploits. He was careful to gloss over details and keep it blandly vague. Despite his comfortableness with her, he remained skeptical of everyone. For the moment, anyway.

"I need this ship," the general said after wrapping up his story, finishing with the encounter with the Vesuvians.

Fletcher nodded. The general figured she had been around him enough to know he wasn't exactly asking, but issuing a not-so-subtle demand. "I can fly you there," she offered. "I came all this way, after all."

"No," the general said. "You might get implicated with me. Better I commandeer this. I can hit you over the head to make it appear you were hijacked."

Fletcher considered the general's kind offer. "No thanks," she said. "I've seen your strength. I'd prefer to be tied up."

She was neither hit over the head nor tied up. She stood outside the shuttle as the general prepared to disembark. The cargo door slowly closed. "Keep your blaster at the ready," he said. "There's plenty of dirtbags around here."

After buckling himself in and running through an abbreviated pre-flight check, the general fired up the *Pigeon*. The auxiliary power unit spun up with a high-pitched whine, which fired up the engines. Meanwhile, the general plotted an uncomplicated route from the port to Erudia, the next planet over.

Then the ship lifted, blowing trash and nickel-sized debris, and, after ascending well into the Wudenan sky, sped away.

Yellow electric clouds wrapped half the planet in a blanket. Erudia had been in a death grip of static for months. The brutal assault of the lingering ion storm had begun to alter the atmosphere to the point many began to wonder if the storm itself was some type of atmospheric planet-crushing weapon wielded by an unfathomable enemy.

The *Pigeon's* controls were sluggish. Twice the general thought it was going into a free fall. The storm was to blame.

It didn't escape his thoughts that the last time he'd piloted a spaceship was when he crashed through Wuden' atmosphere, turning it into a smoking fireball—crashing into a planet was immensely easier than trying not to crash.

For the most part, once the general made it into Erudia's gravitational pull—on the far side of it all and away from any American Forces ships orbiting—he let nature take its course, guided by autopilot.

Shaking—bulkheads rattling loose and buffeting wildly about—the *Pigeon* dropped through the upper atmosphere. Once below the storm, about 10,000 feet above ground level, the turbulence diminished considerably and the general managed to level the ship out.

He'd made it through the worst part.

Now maybe the storm would benefit his cause. Which was to remain obscure.

Since fleeing the *Countervail*, he'd kept his internal comm disabled so the Sixth's cyber ops wouldn't find him easily. Being this close to the Sixth, having the extra bit of insurance in the form of a raging ion storm to hide potential comm emanations didn't hurt. The last thing the general wanted was to be forced to face his brothers and sisters. Like back on the *Countervail*. He didn't seek hand-to-hand combat with them.

For their sake, not his.

He hoped the storm's disruption would mask his arrival on-planet.

Being a VIP shuttle, meant to transport stuffed shirts and media from ship to ship, the *Pigeon* lacked complicated offensive or defensive systems. But its navigation systems were top notch. Taking the transponder he'd collected from Shenko, the general patched it into the ship's navigation inputs.

After a second of processing and deciphering, a display materialized across the *Pigeon's* view screens, which overlaid the wrap-around port windows.

Planetary maps of Erudia came up in the display. They showed mountain ranges, streams and rivers, hilltops, and city streets in minute detail. The transponder coordinates popped up on screen: the location was near the Exaton Mountains. This was where the Vesuvians were encamped on Erudia.

An info box on the display said the mountain range was named after the first brave explorer to traverse the treeless, rocky range. He'd met his end when one too many celebratory drinks of crushed wildfire berries had shot his balance. Leaning over an edge to take in the view, he'd plunged to his death to the delight of his travel slaves.

On the western slopes of the mountain range a gigantic ridge—

of which the Mystic Shelf made a small portion—spanned a few hundred miles. Once a massive fault line of volcanoes. The Vesuvian encampment was north of the Shelf, a hundred miles away.

As the general kept his ship skimming the underside of ion-bred clouds to keep his engine signature muddled, he scanned the ground below.

Erudia, nearer to the center of the Erdine System's sun like Wuden, was compromised of large swaths of desert. Sporadic trees, weather hardy with knotted limbs and thick bark, dotted the landscape. Around desert cities Erudians had built intricate irrigation systems, bringing water to the desert.

As he neared the Mystic Shelf, he passed over dunes that bore black scars. Personnel carriers, ripped to shreds like soda cans tossed on a highway, were half buried. Vehicle tracks crisscrossed the sand. Occasionally, he caught glimpses of bodies. Damaged battle suits and torn bodies. All grim memories of the war.

The Sixth had fought here. And the Sixth had died here.

Despite the order to apprehend him—because now the growing suspicion he had was that the order was, in fact, nothing more than a hack of the Sixth's data systems—he felt a deep sense of guilt at the carnage. Not necessarily the loss, but he was heartbroken because he hadn't been there to fight alongside his brethren.

The *Pigeon's* onboard navigation system broke into his reflections, warning him of a ship nearby.

Gripping the ship's control yoke, releasing autopilot, the general tapped the floating control strip on a holo display to zoom in. The rear view showed a glint of sunbathed metal. An AFSS CF-3720, *Wraith*—a light duty interplanetary interceptor—was on his tail. And it was close. Way too close for someone traveling a little over Mach 1, a low cruising speed for the *Pigeon*.

"Blast," the general said. The Sixth had found him.

And so close to his destination. The general set his jaw in determination. He couldn't allow himself to be stopped this close to his goal.

The only asset the *Pigeon* had over the *Wraith* might be speed. Possibly maneuverability. But that all depended on the pilot. So the general decided to take the gamble and opened the throttle on the ship to separate himself from his tail.

A warning alarm sounded.

Immediately, red outlined the holo displays splayed across the windscreens. The *Wraith* was firing on the ship. But it wasn't missile locked. Whoever was flying the interceptor was using the fuselage mounted pulse cannon.

This invalidated the *Pigeon's* paltry countermeasures, since they were geared for missiles.

The shuttle shuddered violently with gunfire turbulence. Warning lights screamed from the console. Damage to the engine.

In reaction to the trauma, ship safety circuits kicked in. The *Pigeon* slowed momentarily as Next-Gen safety circuitry healed itself, so to speak. Systems had redundant paths and were networked so there was never one point of failure. Power could redirect through a hundred paths of multipurpose hardware.

But that didn't matter as another round of bursts tossed the ship to the left. The general fought the control stick that no longer operated engines or terrain flaps. Warning chimes continued blaring.

It became obvious the shuttle didn't stand a chance against the interceptor. If he stayed in the air, it would be a losing battle.

He needed to see about evening the odds.

And, the general knew he'd rather draw his pursuers down to the ground, as they obviously didn't want to kill him. At least he thought they didn't.

Not at this time, anyway.

The *Wraith* had missiles, cannon, and magna pulses at its disposal. It could turn the shuttle into a smoking hole at any moment. But it hadn't, yet.

Once he rolled out of a left bank he quickly descended and adjusted his thrust vector so that the *Pigeon* hung in the air temporarily before slowly lowering to a flat expanse of granite-like rock.

To the general's surprise, which he honestly hadn't thought would happen, the *Wraith* followed suit, touching down on the opposite end of the rocky plateau.

Taking his sword, the general raced from his shuttle to meet whoever had shot him out of the sky.

The *Wraith's* door opened and out stepped Glass in full battle gear.

"Here I am, cyborg," the general said, his voice sounding more like the cruel hiss of a snake. "Come and apprehend me if you think you can."

"This isn't what I want," yelled Glass as he backed up, his hands away from his body—he made no sudden moves.

For all the trust that could be earned in battle, the tenuous trust Glass had earned, could it so quickly be discarded by the general in a moment of anger? The fact that Glass had attempted to blow him out of the sky was all the justification the general needed at that moment, right or wrong. Especially in the heat of battle.

"Why are you tailing me?" Demanded the general. "You tried to shoot me down."

"Because," Glass said, like he'd never considered his actions as anything but noble, but taking a quick step backwards nevertheless, "I was concerned about you. I wanted to get your attention, but," he turned back to the *Wraith,* "I don't know this ship. It locked onto you because your Friend or Foe was disabled. I couldn't hail you on any frequencies." He continued looking at the ship like it was expected to voice support for his explanation.

And for the general, the old robot who'd learned cynicism from sitting front row to hundreds of years of treachery and deceit, didn't quite believe the explanation. "You lie," he responded, his jaw set firmly. But his monotone voice didn't carry the typical angry, passionate inflections that he liked to pepper his voice with. He had momentarily lost his conviction, unsure of Glass' motives.

"I've pleaded with General Rivera," Glass said, speaking of the Sixth's Wing Commander. "He didn't issue that order. But before he could squash it, war broke out here. The matter took a sideline to the war. I'm risking court martial looking for you. So is Captain Fletcher."

Certain humans were able to broach the general's hardened exterior, intentionally or unintentionally. Even he didn't know why, but he attributed it to some esoteric workings of his emotive chip. "Playing favorites," as Daniel Jacoby had explained it during the general's early days of life.

Fletcher was one. With Glass he still wasn't sure. He remained dubious to the cyborg's intentions. But the mention of Fletcher indicated they were working together on some level. If so, why had Fletcher told him she didn't know about Glass?

"How did you find me?" asked the general, keeping his sword at the ready.

"On Wuden," Glass responded. "At a market some mercs mentioned mysterious things falling to the planet. That led me to a guy named Winder. I got to his house and found enough evidence to make it clear that you were heading east. Then, on my way I met this Vesuvian desert rat named Shenko about to become lunch for a pack of desert rodents. He was ready to cut off his hand for a drink. For a sip, he spilled pretty much everything about the Vesuvians."

Glass looked away from the general to the damaged shuttle. Black and bubbling char on the wings spoke of where the high energy blasts had struck. As he studied the damage he shook his head, an apologetic look crossing his face. "I want to help you," he said.

"I'm headed north," the general said, "to find the Vesuvians. Hatch is behind this treachery, along with the jackals. I'd be there now splitting skulls if you hadn't shot me out of the sky." Then it occurred to the general he'd first heard about Hatch from Glass.

"Yes, Hatch," Glass said, nodding. "My own detective work points to him. Looks like he fooled many of us. You found him?"

"I think he's cowering with the Vesuvians like a kicked dog," the general said, playing along for the moment.

"I can help," Glass said. "I owe Hatch too."

"Why not," the general said.

A struggle raged within the general. He'd never admit it, but the sound of this brought a little relief. He'd been so battle damaged by the bounty hunter and the time jumping witch that he questioned whether he could endure another fight.

But could be trust Glass? That was the million credit question. At the moment he was limited on help. He'd accept the extended hand, but would keep an uneasy eye on the cyborg. Having him nearby would help.

Even so, nothing could turn the general away from his task. He would burn out every last processor, shred every last wire bundle, break every last hinge.

He would find those responsible for causing this mess.

Ang-Thoth licked his dry lips in the same manner a mother lion would before taking the first bite of a throttled gazelle.

Carelessly kicking pillows off his divan onto the dirt-covered rugs that made up his floor, he sat upright in his tent.

The monstrous pavilion on the Wudenan plain had been cleared of time jumper groupies and those hoping to barter for some rare artifact. All that were left was the baron, his mercenary bodyguards, and a monkey. Outside the tent, the time bazaar went on, but without the main attraction.

Standing uneasily before the patriarch time jumper, Kento-Gala didn't show so much as a drop of the disgust that churned inside her.

The Mercurian cloth that made the pavilion was worth a fortune, monetarily and historically. Dirt had been tracked into the pavilion, clouds of fine silt from where a million merchants had stamped the plains grass down to nothing. Everything smelled of dirt, of sweat, of... *on-planet.* Even the heavy rose perfumes wafting from clay pots didn't mask the stench of life.

The time jumper's tent and his lavish throne didn't impress Kento-Gala in the least.

She lived on the *Erio-Magus,* the Queen of Heaven, as many called her. Rare gemstone plates dug out from under the desolate mountains of Titan IV adorned the bridge. Gold accented walkways and handholds. After the Skirmishes of Nabul, the priceless treaty tapestries of living light detailing the life cycle of the Nabulites had been hung just outside her private quarters. Legends were spun and songs written over the contents of the baroness' Victory Gallery alone. Each year the ship's electronics were upgraded. Unheard of tech powered the ship. The Slipstream drive tucked in the engine bay was second to none.

She compared this to the pavilions Ang-Thoth preferred, wallowing in the dirt on a semi-arid planet—there was no comparison in Kento-Gala's mind.

Overhead, intricate material baffles and vent holes in the pavilion roof gave the impression the tent was alive whenever a gust stirred. The roof billowed and heaved like they were standing inside the lungs of some long-forgotten demigod.

Too bad the vents didn't get rid of the stench.

"If I ever lived to see the emergence of Casoy-wu from the pits of hell," Ang-Thoth declared, half to himself, "have I unwittingly jumped into paradise?"

Kento-Gala would've just as soon ran her battle glaive through his disgusting, black heart than endure another moment of his eyes scouring every curve of her armored body. But it would be bad form to dispatch him before asking for his assistance. Since setting her armored foot in his tent she regretted the decision of requesting his audience. But she was here, and she couldn't back out now. "Baron Ang-Thoth," she said as she bowed low, the very words tasting like vomit, "I've come to you bringing the most dire news."

"Unless you've come to accept my offer, I'm not interested," the baron said, casually. "Certainly I don't care about anything my sister has to say." His skeletal body shook as he laughed. It sounded like the death rattle of a hyena. The ever-present monkey chained to the divan slung its leash and chattered, imitating his master.

"That's it precisely, baron," Kento-Gala said, eyeing the monkey with curious fascination. "Your sister."

The baron shrunk back a bit, his countenance taking a suddenly serious tone. "I think you're here to spy for her. Sin-Jalek," he called out in a new burst of animation as he glanced to his right. "She's here to spy on us. Disarm her."

And like a machine that doesn't question the motives or whims of its programmer, Sin-Jalek, one of Ang-Thoth's bodyguard mercenaries, sprang into action.

His blue power armor crackled with life as he drew his sword instead of his blaster.

Professional warriors always looked for opportunities to sharpen little utilized skills. It wasn't everyday he would have a chance to have a good old sword fight.

That's what Kento-Gala would've done.

But before Sin-Jalek could even mount any semblance of a reasonable attack, Kento-Gala had already reacted to the baron's edict with surprising speed. Although within seven feet of her opponent, she had somehow spun her battle glaive so that it now separated the two. Red witch fire emblazoned the tip.

A flurry of silent movements and countermovements filled the baron's pavilion. The only sound metal crashing against metal and an occasional breath.

Amazed at the display of skill and swordsmanship, onlookers watched, mesmerized.

In seconds it seemed like a hundred sword strokes and jabs were thrown. Then, with one mighty spin of the glaive in Kento-Gala's dextrous hands, her blade knocked away Sin-Jalek's sword. Then she cleaved through his breastplate. The uncanny effect of the blade cast him back, almost knocking him off his feet. He dropped to one knee as all his armor went haywire, the circuits burned out, infected with the strange fire.

"Hold!" Ang-Thoth exclaimed, his voice thin yet powerful.

Just as suddenly as Sin-Jalek had begun his unsuccessful attack, it ended. He stood as upright as he could in his malfunctioning armor. Then, with a slight nod of his head in acknowledgment of Kento-Gala's superiority, he moved back to his position, to the right of the baron's divan.

There, he appeared to skulk as his breath returned to him, as ragged as the baron's own labored breathing.

Fascinated by a society that put such value in killing, Kento-Gala had spent many hours studying the southern mercenaries.

She hadn't just defeated Sin-Jalek—she'd brought shame to his family, instructors, everyone who'd devoted long days teaching him weapon play.

And his embarrassment had been put on display for his peers and his employer to see.

Aware of the strict code the southern mercenaries lived by, Kento-Gala knew his pride would haunt him through the night. And in the morning they'd find him with his own ceremonial poignard jammed into his heart.

This is why she appointed double guards over Bar-San as he recovered. The baroness would want him kept alive. As much as she disliked sharing the baroness' attention with others, her loyalty outweighed her jealousy.

"Just beautiful," Ang-Thoth exclaimed. "You haven't lost a step."

Kento-Gala took her position in front of the baron's divan, her battle glaive at a pike ready position. "No more games, baron," she said through quick gasps, her cheek muscles flexing to restrain her anger at the thought that Ang-Thoth could so recklessly toss away a good soldier. "I'm not here to entertain you. Ang-Palius is gone."

She blurted out before he decided to play any more ridiculous games with her.

Ang-Thoth stopped mid-chuckle. "Gone?" he asked quizzically.

"She was pulled into an errant jump," Kento-Gala added.

Stroking the frazzled beard on his razor chin, Ang-Thoth mused. "She's not impetuous enough to make bad jumps. I've made at least six bad jumps in my days. She hasn't made one." He came to his conclusion. "Impossible," he stated.

With a saddened shake of her head, sweat-soaked hair strands clinging to her cheeks, Kento-Gala said, "The baroness was locked in battle with General Mikeal. He caused it."

The baron, up till then stroking his chin, decided to chew on a fingernail as he contemplated Kento-Gala's words. "She went against the general? Looks like the old robot got the best of her," Ang-Thoth said. "I knew she'd become headstrong… What of the *Erio-Magus*?"

Just like Kento-Gala had expected, the time jumper's thoughts quickly moved from mundane things such as family to baser issues. Material. "My sister has it secure," Kento-Gala said. "The Red Guard is on watch. Anyone would be foolish to try and take it. Just like the baroness would want."

The baron nodded, considering her words. Finally, after thinking a bit more he said, "So what do you want from me?"

"To find her," Kento-Gala said.

He laughed again. "You and I both know she'd rather be stuck in eternal damnation forever than have me guide her back," Ang-Thoth said.

"I'm asking this as a personal favor," Kento-Gala said. "If not, can you at least rain hell down on top of General Mikeal? Sources tell me he's on Erudia."

The baron pointed a thin finger at her. "Now I like your thinking, my precious flower," he said. Tossing one hand in the air, he continued, "I suppose I can search for dear little sis. That's going to cost me some spots." He pulled back one of his sleeves to reveal a rail-like arm riddled with time burns. "I don't have much left. You know I'm doing this for the Commandant of the Red Guard, not Ang-Palius."

To which Kento-Gala nodded. The price for rescuing the baroness would be steep. Disgustingly steep.

"I'll even throw in the *hell rain* you asked for free," Ang-Thoth said. "Because I'm a nice guy like that. And it'll be fun."

To which the monkey clattered his teeth before biting the end of his own tail with reckless abandon.

A day after the run-in with Glass, the general hunkered behind a boulder with oxidized veins of ore, watching the Vesuvian encampment on Erudia. The transponder from the worm Shenko had proven true in guiding him here.

Julianna Darrisaw, a cyborg, crouched next to him. She pulled from her cargo pocket a tube of protein-steroids, trying to downplay the event. She turned away from the general as she took in a mouthful of paste.

He pretended not to notice.

A year ago, when the mech had shorted and blew its ammunition stores in the *Countervail's* maintenance bay, Darrisaw the maintenance technician had been right there. Even with her mangled arm and a torso and face full of shrapnel, she'd raced back into the fire to pull fellow airmen out.

Her token for this were third degree burns all over her body and scorched lungs from breathing toxic chemical fires.

The paste helped ease her internal pain.

Once evacuated to the *Sam Houston,* the Sixth's medical ship, she'd begun receiving treatment. Twenty operations later, skilled doctors had grafted sim-skin over the worst areas.

Her face, while repaired, still showed scars and at times looked unnatural. Like when a movie star past their prime thinks plastic surgery or *New Asian* nanite skin cream would fool everyone. They resembled their younger selves. But not quite.

She'd fought medical discharge, pleading her case to the bureaucrats. With the support of General Rivera and countless supervisors, including the general, she was allowed to join the Wounded Veterans Program. An organization to reintroduce the combat-wounded to military service.

The general had become her sponsor in the process. But many of the general's peers had questioned why he would waste his time with a lowly private maintenance technician.

Taking another cyborg on board was the last thing anyone had expected the general to do. He'd respond to her detractors that her skill as a mechanic made her valuable to him.

He remembered the respect Darrisaw had shown him in the past. He also knew her as a gifted technician, able to fix every mechanical problem, every battle damaged armor plate. Even though that's what the general said, he wasn't sure even he believed that was the whole story.

Darrisaw was different. From the moment he'd met her he'd known this. She brought back old but familiar memories to him.

From the general's vantage point over the encampment, hidden behind a boulder and a cluster of sun-dried trees on a small rise, he watched Glass make a strafing run. Glass, having already temporarily 'borrowed' the *Wraith* to find the general, was being put to good use in the plan the general had come up with the day before.

The interceptor made a clumsy bank as it came around. Glass understood the mechanics of flying, but didn't quite yet have the art like Fletcher. But as long as he was able to drop a bomb, he didn't need finesse.

According to Glass, shortly after the general had fled the *Countervail*, Darrisaw, who had h a sneaking suspicion that Glass knew more about the general than he had let on, had invited the cyborg to the ship bar after a particularly grueling day of practice.

It was easy enough for her to ply any information from Glass after his second margarita. He might've been a great teacher, but he sucked at operations security. And holding his liquor.

So when Glass and Fletcher had decided to track down the general, Glass knew Darrisaw would jump at the opportunity to help.

The transponder Shenko had given the general dispelled the Vesuvian cloak, revealing where a hundred sweeping planetary scans had indicated nothing but bone-dry desert.

After some quick recon, the general had put together a plan. And a skinny ziggurat of metalwork framing at the center of the Vesuvian camp was the first target.

Over six stories high, the uppermost reaches of the antenna emitted a ghostly green swirl. Occasionally, a soundless spark of green lightning scrawled into the sky. The general had surmised this antenna as being at the epicenter of the cloaking field.

The *Wraith* circling in the sky had been reconfigured for bombing runs.

Swept back wings moved forward to form an oblong semi-circle around the body of the interceptor. Grills and actuating panels perforating the wings gave the ship excellent maneuverability.

Five GB-605 *Beehives*—fat, stubby-body mass personnel dispersion bomblets—dropped from mounted rails on the underside of the ship. The bomblets plummeted through the Erudian sky until they hit one thousand feet above ground level. The outer shells cracked open. Hundreds of ball bearing size *bees* swarmed from the shells. The low level intelligence of the bugs tracked onto the ziggurat.

Pulse cannons set along the perimeter of the camp must've finally detected the *Wraith*—they spun to life, swinging double barrels upward. Flashes of lightning arced from the cannons as they drummed the sky in ear-splitting blasts. Blue explosive flak clouds chewed through the bugs. But there were too many.

The swarming mass shifted and swelled around blasts, moving like it had one mind but consisting of many bodies. Finding their target, the bees zoomed in and detonated.

The hundreds of micro explosions rattled the tower to its core, ripping it apart from every conceivable angle. Compromised metal crumbled, collapsing onto itself. The ghostly green swirl snuffed out like a wet candle flame. With the death of their cloaking antenna, the Vesuvians knew they were found out.

Now the Sixth would be able to detect the Vesuvians.

This encampment, made of squat pre-fabs like the encampment on Wuden, was about the same size. Twenty buildings or so. Except for one glaring difference—at one edge of the encampment was a gantry of scaffolding that reached over ten stories, dwarfing the other structures. A gargantuan skyscraper in a sea of hovels.

But it was difficult to tell what was inside of the gantry; it was covered with tarps and flexi panels. This structure oddly contrasted against the pre-fabs and tents. Everything else appeared temporary, quickly constructed. But this gantry seemed a more permanent structure.

The general figured it was significant, but he didn't know how much, and he wasn't sure if it needed to be leveled.

After a moment of contemplation, he decided it needed to be razed to the ground.

The general needed to communicate with Glass, and the only way was through line-feed. Once he enabled his comm the Sixth would see him, clear as day. It was time to quit hiding.

Finally engaging his line-feed to tell Glass to hit the gantry, the general was instead flooded with battle chatter from the Mystic Shelf War, happening miles away.

...a captain called for medics because his sergeant had just taken a ballistic to the chest. But the medi-bots had just been incinerated in a plasma bomb...

...Fire Team Echo's lead stumbled across a dug-in pillbox on the left flank. Blaster fire and mortars pinned them down...

...a boy screamed in blood-curdling terror which turned into wet gurgles for what seemed an impossibly long time...

The Sixth's front lines were crumbling. The general couldn't stand the thought of his brothers and sisters in hot combat while he was so near.

His anger at Hatch, his hatred for the Vesuvians, and his overall disgust of the aliens boiled his motor oil blood. Instead of waiting for Fletcher to return with reinforcements like they'd planned yesterday, he made an on-the-spot decision to charge forward. He didn't need help waging war. That he could do on his own.

"Let's see what you got," the general said to Darrisaw. Then, drawing his sword with one hand, taking his nail gun in the other, he charged the encampment, hoping the Vesuvians were in disarray now that Glass had blasted their cloak.

"Wait," Darrisaw called out, but the general had already gained twenty feet on her. She bolted into a full-on sprint. "What am I doing here?" she wondered out loud.

The first man the general came across was leaning against a pre-fab, smoking some type of home-rolled Corinthian tobacco from the smell of it. His bright red and yellow pantaloons and the similarly painted scraps of power armor covering his wide torso told the general this was a Corinthian pirate—they often signed up as Vesuvian mercenaries with the promise of loot and the chance to freely kill.

The pirate eyed the sky indifferently, probably looking for the source of the explosion and the reason why the anti-air pulse cannons were lighting up the sky. A lifetime of fighting had made him complacent.

Seeing General Mikeal sprinting across a strip of barren land, he reached for his standard blaster, but was painfully slow in his reaction.

Without slowing, the general raised his nail gun. A quick squeeze of the trigger and roughly a hundred nails ended the Corinthian's mediocre pirate career. He slipped to the ground even before blood began pumping from his wounds.

Not looking back, the general trained his rifle toward four Vesuvians thirty feet away. Amplifying his voice to terrible proportions, the general bellowed in the Vesuvian tongue, "Come meet *Anura Delo Mek*, you miserable jackals. I'll send you to roast in hell with your cousins."

"It's *Anura*!" one of the men yelled, fear quaking his voice. "To arms you dogs."

Before they could act, the general sprayed the team with nails. One was quick enough to dodge behind a metal shipping container, but his companions were eviscerated where they stood.

Blaster fire responded, erupting from multiple pre-fab doorways. Bolts indiscriminately struck walls as the general brought his sword up to intercept a blast heading for his torso. It ruptured on his blade, energy dissipating. Subconsciously, the general leeched some of the energy traveling through his blade to recharge his own power cells.

He raked the squat houses with nails as he continued dodging blaster bolts.

Darrisaw moved to his left. A squat box on the back piece of her power armor snapped upward and rested on her shoulder.

Seven fist-sized pucks shot from the modified rocket box and spun through the air. Each puck independently targeted warm bodies or flew through open doorways, depending on where her eyes lingered on her HUD display. Once they neared their targets the pucks whirled violently, fracturing into millions of incendiary fragments. Vesuvians and pre-fabs ignited in white hot fire.

Many infantry called the GR-210 Multi-directional Fragmentation Incendiary Pucks MFIPs. But after witnessing their utter devastation, many simply called them "Satan's Breath".

Taking advantage of the sudden conflagration, the general crashed through a crackling wall of flame, intercepting a group of Vesuvians headed to the fray.

Three of the ten enabled their ragtag power armor. Blue and red shimmering hues enveloped them. The general swung at the nearest and his blade glanced off, sliding downward and digging into the ground. The Vesuvian unloaded his blaster, catching the general square in the chest.

The charge enveloped his body. The severity of the massive blow was too much for his system to absorb and nullify. Stumbling backwards and rocking on his heels, the general re-engaged his gyros to keep himself upright.

A mortal man would've been cut in half by the point-blank blast.

"We've got 'im," one of the Vesuvians cackled in a dirty accent.

"Set your blasters to 'liquify.'" A second Vesuvian proclaimed, following his buddy.

But before they reached the general, Darrisaw, with the help of boot thrusters, intercepted the two. She raised her right forearm and from her armored sleeve sprang a telescopic wall, up and down. Extended, it formed a scutum, a curved rectangular shield as tall as her.

The shield caught the blaster bolts, which lit the carbon-fiber and metal composite material but didn't penetrate it, thanks to the state-of-the-art energy absorbing tech built in.

Darrisaw's other arm was an arm in the rudimentary sense of an appendage sprouting from her left shoulder. Instead of a hand, though, she wielded a chained bar.

She's taken an off-world miner's chainsaw—which functioned more like a rock cutter—and tweaked it into cybernetic weaponry.

As she revved her close-combat weapon the chain crackled with yellow intensity, flashing white at its core.

She brought her chainsaw around her shield, catching the one cocky Vesuvian on his side. His energy shield blocked the blade from touching him, but it didn't do much to stop the crackling field.

Fingers of raw voltage played over his power armor's energy shield, arcing in strange ways. It shorted the circuitry, and with a loud bang and whiff of fried ozone blew up his armor. The blast sent him hurling backwards as Darrisaw's weapon recoiled wildly.

"Holy crap," she exclaimed, bringing her weapon back under control.

Never one to waste a precious circumstance, the general utilized the momentary blast and the surprise it brought to his advantage. Leaping over Darrisaw's shield and the partial obscurity it provided, he landed almost on top of the group of Vesuvians.

With a gigantic roar that would've made any sensible man tremble, the general thrust his sword violently, catching a Vesuvian pirate square in the chest. The force of the direct blow shattered the pirate's breastplate and severed his spine, the sword tip erupting out his backplate.

Swinging his rail gun like a club, the general knocked the shoulder blaster from another stunned Vesuvian. Then, tossing aside his own rifle, he grabbed the man by the neck and flung him backward, where he crashed into stacked crates that splintered under his weight.

Rage now drove the general forward, maybe even recklessly. A bloodlust had taken control of him, driving him relentlessly forward.

Too near for the remaining three to effectively use their blasters, the remaining Vesuvians made the rash, poor decision to grapple with the general.

But Darrisaw, having retracted her shield back into her forearm, punched the face shield of one Vesuvian with her brass-knucklegauntleted fist while using her chainsaw to sever another's arm just above his elbow. Electricity rippled over the man, his silver fillings acting as a conductor. His head was thrown back as sparks poured from his mouth and nose, a demented roman candle.

Wisely, the last Vesuvian in the group turned and fled.

"He was obviously the smartest of the group," the general said as he watched him disappear around a building corner.

For the moment no other Vesuvian pirates were near.

After a couple quick lungfuls of cooling air, the general slid his sword from the dead Vesuvian, using his foot to keep the man's lifeless body from lifting off the ground. He noticed Darrisaw conveniently turn away to tend to her chainsaw as a look of revulsion passed across her face.

"You performed like any soldier is expected to perform," the general said in a surprising moment of candor. "You had a job to do and did it with tenacity and thoroughness. On paper, weapons are great. But in use, they're terrifying."

Before she could respond, a particular high-pitched whine got the general's attention. He'd heard it at least a thousand times before.

Leaping with all his might like a pouncing tiger, the general caught Darrisaw by her waist and rushed her underneath an overhang.

The ground where they had just been standing exploded in a rooster tail of dirt and dead Vesuvian body parts. The general turned his back to the blast, breaking the concussion wave.

"Mortars," the general hissed.

Peering from underneath the overhang, the general's hawk-like eyes searched the sky. "Glass, location?" he asked, wanting to get a fix of the only air support he had at the moment. He could hear the ambient engine roar of the *Wraith* but couldn't spot it in the sky. Anti-air pulse cannons still hammered away all around him. He was sure they were tracking Glass.

Several buildings burned, victims of Darrisaw's incendiaries. Voices carried over blaster fire—the Vesuvians were still trying to figure out what was happening on the ground.

"General Mikeal," came a familiar, bombastic voice over his line-feed, the southern Georgian drawl unmistakable. "I thought you'd be hiding with the criminals," General Stinson, the Sixth Infantry Commander, said. The general pictured his smug, punchable face on the other end of the comm.

"Stinson," the general responded with a certain amount of manufactured loathing in his voice he'd created specifically for the man. He switched to a private channel. "I find you just as annoying through comm as in person."

"You're wanted," Stinson said. "A fugitive," he added, his barrel voice now sober. "You caused a lot of tension on the *Countervail.*"

"I've heard your skirmish line crumble," the general responded. "I may've upset some people, but you've lost lives."

"I have your coordinates," Stinson said, all mirth gone as his voice grew thick with anger. "I can spare enough men to apprehend you."

"There's no time for this pettiness," the general responded. "I'm disabling a Vesuvian encampment. They've been secretly feeding mercenaries into the fray to protract this war on the Mystic Shelf."

"Stand down, General Mikeal," Stinson ordered.

The general responded by cutting his line-feed. "The fool." He turned to Darrisaw. "We need to finish up here. I have a feeling we're going to have company soon."

Just then blaster bolts sliced into the ground, sending the general and Darrisaw scrambling from their temporary safe spot.

A smallish terrain scrubber—a highly mobile rocket cycle with quad needlepoint lasers—zipped overhead, ten feet off the ground. It banked sharply before heading toward the general and Darrisaw.

The cycle's pilot, dressed in flexible carbon armor with spikes and an elongated aerodynamic helmet, revved the cycle as it turned sharply, drifting.

"Take cover," the general yelled as he rolled out of its path. Darrisaw's boot thrusters kicked in and she flew to the right as she telescoped her shield.

The cycle unleashed its lasers in short blasts. They chewed into the ground, heading toward the general. He wasn't able to move out of the path in time, the damage he'd taken over the last days slowing him, but he was still quick enough to intercept the blasts with his sword.

He underestimated the force of the blasts, and his sword went spiraling away to embed into a cinder block wall of a storage room. He rolled again, this time positioning himself to within arms' reach of his nail gun.

But Darrisaw was already responding to the surprise attack.

Three more pucks erupted from her back and took converging paths, targeting the cycle.

The cycle driver began defensive maneuvers. It cut left, then right, dispensing in its wake a blanket of ultra-sonic disruptors and flares. Two pucks detonated on the flares, but the third successfully navigated the countermeasure maze. It had almost reached its target when a second cycle blew the puck out of the sky.

Scrambling for cover, Darrisaw exclaimed, "Great, two of 'em. And here I am with a chainsaw." She ducked into a pre-fab cubicle to escape cycle fire.

Inside, a man sat on the edge of his cot fighting to get his left boot on. Once he saw Darrisaw he cursed and dove for his weapon.

Darrisaw, senses already on high alert, beat him to the draw. In a smooth, practiced motion, she pulled her disruptor, a thin, unassuming pistol. Her shot caught the man in his bare chest. He yelped as his body flipped over the cot. The smell of burnt chest hair filled the room.

Back outside, the general sprayed the air with nails as one cycle made a strafing run just above the rooftops. Slivers pierced the cycle but didn't bring it down. It turned from its path, however, diverting away from the general as black smoke billowed from its tail pipes. The cycle began to sputter.

Just then, an unquantifiable warrior's battle sense told the general the gantry was where he needed to go. There he'd find Hatch or Horvoth. Or both.

Yanking his sword from the wall, he charged in the direction of the gantry, a beckoning skyscraper. Minutes ago he'd wanted it destroyed, but he was now pleased Glass hadn't had the chance.

It just so happened that a great clamor of yelling and trampling feet also came from this direction.

His grip tightened on his sword, he stood more upright with his chest out, and he consciously made himself not limp as he rounded a corner of an elongated temporary hangar, a clam shell.

His keen eyes identified at least thirty warm bodies. And these were only the ones he could readily see or pick up on infrared. Countless blind corners, propped up blast shields, and stacked crates probably held double that. But his conviction was such that he wouldn't turn away. He'd never show his back to the jackals.

Several of the Vesuvians, tucked safely behind defensive positions, trained their blaster rifles on him. A hovercraft with a wicked-looking gatling cannon swung about.

Numerous targeting reticules lit in the general's eyes, along with many warning klaxons.

Just then an unhealthy engine whine rumbled through the sky.

The *Wraith* came crawling by, dirty smoke pouring from one wing tip as flames flickered out of the engine.

Before the ship could do anything more than pollute the sky, a Vesuvian anti-flak battery caught the unsteady craft in a hail of pulse cannon fire. This finished the job the other cannons had started.

The blasts shredded the wings and blew fuselage panels off. The *Wraith* rolled as the tail section swung to the left. The crippled ship disappeared over the buildings. Tense seconds later a crash and explosion rippled through the encampment.

So much for air support.

"Darrisaw," the general said through his line-feed. "Fall back. I'm about to become overrun," he said, thinking his charge would end up turning into a no-win situation. The last bit of immediate support the general had hoped for had just become a smoking hole in the ground. Fletcher needed to show up now.

"No way, general," Darrisaw responded. "No way I'm leaving. I'm your backup."

Within a blink, Darrisaw exited the pre-fab and came up behind the general to stand next to him, ready to face the horde of jackals. She revved her chainsaw.

The general gave her a glance and saw her jaw set just as firmly as his own.

"Well look what we have here," came a rough voice from among the surging mass of Vesuvian paramilitary, gun-for-hire mercenaries, and pirates. The voice carried a heavy Vesuvian accent and reverberated above the rest of the noise.

From behind the hovercraft strode a man a full head taller than the rest. He wore armor that seemed to fade into the background, become translucent, and emit wispy smoke, all at the same time. The general had seen the armor before.

Nether War Gear.

The general had encountered countless foes across galaxies so diverse that a planet-bound man would hardly be able to reason with everything the general had seen. And for all his opponents, just as many types of power armor had shattered under his sword. Only twice he'd met a foe wearing Nether War Gear. And each of those times the gear, the almost mystical collection of protective plates, withstood his onslaught.

The first encounter had happened eighty years ago on Artemis, a twin moon circling high above a cold, uninhabitable planet with a toxic atmosphere. Bramber Tarcus, an illegal arms dealer hunted by the American Forces, had crashed his gun runner there, the general hot on his tail.

After a brutal standoff ending in a stalemate, Bramber had made a Hail Mary play by activating a portable gravity well device he'd been hoping to sell to the Vesuvians. But he hadn't known the odd attraction between the phantom-like armor and the well until he'd gotten sucked into it. No one had heard from Bramber again.

The second encounter with the armor was more recent—twenty years ago on a Martian outpost.

The Sixth had repelled a Vesuvian attack on Outrigger Post Seven. There, the Vesuvian commander, a man known only as Five, had challenged the general. It ended had similarly to his first encounter with the war gear, except the armor had given Five a clear advantage. The armor had turned the general's sword strokes and disoriented him to the point that he'd become almost combat ineffective.

Only when Five's men had crumbled under war ship bombardment did the Vesuvian find himself overwhelmed and forced to withdraw. He'd run away, leaving his men behind.

The captured enemy had been more than happy to tell the general all they knew about the armor: an hour of waterboarding did wonders for communication. Their boss Five had called it Nether War Gear. The prisoners knew nothing else about it, except that after a short excursion on some remote planet their leader had returned with the mystical armor. And he'd gone insane in the process.

Without a doubt, the tall man dressed in the Nether War Gear was General Horvoth.

"I imagine you figured out our little ruse since you're here, *Anura*," Horvoth said, sly laughter punctuating his words. "You must admit, turning your own against you is quite the slap in the face."

"You dung-eating jackal," the general said, "I only expect to get slapped by women." He turned to Darrisaw. "No offense," he whispered. She shrugged dismissively.

"I weary of killing your kind," the general continued, hoping to continue goading Horvoth and his pack of jackals. He needed to stall, thinking Fletcher should be returning at any moment. "But come anyway, wretched dog. Let's see if you can do more than slap." Holding up his sword, he exclaimed, "I guarantee OreCrush is ready to split another jackal skull."

Sometimes the general was stubborn and foolhardy. Even reckless. But above all he was a shrewd military commander, seasoned through battle and fire. Over the years he'd learned he could sometimes steer a battle simply by rattling off a few choice words.

At the back of his mind, however, he wondered if he could take Horvoth, dressed in the Nether armor. Or, more importantly, if was able to defeat the armor. That question had eluded him twice already.

He hoped the Vesuvian general would take him up on the offer, even if he expected the coward to run away like a scared rabbit.

Suddenly, the Vesuvian anti-air pulse cannons renewed their drumming, turning upward to meet some new ship. They painted the sky in flak.

A cluster of missiles broke through the low, tan clouds. Wildly they whistled downward, each on an erratic path only they knew. Each singled out individual targets and unerringly struck. They exploded into fiery clouds which rolled up into the sky. Many of the cannons were wiped out.

An engine roar, quite different than the high-pitched whine of the *Wraith*, shook the ground. An AFSS TR-2300B *Flying Whale*, the largest transport drop ship in the Sixth's fleet, split the clouds, lowering from the sky. On its descent it shot more countermeasures from underside ports: sonic disruptors, radar jammers, chaff and flare. More rail-mounted missiles on the underside of the transport dropped, ignited, and then bolted forward. They found new targets. More fireballs as the ground rocked from concussion.

The Vesuvians went into a mad scramble, racing for cover or to get better views upwards. But they wouldn't get a chance to finish their preparations.

Over a half day ago, when the general had quickly thrown together a plan of attack with Glass and Fletcher, he'd realized he couldn't turn the tide of war on his own. He needed help. And he knew just where to go.

Before Fletcher had taken the passenger shuttle back to the *Countervail*, the general had given her the classified access codes to the Sixth's mechanized network that only he knew. Anyone with these codes could completely command the war machines. Even so, they would be hard-pressed to operate the complex mechs with the ming-boggling, intricate commands.

For the most part the general trusted Fletcher, but there was that small bit of nagging at the back of his mind that doubted her sincerity. But he held that caution for all humans, knowing them pretty well after living with them for three centuries.

He'd also laid out for her a complete movement sequence program for the mechs. Accessing their network was only one piece of the puzzle. They were just metal paperweights without an understanding of how to operate autonomously. That was a key difference between low and high level machine sentience. Only the general had the raw processing power to make them work collectively.

That's why he needed to stall the Vesuvians. Fletcher had needed time to steal the mechs and the large drop ship to ferry them on-planet.

He knew her as one of those pilots who lived full throttle inside and outside a fighter ship. Since Glass had already convinced her to sneak away to look for the general, she was already primed, treading that delicate line between care and law-breaking.

Fletcher had wholeheartedly agreed to the plan. Quicker than even he'd expected. No real convincing needed. They were willing to risk getting court martialed for him. That meant something. Despite his living with humans for centuries, they still managed to pleasantly surprise him on occasion.

The *Flying Whale's* rear ramp swung open, and five ovals each the size of a car slipped out the back.

Instantly, the general accessed their neural networks with a thought and took control of the mechs as they descended in their high-altitude insertion configuration.

On their way down arms and legs unfolded from the ovals. Rocket boxes elevated from shoulders. Disruptor barrels telescoped out of forearms.

The couple of remaining anti-air pulse cannons turned their

attention to the ovals, but didn't land any good blows. They all made it to the ground untouched.

Five AFV ACO-2100 *Jacobys,* twenty-foot high mechs, hit the Erudian ground, disruptor barrels unloading a punishing double-punch barrage of energy blasts from two arms in every direction.

Vesuvians screamed in anger and fear.

Several regained their senses enough and returned fire with blasters and pulse rifles. Burning energy bolts and scrawling lasers charged the air to saturation.

The general controlled the *Jacobys*, and milliseconds ago had already chosen fifteen targets he believed would add some sparks to this fray. Additionally, he assigned one to shadow Darrisaw—her wingman, so to speak.

Two *Jacobys* launched a battery of RM-205 *Swords* from their rocket boxes. The missiles arced and raced into what the general believed to be ammo buildings. The resulting pyrotechnic conflagration and the blanketing of nearby Vesuvians with burning chunks of metal indicated that he had been correct. Multiple shock-waves echoed against the buildings, knocking nearby pre-fabs over.

One man, bathed in some type of phosphorus blast, his armor melting onto his body, hurled by as he sought a cool place to die.

This gave the general great satisfaction.

"Horvoth," he shouted over the particle fire and screams. "Your jackals fry like bacon. Let's see how well you slap now." With that he lunged forward to meet Horvoth, who until now stared in disbelief that his advantage could so quickly dissolve.

Then the Vesuvian general seemed to regain composure enough to yell to his men nearby, "Protect yourself. At him, dogs."

Three Vesuvians stepped in the robot general's path, unloading blasters. He dodged three bolts, caught two on his sword, and took another in his leg. It slowed him but didn't stop him. Like dancing in front of a charging bull would incite it to a blind rage, the bolts had the same effect on the general. It spurned him forward, a runaway train of angry, sentient Martian ore.

Horvoth watched it all unfold with a cool attentiveness that replaced his initial disbelief. Maybe even boredom.

One hapless Vesuvian made the incorrect assumption that the general would slow once he stepped in his path. Without batting a metal eyelash the general sidestepped, cleaving through the man's hip, shattering his pelvis and spine into a million shards. Each sliver of bone acted as a missile, cutting through tender, fleshy vitals.

Six other Vesuvians were cleared out of the way by the *Jacoby's* hammering disruptors, which burned holes through armor and men alike.

As the general neared Horvoth, he had a chance to regard him closer.

The man was every bit as tall as the general's seven feet. Possibly even taller. The Nether War Gear, plates covering arms and legs and his torso, threw off thin wisps. Like the armor was dipped in liquid oxygen. But the chill it threw off wasn't cold. It was the chill of another dimension.

Already the gear was playing with the general's eyes. They lost focus several times. Only through continually refreshing his optic sensors was he even able to keep the Vesuvian in view.

"What kind of witchcraft is this?" the general muttered as he slowed.

With his focus so intently on Horvoth and his demonic gear, the general temporarily lost sight of the hovercraft.

Its gatling cannon unloaded a hellish storm of fiery projectiles on the general. Sun-baked Erudian clay and trampled dirt exploded underneath the general's feet, sending him sideways. But as he contorted and established a trajectory that would reduce catastrophic damage to himself, he was already redirecting one of his *Jacobys*, serial number NM-156, to intercept the hovercraft. *NM-156* had a defect in its left hip rotator due to a faulty circuit board which caused it to move fractionally slower than its brothers. It wasn't the most qualified for a flat out bum-rush, but the fully stocked rocket box on its shoulder and its 98% charged disruptors would make up for its lazy leg.

NM-156 received the general's coords and used them to target the hovercraft four hundred feet away, unleashing a teeth-rattling barrage of RS-105 *Daggers,* compact missiles the size of a man's hand. The cluster spread out to avoid blanket detonation defenses.

Each squirreled through the air in erratic corkscrew patterns before one missile found its mark on the hovercraft and ignited the stores of ammunition belts stacked knee high. The resultant discharge split the hovercraft apart, immediately disintegrating the five occupants while sending a shrapnel-filled concussive wave through the surrounding Vesuvians.

The explosion was such that even Horvoth—dressed in the Nether War Gear but so near the blast—didn't escape the raw ferocity of the nearby explosion. Knocked off his feet, he tumbled like a dry weed caught in a dust devil.

Used to being wrapped in concussion blasts and being peppered with shrapnel, the general could shake off most of the effects. He didn't have tender flesh to lacerate, guts to rattle loose from blunt trauma, or fragile eyes that would weld shut with only a few grains of blown dust.

Springing back to his feet, he shook his head to knock the dirt from his ears.

The other *Jacobys* likewise weathered the explosion, taking advantage of the Vesuvian's momentary lapse of reason. The mechs began to pick them off, the ones that hadn't had the breath ripped from their lungs by over pressure.

The battle was becoming a turkey shoot, a term the general had learned from one quiet, strong woman named Xerxan, a fifth gener-ation weaponeer, on Earth. She'd always said there were two types of death in battle: active and passive.

Good field commanders knew when to stop one and allow the other to run its course.

The general dispatched a command for his *Jacobys* to stand down.

"If you value your miserable hides, then flee," the general said aloud, mirrored through each mech. The thought of allowing his enemies, especially these jackals, to live, irritated him. But his eyes were set on a bigger prize anyway.

He turned to engage with Horvoth again, but the man had disappeared.

He extended his visual scanners to locate the fleeing man. But hot spots from a hundred burning fires and blast haze clouded his reception.

The few surviving Vesuvians that could walk scampered away. A couple dragged their wounded buddies, but the majority were left for the vultures, or whatever beasts inhabited this planet.

Presently, the terrain scrubber cycles that had been strafing the camp turned south and sped away. Across the encampment, barely audible through the smaller ammunition and pulse rifle battery explosions, an engine whined.

A ship kicked up a dust storm as it lifted from the ground. Another followed. Vesuvian personnel carriers.

Those that were too slow to make the drop ships grabbed parked terrain scrubbers and personnel hauling hovercraft, scrambling from the camp in whichever direction their vehicle pointed.

Two more various sized personnel carriers lifted off, and the general had no doubt Horvoth was on one of those ships. "Coward," he said as he watched the yellow blasts of engine exhaust climb into the sky.

The battle was over and all that was left was cleanup.

He accessed his line-feed. "Darrisaw, how are you?" Once she responded she was fine, just out of breath, the general sent her a coord that he thought would be close to where he'd seen the *Wraith* plummet to earth, and told her to look for Glass.

"Yessir," Darrisaw responded in her feed.

He watched the blip that represented Darrisaw as it moved over the image map in his mind. He couldn't detect Glass' Friend or Foe beacon.

Any hopes of getting to the bottom of Hatch's treachery faded as easily as the Vesuvian personnel carriers which disappeared in the cloudy sky. Horvoth's admission and the evidence here reasonably proved the general's innocence.

While here, he figured he'd make the most of it.

<*Raze this rat hole to the ground*> the general told his mechs.

Immediately, the *Jacobys* went to work complying with their general's orders. They turned their disruptors on all the rudimentary buildings and tents, blasting what could be blasted, burning what could be burned.

One *Jacoby*, red flames painted down its side,--nicknamed *Hot Shot* by its crew chief— lowered its arms. From its shoulders extended what looked like thin wings. But they were actually launcher racks.

A hundred golf-ball sized objects shot out of the launcher racks at various heights and distances. The volatile objects split and immediately ignited in hellish white fury as the chemicals mixed with air. A phosphorus blanket of unquenchable fire ate through cloth, wood, and steel. They tore through the camp like a chubby kid tears through his trick-or-treat bag.

Everything became a target except for the gantry. The general wanted to inspect it a little closer. And he did.

The gantry could've been a skyscraper under construction for all the general knew.

Crates upon crates were stacked nearby, full of metal plating, rolls of stock alloys, bolts, and other construction material. Disused scraps of metal were in piles nearby, alongside overflowing trash cans, spoiled food spilling over onto the ground. It smelled like cooked death—obviously cleanliness wasn't a priority for the Vesuvians.

Circling the gantry, the general saw scaffolding secured with braided cabling and a hodgepodge of interconnected beams and metal banding.

As he circled the skeleton of a skyscraper, the general noticed a dim, greenish swirling light emitting from cracks in the paneling. Then he found a door. With his nail gun on full auto, he entered.

Immediately he came to a stop, staring, astounded.

A massive beast, at least a hundred feet in length, hung suspended on ropes of nothing. A layer of water, at least two feet thick, encircled the beast like a liquid force field.

On the long journey to the Erdine System, the general remembered reading about this legendary beast as he was orienting himself to planetary environments.

If a human were to see this monstrosity, they would immediately think they were staring at some type of mutant whale. But, unlike its earthly cousin, this beast was much worse.

Most of its body was covered in thick, bony-like protrusions that functioned as scales, tapering down its thick tail to end in long, bony spikes. Rudimentary, underdeveloped arms were perched close to its gaping mouth, and at its opposite end were paddle-like legs. The beast more closely resembled dragons of old than a whale.

They inhabited the Wuden coastlines, often seen from the beaches of the archipelagos feeding on any bird or fish foolish enough to get in its monstrous path. Or occasionally plaguing some lone fishermen, mistaking the boat for a big fish.

Eventually the southern mercenaries, always looking for opportunities to prove their weapon skills, had incorporated the hunt of these beasts as one of their many trials. While the beasts claimed many hunters, eventually they yielded to the generations of battle.

A hardy warrior could only take so many blows before eventually succumbing to the wounds of years and time. So it was with these beasts.

Their gift of long life became a curse, as decade after decade of fending off attacks and suffering non-fatal injuries eventually took a toll on even these strong water beasts. As their numbers dwindled, they'd pushed further out into the great southern ocean to find safety away from the long reach of men needing to prove their manhood.

Given time, the scarce beasts became legendary, with many of the southern mercenary clans worshiping them as *Hysa-De-Wu*, the water demigod of the archipelagos. Warrior clans revered them for their death-sacrifice, as through their suffering they strengthened the mercenary nation.

Apparently, the general reasoned as he stared at the beast, the

Vesuvians had managed to capture one and cargo it from Wuden to Erudia.

The general didn't need to look far or to expend many neural processes to understand why.

On several portions of the beasts' body were mechanical and electrical coverings. Metal plating, molded to contour the massive body, covered most of its soft underbelly. One end of a multitude of plastic hoses were jammed into the beast, while the other ends were connected to the gantry walls. Colored fluid bubbled through clear hoses. Scaffolding of flimsy rails and narrow walkways at ten-foot spans allowed the Vesuvians access to virtually every inch of the beast.

The jackals were turning the water beast into a cyborg.

This nauseated the general in the same way a first year med student is sickened when witnessing their first autopsy. If he produced bile it would've risen up his throat to choke him.

This gigantic monstrosity was a Clockwork Orange sensory experience of epic disgust. The decades—*centuries*—of hatred and revulsion he held for cyborgs wasn't easy to forget. Especially for a robot. And this thing encapsulated all the disgust he'd ever held for them.

Then he remembered the slimy weasel Shenko's words on Wuden.

This had to be *Levatha Hydraus*.

He could not imagine what Horvoth was planning on doing with this spawn from hell. But he understood why he'd wanted a cyborg.

Robots, by their very nature, are not as random as you would expect.

Daniel Jacoby, lead engineer for Dynamo Robotics and General Mikeal's designer, called the term *The Rule of Artificial Non-Entropy*. During many of his early experiments in artificial intelligence and random cognition, he'd noticed peculiarities. Consistencies in robotic thought.

Despite neural nets and billions upon billions of synaptic firings in a robot's brain, eventually they would fall into systematic patterns of thought, action, or deed. The Second Law of Thermodynamics in a warped, reverse kind of way.

No one knew why or how.

But when inorganic artificial intelligence was combined with organic intelligence, that minimized the rule of non-entropy, allowing the beasts to think without becoming repetitive in thought.

Cyborgs.

The general's revulsion of cyborgs, which he believed had gained its footing from his first fight with the Mexican spiders on BattleSat, was rooted much deeper than even he could imagine.

He may not have understood the complete source of his revulsion, but he knew what he had to do at this moment.

This blasphemy could not be allowed to live.

Pulling his sword, he cleaved the hoses within reach. They ruptured like firehoses, spraying fluid wildly. He smelled a heady metallic aroma, blood or plasma.

Until now the beast, curled in a semi-embryonic position with arms and legs tucked close and eyes shut, slightly twitched at the disruption.

Already, *Hot Shot* was on its way to the gantry at the general's command, preparing another salvo of phosphorus balls of death.

The general exited the gantry just as the *Jacoby* launched its payload. A hundred golf balls slammed into metal I-beams and pre-fab walls at the base of the gantry. Fire burst out, quickly scaling the building like it was rotten oak.

From a vantage point sixty feet away—arms crossed against his gouged and blood-stained chest—the general watched the gantry burn. It didn't take long for the phosphorus to eat through the foundations. The building groaned, leaning several degrees off kilter. Then, as loud snaps indicated the weight couldn't be supported anymore, it partially collapsed in upon itself before plunging lengthwise into a small pond that cycled cooling water into the gantry. The building and all its burning contents crashed down, the pond hissing in fury and throwing clouds of steam as the liquid fire burned even the water.

At one point the general thought he heard the beast cry out. If so, that would be the death note for *Levatha Hydraus*. The general made sure of it.

The stench of cooked flesh replaced the smell of chemicals and expended ordnance.

"Sir," Darrisaw said, coming up behind him as his mechs were wrapping up his scorched earth policy.

He turned and saw that Darrisaw had found Glass. Glass leaned on Darrisaw's shoulder as he favored one leg. Soot and ash covered them both.

"You lived," the general said rather impassively, the image of the beast still troubling him. The ghastly distraction colored his speech, making his already monotone, mechanical voice sound even flatter and sinister in tone.

"Yeah, I lived," Glass responded, in just as mechanical and terse a tone as the general's own. "The ejection pod didn't make a graceful landing though, bailing out so close to the ground. But I'm alive."

The general didn't respond in any way, having already turned his attention back to the smoking ruin, partly submerged.

Just then, Fletcher brought the drop ship to land squarely on top of a dirt expanse near the center of the camp. Secondary thrusters stirred up loose topsoil and ash. The general finally pulled his eyes away from the ruined gantry and the well-done water dinosaur.

"What's next, general?" Darrisaw asked. She looked his battered body up and down with her keen, skilled eyes. "You've taken some serious damage. I think there're some scanners in the ship. I can run diagnostics and repair—"

"No time to rest," the general said, cutting her off. "We're going to the Mystic Shelf to pick a fight. The Sixth is getting their heads handed to them." With no chance for any more discussion, he headed for the drop ship as Darrisaw and Glass fell in behind him.

"By the way, sir," Darrisaw said, "I didn't know your sword was named OreCrush. When did that—"

"Don't ask," the general cut her off again, regretting his use of the term—sometimes even robots slipped up.

The cargo door dropped, and, with the dirty business of leveling the camp complete, his mechs stepped up the platform inside.

Taking one last look behind her, Darrisaw asked, "what was that thing anyway?" pointing to the gantry that still crackled with white hot fire.

"Something unholy that'll never see the light of day," the general responded as he stepped onto the platform.

He had no idea how wrong he would be.

Senior airman Rhonda Rudderham prayed for her power armor to hold as she crouched in a trench, gouged out three days ago by an excavation bot to form a phase line.

Blood turned the dirt muddy red. It caked onto her armor and plastered every crevice. Everything, from her armor to her service rifle to surveillance drones, was covered. The blistering Erudian sun baked the mud tight onto whatever it clung to. Her boots, one size too large for her tiny feet, constantly stuck in the sucking mud. The only thing keeping her from walking out of her boots was her shin guard's armor plating. One of the latches circled under her boot heel.

To make this miserable moment just a little more overwhelming, the relentless ion storm raging over Erudia played havoc with her electronics.

The HUD overlay in her helmet visor flitted, threatening her that at any moment it would drop offline. Again. Friend or Foe beacons, icons showing the location of nearby soldiers and airmen hazed out, then with a snap came back into focus, significantly dimmer than before. They finally settled into two distinct images, which made

Rudderham go cross-eyed trying to look at them. Finally, she tapped the control on her info sleeve to shut off the malfunctioning display.

Many believed the ion storm that had been ravaging the semi-arid planet of Erudia for weeks to be more than natural phenomenon. Speculation trickled through the ranks that the Vesuvians were behind it, having found some new weather control tech.

Anything to make everyone's life miserable.

Two days ago their on-planet commander, Captain Buck Gunwald, a shrewd captain who should've been a major but didn't have the intestinal fortitude to play politics for rank, said the storm was finally letting up. But the damage was already done. He'd assumed command once a bomb-carrying Vesuvian terrain scrubber had performed a kamikaze on the command vehicle because Colonel Dexter had to be in the thick of it.

The Sixth had been caught between a rock and an even harder rock. On one front, a city with several thousand residents, now full of mostly raving murderous lunatics. Driven mad by the Shamblers.

On the opposite front, a Vesuvian sneak attack.

The Sixth couldn't get reinforcements on-planet through the storm to support the two battalions on the ground. So the troops, less than 1,200 warm bodies—many of those injured— had to dig in and hope their power cells stayed charged and their ammunition belts didn't run dry.

Despite her crouching in a foxhole, a trench at least fifty yards long, on the verge of getting overrun, or worse yet, buried alive, she still preferred this to spending another moment with Master Sergeant Bol, her flight chief.

With alabaster skin, a light dusting of freckles across her nose and bright, wavy copper hair that seemed to shine even in the dark, Rudderham had arrived on the *Countervail*. Two months ago, reassigned from the Tenth Space Wing. Half of the Tenth's fleet was at

AFSD-5, *Space Dock Aldrin*, due for depot maintenance. Just on the other side of Mars.

Rudderham had been assigned to the security police flight on the *Countervail*, and, immediately upon arrival, she'd had the unholy displeasure of meeting her supervisor, Bol. Within a half hour of her coming on board he'd already made eight passes at her, even though he'd buried his latest wife less than six months ago.

Once she spurned his blatant sexual advances, he quickly labeled her as *Dirty Rhonda*, alluding to some imagined situation only he knew about. Not wanting to bring attention to herself, she put up with it by staying as far away from him as possible.

Her moment of hesitation in apprehending General Mikeal in the *Countervail* docks was all the justification Bol had needed to send her on-planet. When the wing-wide line-feed channel put out a request for battle augmentees, her name magically appeared at the top of Bol's 'volunteer' list.

As Rudderham had hopped a drop ship headed on-planet to war, she imagined anywhere was better than being around him.

She found herself reconsidering this thought as another explosion fifty feet overhead showered her in burning fragments. Pressing against the trench wall, she found the smell of fresh dirt and ozone mixed in an oddly comforting way. A thousand chemical smells filled her nose. At least she wasn't dead. Not yet, anyway.

A chunk of burning slag the size of a fist slammed into her shoulder, making her teeter. Immediately it hissed, beginning to chew into her armor plating. She shook frantically, using her gloved hand to knock it off before it could do any damage. Then she adjusted her helmet, which had shifted on her small head.

"Hold the line," came Captain Gunwald's voice over line-feed, slightly distorted to autotune, his comm equipment damaged from the ion bombardment. "Badger team, kooks headed your way."

Here comes the kooks, Rudderham thought. The name derived from "kooky," meaning strange or eccentric. That's what the murderous, raving mad people were called by everyone. Murderous became strange. An odd, funny name for something that was anything but funny, but definitely odd. Others called them zombies.

Maybe that was the point, to avoid looking at them as what they were; families and neighbors, now driven to bloodlust until a bullet was put through their head. Call them kooks instead. Reduce all that messy 'these were once people just like you' into a silly word. Kooks or zombies.

It made pulling the trigger a little easier. But not enough for Rudderham.

She was one of the few remaining members of Badger able to fight. The last casualty, Staff Sergeant Jenson, squad NCO, had been mobbed by a group of 'infected' tourists not long ago. A blast from an alien Shambler's pole weapon drove the citizens insane with rage and the desire to kill.

She shuddered as she remembered his high-pitched cries for help as they bit, clawed, and ripped him apart. Once finished with him, they turned on each other until only the father remained. Then he charged into a crossfire of disruptor blasts that promptly cut him in half.

Swallowing the rising horror in her throat, she checked her chin strap, then lifted her barely five-foot frame onto the ammunition boxes she had stacked on top of each other to see over the artificial berm.

In the background, the city of Eradda, sitting between the edge of the desert and the city nearest to the Mystic Shelf, burned. Smoke —dirty, greasy, full of organic and inorganic ash— blew over the entrenched ragtag remnants of the Sixth's battalions. Black clouds, more like sentient beings of rolling ash, obscured much of the battlefield.

Without giving it a second thought, her jaw shifted in a particular way. This simple action brought the rebreather cup in her helmet over her nose and mouth. She sucked in fresh oxygen, fed from the slim oxy tanks on her back. With another motion the cup moved away from her mouth. As much as she wanted to suck in more air, she knew she needed to keep a full tank. Just in case—you never know when you'd need a fresh breath.

She caught glimpses of the city through breaks in the raging fires and chemical smoke. Her head shook in disbelief. Once the alien rift at the Mystic Shelf had opened, the nearest town of roughly twenty thousand citizens, Eradda, had been the first target.

Rudderham could see skyscrapers burn. Distantly, the sounds of war and destruction rang through the smoky haze. Occasionally she could make out figures, only silhouettes, moving through toxic plumes of smoke and ash. She couldn't tell if they were friend or foe, and her malfunctioning detector in her helmet wasn't reliable.

Climbing out of the ditch to investigate wasn't going to happen, either. Plus, Jenson's last command was for Badger to hold this position. That was before she'd heard his life end so gruesomely.

Mortars exploded indiscriminately, not caring who was nearby. Disruptors flashed occasionally through the hazy sky, temporarily illuminating the smoke with strobes in some evil caricature of Christmas lights. Ballistics zinged near and far. Every so often, she imagined one whizzing inches from her head.

Her eyes watered from the countless fires. She checked the seal on her helmet and tightened the straps—if they tightened any more she'd probably choke herself out. Fingers covered in hardening blood-mud made this simple task more difficult.

Two figures appeared in the haze in front of her, at least a hundred and fifty feet away. Fuzzy edges, possibly an adult and child. She checked her disruptor rifle charge. Eighty-two percent.

They stumbled over the field, pockmarked with blasts and strewn with bodies. They tumbled, slid, fell, then got up and stumbled more as they moved forward. Rudderham swallowed hard as she aimed her disruptor. "Two citizens, forty yards, at my twelve," she yelled out to the rest of her squad, if any could hear. If any were alive.

Through the chaos of fighting on two fronts, the Sixth had been spread thin along the phase line, separated so much Rudderham couldn't see anyone anymore. That wasn't standard procedure.

For the last twenty minutes, she'd felt like the only one left on the field.

As the two figures materialized from the fog, Rudderham saw the couple were, in fact, a woman and child. Probably a mother and her son. Still, she couldn't tell if they were… *possessed* or not. Kooks. Zombies. With her visor HUD off, she had to manually aim her disruptor. Which she did, squarely at the mother's midsection.

As the two got closer, the mother obviously noticed Rudderham, becoming animated. "Help us!" the woman cried, her inflections accented to the point that American was probably a second language to her. With a burst of new energy, she scooped up her child and made a beeline for Rudderham.

Thankful the lady had spoken and that Rudderham didn't have to smoke her, Rudderham frantically waved her hand. "Over here. Get over here," she called out. Possessed never spoke once driven mad by the alien Shamblers. At most they screamed, cried, or growled. Like a zombie instead of a human. A kook.

The mother handed her son to Rudderham before climbing into the trench herself. Rudderham handed her son, eyes wild with crippling fear to the point that he didn't talk or blink, back to her. She turned the mother's shoulders, pointing her in a direction to the rear, to one of the trenches winding back to safety. "Go. Now," Rudderham yelled, giving her a shove to help her along. With a look back, the mother took off with her son clutched to her chest.

Sweat dripped off Rudderham's forehead as she got back on the boxes and looked toward the burning city. Instead of finding the city, she saw a line of fifty people twenty yards away, climbing over dead bodies and crawling along the ground. They were screaming, crying, and growling.

Her disruptor lit up the haze.

A man dressed in the fine white robes of an Erudian diplomat took a glancing blast to his side, enough to ignite his tailored linen. His clothes engulfed him, but he seemed oblivious at becoming a human torch. He roared with anger, hands clenched, plodding forward. Only when his nervous system began shutting down did he drop to the dirt. But a little thing like that wouldn't stop him. He grasped at the ground to pull himself along, determined to reach Rudderham.

The alien-manufactured hatred and madness that drove him along terrified the young airman.

Her previous feelings of being alone on that battlefield ended as other disruptors unloaded somewhere on her flanks. Muzzle flashes and tracers lit up the smoke. More of the mad kooks dropped, smoked indiscriminately. Disruptors tore into the crowds. The air became electrically charged: battle static.

Power armor worked as a ground to disperse this static. Even so, a slight tingling could sometimes be felt in the chest and arms. Similar to gliding across carpet to build up a charge.

Normally this sensation irritated Rudderham, but now she welcomed it—she wasn't alone.

"*Wiggler* at these coords," came a voice over line-feed, ballistic fire in the background. Since her HUD was off, she couldn't see the coords painted. She just hoped it wasn't near.

Off to her right, contact was close and engagement picked up in in the form of disruptor blasts and ballistics. The sky flashed like a thunderstorm, erupting brightly in flashes of battle over the course of ten seconds.

"Overrun—" came the voice again, but this time frantic, before getting prematurely cut off.

Rudderham could do nothing more than grimace as her imagination ran wild with the types of horrific death the unnamed soldier had just encountered.

"Mighty Sixth!" came a mechanical voice, roaring over line-feed, startling Rudderham and all others listening. She didn't know where it had come from.

"This is General Mikeal. There's been much speculation as to my loyalty. I've put up with humans for three centuries. That should be enough to testify to my loyalty."

Anyone who had spent any time with the general knew this was as close to an apology as you could expect from the temperamental robot.

"Identify yourselves," the general commanded, which meant for the Sixth to ensure their Friend or Foe beacons were lit. Nothing was worse than smoking your buddy in an unfortunate friendly fire incident. "Soon your enemy will be exposed. There is no more safety for them this day. Prepare to run down the jackals!"

With a surge of enthusiasm, Rudderham checked her non-functioning HUD. It now worked. And she couldn't help but smile at the general's voice, enraged as usual—there are times those qualities are desired.

Then embarrassment washed over her as she thought of the last time she'd seen him on the *Countervail*, when Bol had ordered his apprehension. The general could've killed them all, she knew that without a doubt. So did everyone else. But he hadn't. Many said he'd gone out of his way to *not* harm anyone. That had to account for something.

A low rumble just underneath the hot sizzle of disruptor blasts and ear-shattering mortar explosions indicated a ship approaching.

Suddenly, the cloaked Vesuvian *Wigglers* that had been taking potshots on ground troops became visible, first flowing as they materialized as though submerged underwater, before forming and becoming solid. Their cloaks now disabled.

Vesuvian mortar-x batteries and hover missile platforms that had previously had free rein on the battlefield suddenly lit up on Rudderham's HUD with exact locations. Their radar jamming devices no longer jammed radar.

Then, through the smoke of a thousand war fires, descended a *Flying Whale* drop ship, its engines roaring and making the ground rumble as it performed a combat landing.

The Sixth Mechanized had arrived.

From her trench, Rudderham watched the *Flying Whale* drop rapidly from the sky, vectoring its wing thrusters to kick up a storm of debris and topsoil. Whirlwinds danced off the wingtips. Eddies rolled over the ailerons.

The cargo door on the underside dropped open, revealing a large, gaping mouth.

Under Fletcher's expert and steady hand, the drop ship performed a textbook touch and go, kissing the Erudian soil only long enough for two massive ferro-tanium balls, each thirty feet across, to dump out the back.

Immediately the general, probably still onboard the ship, would control them. Only he could wield any of the collective mechs of the Sixth Mechanized.

The Machine Accords after the great A.I. War banned any completely sentient machine. High-level A.I. Like the general. But his saving grace was that he'd raised the alarm when War God, a mining A.I. mainframe gone rogue, attempted to kill mankind. Plus, he was the one to kill War God, saving the human race from extinction.

Mechs operated semi-autonomously. The general gave

commands, they followed orders. This ensured that machines couldn't rise to god-like status.

For this, many called the general the *Grand Conductor*, likening his control of the mechs as orchestrating a symphony of steel. Deadly, pain-inducing steel.

Rudderham had learned such things not only in basic training, but also in grade school.

The two gigantic ferro-tanium balls were covered in overlapping scale shingles. They slammed into the ground, momentum slinging them forward helter skelter. They thundered along, billiard balls on a giant's table. They skipped over trenches and barreled through a line of citizens gone wild, as easily as a rock punches through a wet paper towel.

Well into enemy territory, they rapidly ground to a halt. Many kooks inched close to inspect the oddity before them, curious even in their maddened state.

The balls unfolded themselves into arms, legs, and a tail to stand upright, each forty feet high. Rudderham had learned about them through deployment training on her way to join the Sixth.

AFV ACO-4604 *Pangolins* were siege mechs, named because of their striking resemblance to the slow-moving earthen creatures. Equipped with reinforced battering ram arms the size of a full grown, hefty man and a monstrously sweeping tail, they were originally designed to breech hardened Tangene fortifications.

A collage of misfits, criminals on the run, and assassins for hire had banded together into a paramilitary group, calling themselves the Tangenians. They'd begun a campaign of piracy and murder, spreading discord across planets and inhabited moons in the Tangene group.

Tasked with stamping out this menace, the Sixth had traced them back to Tangene Sav, a wasteland planet of rocky mountain crags and plantless valleys.

The general had led a squad of mechs onto the frigid planet, and they'd fought up the hardened, jagged crags of the western mountain chains where the Tangenians had built reinforced structures and holed up under the mountains, dwarves battening down for the winter months. There the general had come to a stop, because neither he or his mechs could penetrate the fortified hideout.

What they'd needed was a nutcracker to crack the nut.

Back on the *Einstein*, the Sixth's research and development ship, the general, working with engineers, had modified the existing heavy-duty chassis of Martian Ore Slammers, transforming the rock-crushing mechs into a head-crushing siege engine.

On Tangene Sav once again, the *Pangolin* siege engines—the ore slammers' new name, based on their scales, physical resemblance, and waddle as they walked on hind legs—had shattered the fortifications, and the general, leading *Iron Zoo Platoon,* had been able to extract the Tangenians that hadn't escaped off-planet hours before their empire had fallen.

Instead of battering thick granite-streaked boulders and hardened strata, the *Pangolins* now worked crowd control.

Launched into the thick of Erudians given over to the alien-induced madness—now zombies—the twin beasts roared with electric life. Arms swung, catching five and six bodies in jaw-dropping sweeps. Tails meant to help counterbalance arced behind each, tossing crowds away with such gut-wrenching force they were dead before hitting the ground from internal trauma.

Their tree-trunk thick arms punched mercilessly, reinforced with electromagnetic weights that amplified the force by a thousand. Each blow drove six bodies into the dirt.

Many of the possessed could only understand killing. With no regard for their own fragile lives, unable to comprehend the scores of others already trampled and smashed by the *Pangolins*, they hurled forward recklessly. Some with blasters, some with sticks, some with blood-stained hands. They clawed and scratched with futility as they reached the mechs, trying to rip their scales off.

But the machines, decked in plate armor, didn't bat a mechanical eye. They simply shook like a dog getting a bath, sending bodies flying to crash hard on top of each other.

By now the *Flying Whale* had come back around, making a hot landing ahead of the shifting skirmish line. Rudderham, within sixty feet of the craft, unconsciously squinted even though her helmet's visor kept wind-whipped particles from etching her face.

Five-foot sword clutched tightly in one hand, a nail gun chewing through rounds in the other, General Mikeal exploded from the drop ship's cargo ramp. With a deafening amplified roar, the general hit the ground in long strides, not veering or turning from his path. He made a straight path for the enemy.

Two of the general's cyborgs followed. Sergeant Glass emerged, riding his rocket boots. Airman Darrisaw came next, revving her wicked chainsaw. Then five *Jacobys* plunged down the ramp, followed by a slower moving AFV ACO-4001K *Beholder.* The drop ship rocked with that behemoth's thundering footsteps.

"The jackals can no longer hide behind their cloaks," the general yelled, his resonating tone causing the battlefield to temporarily quiet. "At the jackals!"

Over line-feed several voices echoed the general's infectious war cry: at the jackals!

Seeing the general on the battlefield reciting the battle chant and hearing the death screams of the enemy as the *Pangolins* tore into them, was a shot of adrenaline.

Rudderham crawled from her trench, clutching her disruptor, jaw set grimly, ready to fight. And the remaining Sixth also crawled from the trenches where they'd been hunkered down for the past day and a half.

Immediately the *Jacobys* faced two *Wigglers* that had been belching liquid fire onto the dug-in troops. Their stores of RS105 *Dagger* missiles and their larger cousins, RM205 *Swords*, targeted the vessels' ports as disruptors peppered the engines in the hopes of bringing the semi-organic Vesuvian ships down.

An ambush ship, *Wigglers* relied on the stealth of cloak because their undulating movement was slow to the point of almost appearing like they hovered in place. As such, the ships couldn't possibly hope to escape the scores of missiles simultaneously launched in their direction.

One ship took four direct hits to its left main engine. An internal explosion finished shredding it apart. Fire and chunks of metal puked out the exhaust. The ship listed and began a wide unintentional bank, bringing it directly over the trenches. Ground pounders, now able to see what had been haunting them, took the opportunity to respond as a ground pounder does.

Disruptor fire and hand-held rocket grenades raked the bottom of the listing ship. The onboard Vesuvian crew fought to keep their ship aloft, but inch by inch their crippled *Wiggler* corkscrewed downward in a death spiral.

The *Beholder*, a monstrous circular, disc-like mech that was more like a mobile rocket platform on four legs, immediately swept the battlefield with powerful radars, separating friend from foe as it finally cleared the *Flying Whale* ramp in slow, intentional steps.

With its sweeping red eye it would preselect up to a hundred enemy target from within a quarter mile, although it was capable of reaching out to targets three miles out. Once it performed a rigid digital threat analysis, the large protective dome over the top of the cylindrical mech slide apart. Launcher racks went from 'safe' to 'on'. Eighty-five missiles out of the thousand it carried were given individual coords. The *Beholder's* legs braced and the missiles screamed into the air, blasting away in puffs of grey blue smoke.

Each of the missiles reached an apex high above the battlefield, then swung back down, gaining momentum. Smoke trails that looked like intestines hung in the sky. They found camouflaged Vesuvian rocket batteries, pillboxes set up with gauss cannons, and mortar-x pits. Almost instantaneously, mortar fire that had been pecking away at the Sixth's exposed flanks ended without fanfare, except the Vesuvian mortar men getting incinerated miles away.

Rudderham raced onto the open field in the hopes of fighting alongside the general. She thought that would make up for the incident on the *Countervail*. But she couldn't keep up with him. No human could.

The general fought like a starved wolf being released in a field of plump newborn lambs.

His nail gun, a terrifying weapon only the most skilled marksman could hope to wield, he waved like a child's toy. The carbon steel slivers found their mark, effortlessly perforating skin and bone. Sometimes puncturing two and three bodies deep before they even realized their time was up. With a lethal precision only a high level A.I. could possess, the general shredded the ranks of opponents, inflicting countless casualties.

Those foes that managed to get close enough to even hope to lay a bloody hand on the general were met by his sword. The edge didn't need to be ground sharp, because the ferocity of the general's swings was enough to cleave boulders and deeply gouge the hardest steel.

He fought like a madman, leaving a trail of devastation as noticeable as a tornado's path through an Alabama trailer park. He was an elemental force, as raw and unquenchable as a thunderstorm. Nothing could withstand the general unleashed.

Many of the Vesuvians that were noble who had hidden behind cloaking tech now found their safety compromised—as fleeting as their courage, many broke and ran. Pillboxes and defensive positions were abandoned as a creeping sense of fear overtook the paramilitary groups. Momentum had swung.

A few Vesuvian commanders attempted to keep their armies together, shouting curses and threats. But even hired hands knew their limits, and it usually began and ended when their lives were at stake.

The battle-weary battalions of the Sixth Infantry rallied on the general and the Sixth Mechanized.

Soldiers in power armor blasted away at the enemy, oblivious to the overwhelming odds. The air became saturated with battle static to the point that hair on the back of necks stood on end and static discharges rolled along disruptor barrels.

Rudderham could feel the static as she swept her disruptor rifle from left to right, her cheek welded to the stock, searching for another target.

A tall, wild-eyed man holding what looked like a golf club clambered over a dirt mound fifty paces away. Once his distracted, alien-maddened eyes set on her, he grunted like a hungry pig and charged. Calmly, she double tapped him in the chest. The disruptor blast spun him so his club flung from his hands. He dropped, chest smoking, his insides cauterized.

One foot cautiously in front of the other, the airman methodically plodded forward. She couldn't keep up with the general, but she could do her job, just like her brothers and sisters on the field.

The second *Wiggler* managed to dump one more payload. Molten fire spit from the ports to bathe anything underneath in burning plasma. Two *Jacobys* and a fire team were caught in the waterfall from hell. One of the *Jacobys* attempted to maneuver itself out of the way, but instead detonated as the ammo stores inside its body became overheated. The blast knocked the second *Jacoby* off its feet onto its back. Not designed to lie down on the job, it fought to upright itself, but only dug itself deeper into a wet hole.

One of the fire team members, a tall woman with her helmet missing, looked up and saw the waterfall. She threw her disruptor aside and bolted forward, barreling into her two teammates and knocking them over a ridge into a trench. But she was unable to move in time, and the plasma swallowed her. Back on their feet, her teammates scanned the area for their savior.

The listing *Wiggler* finished its wide bank, finally making a rough landing near the *Pangolins*. Before the crew could escape, Glass and a handful of infantry were already lighting up the wreckage with phosphorous bombs and laser blast torches.

Rudderham had watched a video a couple weeks ago, recorded decades before she was born. In it, the general was speaking at the war college. A commencement or a special occasion of some sort.

In it he'd talked about his education. He'd learned doctrine by some of the best war planners in the most prestigious American war colleges. In it, the general had said sometimes a war is fought with exact strategy. An intricate chess game played with lives as the pieces.

Other times it was a barroom brawl. Whoever was left standing, won.

Rudderham pictured this as the kind of battle the general had in mind when he'd said that.

She continued trailing after the general until he paused.

Three Vesuvians, somewhat bewildered after scrambling from their mortar-x battery seconds before it exploded, stared dumbly at the general.

"Jackals," the general said. "I'm surprised you didn't scatter like bugs underneath a boot." His chest heaved with the exhaustion of killing, his five-foot sword dripping wet. "I will spare your miserable lives. But relay this. Tell Horvoth we have an unfinished fight. And tell Hatch I won't rest until he's dead and worms are digging through his brain."

One of the Vesuvians, the youngest from the looks of it, began cursing the general. But the team leader, a man old enough to know to recognize those rare moments when your neck escapes a noose, sternly told the young rogue to shut up before saying, "*Anura*, we'll relay this." Jumping at the opportunity afforded him, he led his men by their collars over a ridge, disappearing from the battlefield.

The general watched them disappear into the haze and smoke. "I'm becoming too soft," he said. But then he stood upright, going completely still, staring into the sky. He held up an arm and inspected it closely.

As Rudderham wondered what was happening to the general she felt a strange sensation. Probably the one the general now felt.

An electric pulse, similar to battle static, crept over her body. But not quite battle static. The pulse seemed to be coming from above.

She looked up.

In the sky, approximately a thousand feet across, a thin circle of blue began to form, parallel to the ground. Crackles of white energy rolled across the circle, and with each second the circle deepened in color. As the circle grew the energy intensified. Several midget lightning bolts shot from the circle, striking the ground.

Now, not only did she and the general watch the sky, but also the rest of the Sixth and the few surviving Vesuvians. Even some of the possessed residents stopped their maddened attacks and peered upward. Heads turned. All fighting stopped as the circle became a spectator sport.

The circle started rotating counterclockwise, veins of dark blue streaking in swirls. And as the circle rotated light bent around the edges, like the circle was sucking in surrounding ambient, distorting it the way an image is refracted on the edges of a convex mirror or prism.

Only one emotion remained in her, replacing all the ones she'd experienced over the last few days. Uneasiness. Involuntarily she inched closer to the general, not taking her eyes off the swirling disc.

"A time portal," the general said to himself, but she was close enough to hear.

Suddenly, something struck her helmet. She slid her visor aside and looked up again. A drop of water hit her cheek. Curious, she searched the spinning wheel of light to see if she could detect where the water came from.

Then, it started to rain.

Ang-Thoth's mercenaries had traced the general's steps to Erudia. It wasn't that difficult, after all. If there was a war, more often than not the general would be there in the middle. And he always left an unmistakable trail or carnage.

Once his cadre of lethal killers for hire had exited the planetary hopper craft and secured the location, a circle around the craft, Ang-Thoth stood at the ship's exit ramp, slightly hunched. Slowly, even feebly, the elder and chief of the Ang clan made his way down, a staff clutched in his hand to steady him and a monkey riding on his shoulder. Ang-Thoth loosely held the golden leash around its neck.

The monkey chattered wildly, hopping from shoulder to shoulder. Ang-Thoth gave the leash a gentle tug to calm down the creature.

Even though the area in the midst of the destroyed Vesuvian encampment on Erudia was secure, Ang-Thoth couldn't help but keep his wary eyes peeled. With countless mercenaries and bounty hunters—also many of his kinfolk—wanting him dead, being overly cautious had kept him alive. He treated his time jumping the same way.

Careful and attentive to detail.

For time jumpers, simply surviving a jump was a measure of success.

Entire time jumper clans had been wrung out to the point of extinction as they learned the hard way that altering the past when it had the potential of affecting current and future time was met with a heavy penalty.

Instead of altering a future event, the jumper would merely wink out of existence. Effectually becoming dead to the universe and the time stream. It took many decades and hundreds of jumpers' lives to discover this simple limitation to their skill.

They called it the Self-Correcting Universal law.

Once this deadly fact had been realized, time jumpers had been reduced to time-bending scavengers, hopping into the past to dig up lost items that no longer held any future impact.

Jumping to the future was too risky, as most actions held immediate and dire consequences for the jumper.

One of Ang-Thoth's thin hands gathered his robes as he descended the ramp. He hoisted them just above the filthy ground as he set foot on Erudia. He held to his nose a scented, silken handkerchief to help curb the stench of cooked meat.

On the ground, he surveyed the ruins of the Vesuvian camp.

His men—the best southern mercenaries credits could buy— fanned away from him, sweeping for potential ambushes. They swung devastating pulse rifles while the planet hopper ran its own scans, auto guns on the top continually swinging back and forth.

Broken bodies littered the ground. The familiar smell of burnt flesh made Ang-Thoth's nose shrivel in disapproval. Carefully, he maneuvered the battlefield, keeping clear of any objects that could soil his silken robes.

Ang-Thoth owed much to textiles.

One day while examining a bolt of Mercanian tapestry he'd found while diving four hundred years into the Wudenan past, a discolored old patch sewn onto a bolt of priceless fabric had given him an idea.

With this new inspiration, he'd diligently studied the history of time jumpers. The innate skill passed through DNA in his family had laid the rudimentary foundation. But that was just the raw talent. It needed to be tempered. Like a sword. It took years to master the art and properly wield that skill.

Oftentimes Ang-Thoth's research led him to offer jumpers from other clans large paychecks to perform dangerous experimental jumps.

For time jumpers, greed frequently overrode common sense.

"Sir," one of his mercenaries said. Ang-Thoth made his way slowly to the man, but he didn't need an explanation to see why he was called.

He stood before the smoking ruins of the gantry and the near-completed beast that lay cooking inside. The smell of roasted flesh and blubber became almost unbearable, and Ang-Thoth dabbed his nose frantically with his perfumed handkerchief.

After decades of tests and sacrifice on behalf of other jumpers, Ang-Thoth had finally gained the skill he needed.

Nine years ago on a rare cold Wudenan winter day when the leaves had fallen and Ang-Thoth had been injected to the teeth with vitamins, pain inhibitors, and various stimulants concocted by the most knowledgeable physicians he could find, he made a critical jump.

Ang-Thoth went *sideways* in time.

He broke the notion that a time jumper was restricted to only forward and back in space and time. Tapping into the possibility of what *might* have been, Ang-Thoth was able to manipulate his talent and skill to search incomplete events. Since they never happened, he suffered no consequence tampering with them.

Like the old patch sewn onto the new material, Ang-Thoth was able to take the *never happened* and sow that onto the fabric of existence. And like any great treasure, he kept this knowledge solely to himself.

On Erudia before him now, the smoking ruin of a monster gave him the perfect opportunity to practice this sideways jump. Ang-Thoth smiled to himself with this secret knowledge and Bobo—a rare monkey that lived in the sky-trees on Tarsus Opal that he'd accepted as payment for a gambling debt from a jungle warlord—detecting a change in his master's demeanor, began to chatter incessantly.

An hour later, Ang-Thoth descended from his ship with uncharacteristic limberness and vigor.

Chemicals pumped through his veins as he now wore a tight-fitting uniform, plates of customized power armor bulking up his thin frame and giving him the impression of a mighty warrior. On his armor's breastplate was his crest, a golden dragon with one broken horn.

A slimline power skeleton built into his armor gave him almost extra human strength. His walk and his movements were completely unhindered.

His men stood back near the ship watching, wide-eyed with wonder, even though they'd seen him jump a hundred times before.

Taking his jumpers' staff, a six-foot lightweight carbon pole inlaid with jewels that glistened every color of the rainbow—a fortune by its own right—Ang-Thoth effortlessly twirled it before him. A blue wheel formed from nothing. Sparks danced on its edges in beautiful arcs. The wheel fluctuated slightly, then became stable, as stable as anything else on the world of Erudia. Without hesitation, he stepped into it.

A fraction of a second later a massive blue, ethereal wheel formed above the discarded battlefield. It was birthed and grew out so rapidly, spanning well over a hundred feet across, that it seemed effortless in creation. Within seconds, the glowing ring descended onto *Levatha's* smoldering carcass.

Ang-Thoth had reached out to a future time that never existed. A time when the beast was complete, if left alone. He retrieved *Levatha Hydraus* and pulled the monstrosity into the current timeline. A patch sewn onto the fabric: overlaying the timeline, rather than manipulating the existing timeline. He cheated the system, bypassing universal laws.

This he did to impress and fulfill his promise to the Commandant of the Red Guard, Kento-Gala, a woman that stirred him in ways no concubine or slave girl, bought or stolen, ever could.

She had asked him to *rain hell* on the general for what he'd done to her baroness, his younger sister. And Baron Ang-Thoth, time jumper, was glad to quite literally rain hell on the robot and the Sixth.

The fat drops thinned, becoming a mist, which then became a gentle spring rain, which became a steady downpour. All this happened in the span of a couple minutes.

The downpour steadily increased into a mini hurricane, as outflow winds from the swirling wheel of light blew the rain at odd angles, pelting the skin and face like stinging needles. Before anyone knew what to make of it all, the rain turned into a tempestuous monsoon.

Soldiers and airmen scrambled for cover from the supernatural downpour.

Hundreds of mortar fires licking at the bones of dead men and broken machines began hissing as the drenching quelled them. Great plumes of steam rose: even the most blazing phosphorus fire couldn't withstand the deluge.

The softened Erudian ground underneath the wheel quickly turned into muddy paste, fresh piles of dirt churned up from hundreds of mortar blasts and explosions and from soldiers' boot heels digging in as they scrambled.

Long trenches dug by excavation bots became compromised under the torrent. Soft dirt collapsed upon itself. The trenches channeled water into impromptu rivers, which began sweeping away the alive and dead, anyone unfortunate to be caught in the six-foot deep trenches.

Power armor, a lifesaver under normal battle environments, suddenly became a burden as every extra ounce of weight made maneuvering the morass difficult. Soldiers fought to keep their head above churning water as they struggled to escape the burdensome helmets and gear.

One *Pangolin* standing near a trench toppled over as the edge gave way. Its heavy-duty chassis now worked against it, dragging it into the muddy rivers, frothing with angry white caps. It attempted to right itself, but it couldn't secure its footing in the shifting trench floor. Although water resistant, the mech wasn't watertight. A hairline imperfection between two belly panels allowed enough water inside its casing to infiltrate vital control mechanisms.

The general, intricately tied to each of his mechs, was notified that his *Pangolin* suffered multiple fault codes. Then it dropped offline.

Water, indiscriminate as a nuclear detonation, washed away soldier and raving lunatic alike, Vesuvian and robot. Mechs struggled to keep their footing while soldiers began to form human chains, hoping to keep their comrades from being ripped away by the driving current across the hundreds of rivers the trenches had turned into. Dead bodies and shattered vehicles swirled as detritus in the water.

The suddenness and the intensity even caught the general flat-footed. As he watched the terrible wall of water erode the entire battlefield, he had a difficult time piecing together a plan of action. All he could manage was a reassuring command to the troops. "Stand fast," he said over line-feed as even he sought higher ground.

An airman in power armor clung to the side of a light duty personnel carrier. As the general's reticule focused on the airman, an info box in his visor brought up the airman's name and battle stats.

Senior airman Tyus Bronski. Bronski scrambled to the top of the cab, shedding helmet and gloves. He began calling for his fire team as he searched rushing waters around the carrier.

A hand shot from the water, wildly clutching for a roller bar on the cab. Bronski nearly fell off as he dropped to his stomach to reach the hand. After a tense couple seconds, he managed to grab hold. Then he strained as he helped the soldier onto the cab.

Senior airman Rhonda Rudderham, according to the general's info box.

He cursed to himself as all he could do was watch. A bystander to devastation. With his sword jammed into the earth to brace him, the general kept his feet planted, raging water at his chest. He felt if he lifted one foot he'd get swept away.

Then an object, on scale like a chunk of mountain, but indiscernible because it was wrapped in the driving rain, dropped from the wheel of light. It slammed to the earth, sending a rumbling shockwave.

An accompanying wave of water, a micro tsunami, knocked the general off his feet, along with most everyone else within three hundred feet.

Sensors flashed in the general's eyes as his heavy frame dragged him to the bottom of a trench. Floundering: he wasn't made to swim.

His core circuitry, built centuries ago, had largely remained unchanged. He'd had minor upgrades, but for the most part his wiring was old. And crude. And this simple fact allowed him to withstand many more environments than traditional mechs.

He'd been able to function in the icy wastes of the moon circling Triad. There he had led an expedition of frost-born mercenaries to recover a plundered freighter's contents, rare Martian ore.

Not more than a year ago, he had led the Sixth through the

desert regions of this very planet. Soldiers in power armor and pilots in mechanized suits withered under the blistering heat. But not the general.

With a quick inventory of his systems, he began shutting off processes that might be compromised.

Submerged, he fought the currents pulling at him in a hundred ways. His grasping hand found a wall of mud and rock. Slippery but stable. Using this, he elevated himself back above the water, now that the micro tsunami had receded.

And as quickly as the flood sprang from the circle, so it ended. In fact, the wheel of light had already begun to fade, dissolving in the sky.

Thankful the mysterious, supernatural rain had ended, the general turned to see what object had caused such a disturbance, crashing to the earth as it did.

As his eyes met the monstrous beast standing in the midst of the water and muck, the motor oil in his metallic bones ran cold.

Levatha Hydraus.

And quite alive.

"Holy crap," the general said as his head craned to take in the complete enormity of the towering beast—as terrible as *Levatha* was in its comatose state inside the gantry, it was downright nightmarish alive.

Cybernetics grafted to the whale-dragon gave it long arms, ending in a complexity of cold metal and steel barrels. Massive mechanical legs granted the beast that was never meant to leave the water land mobility.

And what the general thought was a shimmering force field of water on the hide of the beast remained. In fact, water appeared to weep from *Levatha*, seeping out from between the keratin scales that appeared harder than refined ore.

But like any natural beast with a wild, untamable nature, it refused any attempts to be contained artificially. It struggled against the machines attached to its body, giving it non-graceful, jerky movements.

After a few seconds the general's comm systems came back online.

"What is that thing?" Captain Gunwald said over line-feed.

"Something that shouldn't be alive," the general responded.

"Pa would love that big gator," Gunwald said in his backwater bay Cajun accent. "He'd live like a king after selling that."

"Rally your troops," the general ordered. He sent a message for *Hot Shot* to engage, but within seconds of receiving the order, his incendiary mech went off-line.

Immediately Gunwald sent a status command and his fractured squads began to respond, taking inventory of the missing, dead, and injured. Fire team leads searched for their members as they began to recover from the assault.

Two soldiers used their disruptors as shovels to scrape away mud from their submerged teammate, only a left forearm visible. Calls went out to any available medic bot.

The line-feed jammed with requests for weapons as soldiers and airmen found their disruptors unusable after being near drowned.

The general found himself digging from the mud, trying to find solid ground in which to plant his feet. Three mechs were already in motion, executing his command to regroup. He wanted to establish a skirmish line to concentrate his attack on one area while also distracting long enough to allow the men and women precious moments to regroup.

But the *Jacobys* were having just as difficult a time in the mud as the general. Legs, hydraulically powered, were able to pull from the deep muddy water, but soft earth shifted under their weight. Gyros pitched, nearly overwhelmed in an effort to stabilize.

Fortunately for the mud-seized Sixth, within minutes the water had already receded by a couple feet.

Levatha opened its wide mouth and cut loose a terrible shriek mixed with a dreadful moan. Soldiers shivered at such an ear-piercing noise as a spray of mist and phlegm flew from its mouth.

Then, with no warning, *Levatha's* arms erupted with a thunderclap that rivaled howitzers. Monstrous muzzle flashes stretched eight feet long. Projectiles exploded hundreds of feet away, concussion blasts splitting ear drums.

The powerful cannons appeared to surprise *Levatha* as much as the soldiers. It roared as its dorsal fins flapped wildly. The shots were wild though, not striking man nor mech.

The three *Jacobys* that survived the flood had managed to maneuver to *Levatha's* left flank, near enough to engage. They opened with a devastating barrage of disruptor fire.

The watery shell covering the beast appeared to conduct the high-energy blasts, rolling across its scales in flashes of artificial lightning. In response, *Levatha* shuddered and cried, attempting to back away from the painful stings of energy rippling over its body. One of its gun barrel arms took aim.

Five ballistics boomed from the cannons, muzzle flash making them look like a dragon breathing fire.

The *Jacobys* attempted evasive maneuvers, but the muck slowed them considerably. Two rounds slammed into one of the mechs, splitting it in half. Chunks of gnarled, flaming metal plopped into the mud. Another salvo detonated the mech's onboard ammunition stores. A secondary explosion, much larger, consumed the overturned mech and took out a neighboring *Jacoby*.

Fire teams, muddied but still full of fight, engaged *Levatha*. Gunwald barked commands, and his ground pounders responded. Disruptor fire sprinkled across the beast from a hundred directions. But the beast was so massive the impacts were like fireflies dancing across its disgusting, wet body.

A four-man grenadier team, able to keep their weapons dry, set up a quarter mile away on a rise of dry ground. They called incoming fire.

Sergeant Raul Tivus, a veteran of four battles who had earned a Purple Heart while losing three fingertips and one toe in the Neptune Campaigns, was able to get Fire Team War Horse in position for a clear shot with their GR-490 *Javelina*. The rocket-propelled grenade streaked furiously and slammed into the side of *Levatha's* head. Small pieces of hardened scales broke away. It bellowed in pain before shaking off the explosion. Two more *Javelina* rounds found their mark, each one equally painful.

While the beast was distracted, the remaining *Pangolin* charged *Levatha*. But the siege mech looked like a toy rushing the cyborg, which was over twice the *Pangolin's* height.

Regardless, the *Pangolin* laid into *Levatha*, relentlessly pummeling at its mechanical legs with trunk-like arms. Each blow resounded like artificial thunder.

Lashing wildly, *Levatha's* tail caught the *Pangolin*. But the mech's low center of gravity and relatively small size allowed only a glancing connection. Undeterred, the *Pangolin* began a new assault, which actually caused the towering beast to stagger back.

But with each passing moment the union of machine and mammal grew stronger. *Levatha's* movements became exact and precise as it now comprehended in its own way the purpose of the cannons on its arms. It aimed one arm point-blank at the *Pangolin* and unloaded a ferocious blast.

Then, with its newfound precision, the beast launched an earth-shattering salvo high into the air where Fire Team War Horse were readying another *Javelina* grenade. The salvos fragmented before impact, burrowing through power armor and flesh and eviscerating the team.

The general, eager to jump into the fight, closed the distance to *Levatha*. With sword in hand and rage in his eyes, he launched himself against the cyborg nightmare. Not a shred of hesitation caused him to falter. The fact that *Levatha* shrugged off most of what the Sixth threw at it didn't slow him enough to reconsider. He knew one thing. This beast had been brought here by a time jumper for one reason: to kill.

If he was to die by the hands of a cyborg, he would drag its unholy soul along with him. No matter its size.

Reaching the beast, the general unloaded a flurry of savage sword strikes. His strokes bit deep into its metal legs, but at this rate he'd be hacking away for a week before the beast would topple.

Instead, he struck at the part of its body he could reach, the underside of its belly. But this was where its scales were thickest. As he laid ferocious sword blows, the strikes did little more than gouge out chips. This troubled the general—it would take hours of him hacking away to do any real damage.

Levatha swung a massive leg, knocking the general aside. Any human would've had every bone broken with the force of this blunt trauma. But the general flew through the air to splash down in mud.

Meanwhile, Glass hovered overhead by his rockets, clutching onto Darrisaw. They circled over *Levatha,* taken in by the sheer enormity of the whale-sized monster.

"Where did that come from?" Glass yelled over line-feed.

"That thing was destroyed in the gantry," Darrisaw responded. "But there were two?" she asked, not knowing about the time jumpers' signature wheel of light. "Bring me low," she added, after seeing the general knocked aside.

Glass complied. He dropped forty feet, his arms hooked underneath Darrisaw's arms—she dangled like a mouse from a cat's mouth.

As Glass passed *Levatha,* Darrisaw wiggled herself loose from his grasp. Plummeting for a few feet, she engaged her own thrusters and picked up speed. Her chainsaw, pointed forward like a missile, revved.

In the general's mind he pictured her as a sawfish, falling from the sky.

Right before impact Darrisaw deployed her shield from her forearm mount and tucked her body behind it.

She slammed into the beast's side. Her chainsaw smoked as she went to work trying to carve through its scaly flesh. Hardened cartilage smoldered as hundreds of anodized chain teeth chewed through the scales.

Levatha roared and strained to reach her, but its arms were constructed in such a way that it couldn't reach its midsection. Instead, it spun wildly, its tail flailing through mounds of mud, sending wild sprays of water and silt.

A wave created in the wake of the thrashing beast splashed over the battlefield. Bronski and Rudderham were knocked off the top of the carrier in the torrent: he disappeared in the water as she managed to grab hold of a tree sapling poking from the muck.

Although *Levatha* couldn't reach Darrisaw, it was able to bend enough to reach in front of its legs. There, it snatched the *Pangolin* in its manufactured hands. With arms it was still learning to use, *Levatha* clumsily brought the *Pangolin* up to its gaping maw, and, with one powerful chomp, bit off its head. It spit the useless piece over its shoulder the way a cowboy spits out a tasteless plug of chew.

To remove any doubt the siege mech could still fight, *Levatha* chewed through its body. Mechanical scraps and hydraulic oil poured from the corners of its mouth. It screeched with beastly satisfaction.

The general recoiled at the destruction of his mech.

Finished with its meal, *Levatha* screeched in rage once again, stomping forward. Both arms unloaded salvos, laying a carpet bomb of explosions indiscriminately.

Renewed screams over the line-feed made it clear that many of the Sixth were caught in the wide-area blasts.

"Status!" Gunwald yelled over line-feed, pain in his voice indicating he had taken some undisclosed damage. The general's internal display lit with a massive red *X*. It overlaid *Levatha* with target coords: Gunwald had painted the prehistoric monster.

"Nothing's stopping it," a voice, shaking, said in response. "Bart just got smoked. Looking for Ally now."

The general was about to instruct his broken teams to retreat when his line-feed squawked. *<Attention on the net. War Galley inbound. Fire for effect in fifteen>* The target *X* that was *Levatha* turned green—a lock-in.

With the ion storm finished, the Sixth's assault ships were finally able to make it on-planet to reinforce the ground units. But it'd take time to get there. And the general knew there wasn't much time left.

"Fall back," Gunwald ordered, painting a new location on his map. This position, a rally point, also came up on everyone's visors.

Even though they were inspired by the general's blitzkrieg, the cyborg monstrosity was too much for them to handle.

The general, clearing himself from the mud, watched the troops begin to migrate away from *Levatha* while a few remained in place, laying suppression fire. The nearest, Rudderham, according to his visual Friend or Foe overlay, was having a hard time getting away.

In knee-high water, she attempted to run through the sucking mud. But her small stature and bulky power armor kept her at a snail's pace. Using her disruptor to balance herself, she lost her grip and it slipped away under water. With renewed effort she began churning her legs as her arms flailed, high-stepping to gain momentum. She moved so slowly it looked almost comical.

She was in the path of *Levatha*.

"Get out of there," the general yelled as he moved towards her the best he could through the mud.

With a frantic look over her shoulder, Rudderham tried to double-time. Her arms spun wildly as her legs kicked in the mud. But she couldn't distance herself from the towering beast.

Levatha finally shook Darrisaw off its side. She fired her jets to put distance between herself and the beast before tumbling from the sky to land hard in mud. *Levatha*, now free from any attackers, gave a shortened snarl as it moved forward through the muck with surprising ease. It had its eyes on another prize.

Reaching down, and with articulated fingers, *Levatha* plucked Rudderham from where she'd bogged down. She kicked and punched at the beast in vain.

Levatha opened its mouth and cut loose a ferocious roar. Water spewed from its gaping maw. Then it popped the struggling airman into its mouth, swallowing her whole.

The general, dumbfounded, stopped in his tracks. He looked the beast over, feeling in every way insignificant to damage the water dragon.

He thought back to the gantry when he'd seen *Levatha* in the early stages of construction. He remembered portions of its soft underside, which were now covered in plate steel. Then a thought occurred to him.

"*Levatha Hydraus,*" he called out, amplifying his voice while waving his arms. "Come and feast on me."

He caught the beast's attention. It turned to face him, pausing like it seriously considered the general's offer. Then, when it saw the general didn't move or attack, its natural animalistic ferocity took over and it quickly scooped up the general in its hand.

"No!" Darrisaw yelled, still pulling herself from the sticky mud. "Sergeant Glass," she said through line-feed, "get the general."

Overhead, still riding his rockets, Glass had watched the scene unfold. He hesitated, apparently not sure what to do.

Just like *Levatha* had swallowed Rudderham for its main course, so it swallowed General Mikeal as dessert.

In some wild, primeval triumph, the water beast bellowed. Its victory cry resonated with every last ounce of wind in its lungs. This lasted for a good half minute.

But just as abruptly, the cry stopped. A questioning look ran across *Levatha's* terrible face. The questioning look became a troubled expression. Its face contorted, its monstrous tongue dangling out the side of its mouth, overlapping its dagger-like teeth.

Then its mechanical arms angrily scratched at its chest.

Levatha cried again, but not in victory. This time it was a cry of pain. The cry turned into a low, mournful bellow. On shaky legs it staggered. And as it did, its arms now pulled at its stomach, like it wanted to rip its own guts out.

Then, a metal tip ruptured from *Levatha's* underside. Its belly. Blood came spraying out as the monstrosity clutched at the tip, but the sword tip had already receded back into its body, only to reappear nearby, creating a new hole.

Teetering from the internal wounds and the battered leg, *Levatha* bellowed again in ear-piercing pain before toppling over to splash down hard in waist-high, muddy water. It convulsed and thrashed, each death echo becoming thinner, less forceful. Its whipping tail cast massive waves.

Finally, with one last rattle to indicate its time on the earth was over, it shuddered then became still, its mouth partially open in a silent scream.

Its stomach finally split open from the inside, dumping out the general and a few hundred pounds of guts.

Quickly, the general still holding his warm sword in his gory hand, thrust his other into a particularly large track of intestines. He found what he searched for and pulled up an arm. He lifted Rudderham from the entrails, and the two rushed clear of the mound of guts.

Immediately Rudderham fought with her helmet, busting the chin straps and ripping it off her head. She spit the rebreather tube from her mouth and tossed away the helmet. Then she wretched.

"General," Darrisaw said as she used controlled thrusts of her jump boots to skip across the top of the mud and standing water. "You killed it?" she asked, still not sure what had just happened.

The general leaned heavily on his sword. "I figured if Jehovah could pull a man from a fish's belly after three days, then I could surely last inside the belly of that thing for three minutes."

Not sure what else to say, Darrisaw turned from the general to stare at the dead monster with morbid fascination.

Glass landed nearby on a solid outcropping of rock. His shoulders slumped and he was covered in caked mud and battle grime. "I need to find a medic," Glass said, his voice tired. Without another word or glance, he wandered off.

The general, still completely exhausted from cutting his way outside, didn't think anything of Glass leaving so quickly.

With herculean effort the general stood upright, and after docking his sword on his back he began limping in the same direction as the rest of the Sixth, to the rally point Gunwald had set earlier.

Darrisaw helped Rudderham to her wobbly feet.

The general glanced from one to the other. "That was fun, right?" he said. If his mouth had moved, it would've smiled.

"If you say so, sir," Rudderham said in a mousy, unsure tone. She pulled a strand of intestinal mucus from her coppery hair.

A week after the Mystic Shelf War ended, raucous laughter and glass scraping against glass filled the *Countervail's* bar and mini-casino on deck six, a recreation deck.

The slot machines, dice and cards, and other intergalactic games of chance kept everything lively. Patrons prayed to whatever pagan gods they'd dragged along to the casino in the hopes of striking the right lucky numbers. Occasionally an electronic siren on one of the machines told of another big winner. Their god must've answered.

Sitting at his favorite table—the one tucked away at the rear of the massive gaming room, nearer the bar, far from the main thoroughfare—Glass thought against pouring another shot.

But who was he kidding?

Like his father before him, and his father before him, Sergeant Jeremy Glass thought the answers to his problems lived at the bottom of the liquor bottle.

Nexus IV Redeemer, to be precise.

Distilled from the blossoms of the rare Nexus IV trumpets, a vining succulent found nestled in the southern reaches of the tiny planet, deep in the swamps. The rumor was that for every bottle made, one native harvester died. Most likely eaten by one of the swamp beasts, which were the worst parts of an alligator and snake wrapped together. That's how dangerous the swamps were.

This also meant the liquor came at a high price, a top shelf brand.

Picking up the bottle, Glass gulped down three gigantic swallows. All that remained was a single, shriveled white trumpet blossom at the bottom of the bottle. Eaten in the wild it would mean certain, excruciating, death. After the distillation process, it merely tasted like death.

Glass popped the blossom in his mouth and chewed mechanically. It tasted like death in an oddly comforting way.

But no matter what he took in, it didn't stop Glass' mind from haunting him with another replay of the Mystic Shelf War. He knew what he'd done. He wondered if anyone else did.

"Hey," a slurred voice called out.

Despite the clamor of slots and a hundred drunken voices straining to be heard in this place, Glass could tell this drunken voice was directed at him.

The man, well past the point of comfortably numb, leaned heavily on the table. He wore a high and tight and his face carried the evidence of many hand-to-hand fights. Even with the man's loose-fitting shirt his muscled body couldn't be hidden. His drunken smile had four less teeth than should've been there.

A typical ground pounder.

His buddy, who could've been a carbon copy except for his darker skin, clutched at the man's shoulder to keep himself upright. But they both relied on the table to keep them steady.

"I said *hey*," the man repeated. "I know you," he slurred. His arm extended fully as he pointed with exaggerated, unsteady movements and a wobbling finger. "You're with the mechs. You're a robot," the man exclaimed, like he'd just discovered a great truth.

"Cyborg," Glass admonished, his voice low and steady. "Leave me alone." The grunt wasn't worth the effort.

"You robots are all the same," the man continued, "bunch of rust and crap…" his voice trailed off.

The simpleton's statement obviously struck his buddy as amusing because he snickered, covering his mouth with his hand like a school-age child.

This emboldened the drunk man. He continued, "Yeah, rust and crap, like a metal… a metal… *turd*!"

Glass glowered at the two as the man and his buddy, laughing, drifted away to another table. They dropped onto the chairs, almost missing the seats.

Turning back to his bottle, Glass turned back to his own fragile thoughts.

When the call had gone up to rescue the general he hadn't taken any action. He blamed it on battle static, the emotion of the events, not hearing Darrisaw, not seeing it—any number of defenses. And any of them would've been plausible to anyone on the outside watching the battle unfold. Especially in battle, when things got foggy and muddled. Odd things happened.

But his mind knew differently. He knew differently.

He'd clearly heard Darrisaw's plea as the general was snatched up. Instead of racing to free his commander though, he'd held back.

With curious detachment, he'd watched *Levatha* bring the general to its mouth. His heart had raced with sinful excitement, a voyeur getting a glimpse of a crime.

He hadn't expected this sensation, the thrill of the general getting eaten, and immediately it had begun to haunt him.

Shortly after the fighting he had attempted to rationalize his inaction as just slow reaction. But as the days wore on and his mind settled, he knew that wasn't the case. He hadn't attempted to rescue the general—intentionally.

Inaction meant acceptance of the crime.

Since making it back to the *Countervail*, Glass could barely stand being in the same room as the general.

That led to the larger question: why?

As he mentally probed those thoughts for understanding, trudging through the swamp like a Nexus IV harvester, he wanted to piece together why he felt that way. The liquor would help him focus. Glancing at the label, Glass read Nexus IV's slogan:

He gave his life to redeem yours.

It was anger. Anger at the general, anger at the beast, or himself. He wasn't sure.

Maybe it was because the general could so quickly turn on him. Like when they'd first landed on Erudia, him in the *Wraith*, the general in the shuttle.

Sure, he'd almost blown the general out of the sky with the interceptor ship, but he hadn't intended to harm the general at that point. Or had he?

Everyone knew the general hated cyborgs. Only through congressional mandate would he accept them in his ranks. That didn't exactly make Glass feel warm and fuzzy inside. Even though Glass had saved the general's neck the first time they were on Erudia, months ago.

No matter what Glass did, the general would still hate cyborgs.

Hate him.

That was why he'd hesitated on the battlefield. Some small part of him wanted to see the general defeated. Whether he owned that emotion or not, it was there for him to see.

When Glass realized his bottle was empty, he stood, holding tight onto the neck as he used the table to steady himself. Just like the ground pounders.

The room swayed slightly, and the noise cut in and out. He pushed through the crowd.

Familiar laughter made him pause. At a table the two ground pounders sat, slamming beers.

Gripping the bottle neck tight, Glass shattered it over one of the ground pounder's heads. It sounded like a gunshot and the man, now unconscious, slid under the table.

His buddy leapt up just in time to intercept Glass' alloy, cybernetic arm with his face. His jaw shattered and he fell backwards, squealing in pain.

Their two table mates also hopped up, but Glass was already on top of the table, kicking one in the teeth with his metal foot. He heard teeth shatter. The fourth clutched onto his leg, knocking him off into the crowd.

Wildly he spun about, swinging with his massive arms in a good old barroom brawl.

But it all came to a quick end when the painful touch of a sonic baton made Glass' torso go numb. Two more baton strikes took all the fight out of him, essentially rendering his body uncooperative.

As Glass faded into unconscious, he realized he was mistaken.

Kicking in those ground pounder's heads was totally worth it.

R eturning from visiting Glass in security police custody, the general sat in his personal quarters in the *Countervail.* He finished the can of motor oil on the table.

For the most part Glass hadn't talked. The general figured he would once the alcohol wore off. A few days in correctional custody would do him some good.

As he tossed the can away and grabbed another, his mind wandered to the recent battle. The euphoria of cutting himself from inside a whale-dragon could only entertain him for so long. The story had wore thin after a day or two.

His mind then turned to more sullen thoughts, such as the fate of his beloved mechs and the loss of life that always accompanied any fruitful and productive war.

Frequently the general had said the only way a human could understand the magnitude of loss he felt when a mech died was for the human to lose a brother or sister.

As a true warrior, he could set aside his emotions in the passion of battle. For the most part. But when the last blaster bolt faded and all the mechs had powered down, that's when it was time to reflect on the loss.

There was kinship between him and his machines that could only be understood through the lens of family.

In the fight he'd lost four *Jacobys* and the *Pangolin* that *Levatha Hydraus* had decided to eat as a snack. Most of the others were waterlogged, but salvageable. They now rested in the *Countervail's* maintenance bays. The mechanics were working double shifts and would have them back in commission in no time.

A thousand soldiers and airmen had survived the Mystic Shelf War. But twelve hundred men and women hadn't. The Erudian city had been purged of all possessed inhabitants, driven mad by the alien Shamblers. After action battle assessments, this put their losses at around six thousand civilians. The Vesuvians had been driven off-planet.

The Sixth civil engineers had picked back up on building the outrigger post that had been interrupted when the alien Shamblers had returned months ago.

A couple days ago the Sixth's intelligence, surveillance, and reconnaissance section had discovered that the Vesuvian rail gun on Wuden, *Masso Arcus*, was the cause of the ion storm over Erudia. Its sustained barrage of radiation into Erud's delicate atmosphere had churned it up. The general's destruction of it in the soup bowl had inadvertently ended the storm, allowing the Sixth to finally get reinforcements on-planet.

Once again, the general had played no small part in the war. He and his mechs. That counted for something.

That something was the Sixth Space Wings' staff judge advocate general deciding to not court martial the general. Or those that aided him: Fletcher, Glass, and Darrisaw.

General Stinson, always quick to deride General Mikeal's motives and actions, argued the general needed to be charged because of the damage he'd caused, busting up the docking bays and stealing the transports. Destruction of the *Wraith* and expenditure of millions in ammunition.

But his complaint fell on deaf ears. Instead, the JAG recommended non-judicial punishment for him and his cohorts.

Colonel William Blatt, Jr., the JAG, had pinned on his full birds not but a year ago.

The eldest son of William Blatt—governor of the northwestern state of Sublime Pacifica which had replaced Oregon after it was nuked off the map—young Willy Junior grew up in a political household. Every hiccup and fart made by the Blatt family was scrutinized for context by the media.

Willy's father was in a heated race for the governorship, and the last thing he needed was word to get out that his son had decided to court martial a national institution such as General Mikeal, the robot general.

Colonel William Blatt, Jr. was a politician first, much more than a lawyer.

So the Sixth Space Wing Commander, General Rivera, gave the general a Letter of Reprimand for his actions. This amounted to little less than a hand slap.

The general knew the importance of maintaining good order, so he'd signed the reprimand, accepting blame while offering no defense.

It had been a busy couple of weeks.

Just a day ago he'd finished his last debrief with the wing historians. He was sure they had already crawled back to their holes and were hard at work cataloging the exploits of the mighty Sixth and the war for the Erdine planetary system. Through collection of camera footage and debriefs, data feeds and native inhabitant interviews, they wove a tale of sacrifice and valor. A victory lap to sell back home on Earth.

A knock on his quarters' door roused the general from his deep contemplation.

"Come in," the general said.

It slid open and revealed Darrisaw standing just outside at attention. With a nonchalant wave of his hand, he beckoned her in.

Her chainsaw had been swapped for a cybernetic arm and hand. Her customized power armor had been shelved, replaced by her military greys. Her long, black hair had been cut into a shoulder length bob. She always kept a portion of it pulled forward to cover the burn scars on the side of her face.

The general had always meant to ask her why she'd never gotten reconstructive surgery if the scars bothered her so much. But today wasn't the day to bring it up.

Darrisaw stopped a few feet from him. "Sir, Airman Darrisaw reports," she said in a rigid military voice as she rendered a tight salute.

"At ease," the general said, returning the courtesy.

She started to speak, then paused as her voice cracked. Taking her tube of liquefied protein-steroids from a cargo pocket, she squirted a mouthful and swallowed. She took another swallow of the green semi-liquid stuff before tucking it away, an embarrassing red flushing her cheeks.

As he opened another can of motor oil, the general studied Darrisaw. If he didn't know better, he wouldn't think this shy girl was the same warrior he saw on the battlefield.

Then he thought of Hatch. His mind kept going back to him: from the general's flight from the *Countervail*, to the iron mountain snake and the battles on Wuden, to Erudia and and *Levatha Hydraus*. All because of Hatch and Horvoth, the Vesuvian general. Was there something more intricate at play than just these two men?

His oil blood boiled at the thought of the men who had caused so much trouble getting away. Horvoth, he could understand. The Vesuvians hated him as much as he hated them. That was understood and accepted. But Hatch was an Earther.

The one calming assurance was that the general had nothing but time. He would track Hatch down even if it took ten, twenty years.

He'd find Hatch even after the man retired and was spending his days in a park feeding ducks. The general would find him.

Sometimes the general's revenge was simply outliving his opponents.

Darrisaw cleared her throat to get the general's attention. "Sir," she said. "In a couple weeks I think we'll have most of the *Jacobys* good as new. Preliminary diagnosis shows they're all repairable."

Despite being mangled in a maintenance bay explosion months ago, Darrisaw had insisted on returning to work as soon as she was able. The general figured after losing limbs and being nearly burned alive she would've developed some superstitious fear of the lower mechanic decks. But not her.

He knew she'd been raised by her widowed father and spent most of her childhood helping him at his job, a pulse engine mechanic. Fixing ran through her veins. It was one of the handful of skills a human could possess that would actually impress the general.

As he studied her, it finally occurred to him why he felt so at ease with her. If he didn't know better, Darrisaw was a grown version of Jenny Jacoby, Daniel Jacoby's daughter.

Daniel had been the chief engineer of Dynamo Robotics over three centuries ago. He had drawn up the blueprints for the general and the liaison robots, from the hardware design all the way to the emotive circuitry.

He believed in the promise of high-level sentience so much he'd bet his family on it. As a new liaison robot, the general—Mikeal— had chosen to live with the Jacobys.

One summer he'd spent every afternoon pushing young Jenny in the front yard on a tree swing. At first he hadn't understood how a human child could derive so much joy from something as simple as swinging. That was one of the great mysteries his emotive circuitry had to unravel.

He was the tireless friend that would stand at her window during the raging Martian dust storms. His mere presence kept the static lightning at bay so Jenny could sleep in peace, so she thought.

They would race through the canals, playing hide and seek. When he'd continually won, she'd gotten mad and stomped the red soil, saying he'd cheated. From those times he'd learned the intricate dance of human emotion, letting her win just enough to keep her happy without making it appear he had given up.

With dark hair and sullen features, Jenny and Darrisaw could pass as sisters.

The general nodded at Darrisaw's estimation. He was comforted by the thought of his mechs being entrusted to her. "Good," he said simply.

Another knock on his quarters' door drew his attention. It opened, and a man thin from lack of exercise stood there. He wore the white jacket of a contractor, an engineer.

The general looked at Darrisaw, and she got the hint.

Coming to attention, she popped a salute. The general came to attention and returned it. Spinning on her heel, Darrisaw exited his quarters, unconsciously turning her head slightly away from the man, probably so he didn't see her damaged face.

"Come," the general said, sitting back on his chair.

Quickly, the engineer entered. He held what looked like a suitcase. The weight tugged on his arm, causing him to slouch.

"I'm Dr. Parsus from the *Einstein's* R&D labs. I must say, general, it's been an honor…" Parsus began, the words spilling out. But his mouth ran faster than his mind, and he began stumbling over what to say. "An honor to meet *me*. I mean you, of course…" he laughed nervously. "What I'm saying…"

"Did you find it?" the general asked, being sure to inflect his voice with as much exasperation and annoyance as possible.

"Yes," Parsus blurted. "Yessir." He held out the box. "We searched long, but… we could've digitized it," he said, changing thoughts mid-sentence.

The general tried to ignore him as he took the suitcase.

"It's just like those in mid Twentieth Century," Parsus explained. "Except the power source, of course. We had to—"

"That's enough." The general waved his hand, cutting him off.

"Yessir," Parsus said, wringing his hands.

Before the research engineer could get started on another tangent, the general dismissed him. With a couple of bows as he backed away, Parsus exited the quarters.

Alone, the general opened the suitcase.

It contained a personal project he had tasked the pointy-headed engineers on the *Einstein* to figure out.

Setting the box on a clear acrylic table, the general went to a cabinet in his quarters that was mostly empty except for a Bible and a few metal trinkets only a robot would find interesting.

There he retrieved the eight track he'd brought back from Wuden.

He checked the slack on the tape before inserting it into the player deck built from scratch by the Sixth's engineers.

Led Zeppelin IV played as he reclined in his chair, feet propped on the table. He took another sip from his can of motor oil as he remembered driving Winder's Nova across the plains.

Then, a sudden and quick thought occurred to him, so clear he almost dropped his can of oil. The exhilaration he'd felt in the Nova was the same feeling Jenny had felt in the skimmer.

And he knew without a doubt Jenny would've loved sitting alongside him in the car. He imagined her throwing her arms up in the air, laughing in delight.

THE ROBOT GENERAL
BOUNTY HUNTER BREAKER
MOLECH'S CHILDREN

GET 3 BOOKS FREE!

...as a thank you for reading *The Robot General,* book one in 6th Mechanized.

We hope you enjoyed it! Please take a moment to encourage you to review the book on Amazon and Goodreads. Every review helps further the author's reach and, ultimately, helps them continue writing fantastic books like this one.

Check out the rest of our catalogue at www.aethonbooks.com.

To sign up to receive a FREE collection from some of our best authors as well as updates regarding all new releases, visit www.subscribepage.com/AethonReadersGroup.

JOIN THE STREET TEAM! Get advanced copies of all our books, plus other free stuff and help us put out hit after hit.

SEARCH ON FACEBOOK:
AETHON STREET TEAM